# MISTER LUCKY

To Dee —

I've known you for years and based a character in this book on you. Guess which one —

Roger

Booklocker.com, Inc.
2007

# MISTER LUCKY

**Roger Poppen**

# Table of Contents

# PART I

# WELCOME TO WESTERVILLE

# Chapter 1: You Got the Job

"Ladies and gentlemen, the President of the United States."

After perfunctory opening statements, President Jimmy Carter, in his slow, Georgia Piedmont accent, announced, "I have given notice that the United States will not attend the Moscow Olympics unless the Soviet Union forces are withdrawn from Afghanistan before February twentieth."

Robert Rochmann, watching the flickering image on the small television screen in his hospital room, clicked the remote control. "Well, that's that. The bastard. You know the Ruskies aren't going to leave in a month."

"It could be worse. You could've made the team." Bill Chappell, Rochmann's best friend, roommate, and all-around expert on the good things in life, could be counted on to put matters in perspective.

"Screw you," Rochmann said.

Chappell laughed. "Think about it. Suppose you hadn't torn your knee. You're doing your lifetime best lifts, maybe even looking at a national record at the Olympic trials this spring, and President Peanut pulls this. You'd be another Lee Harvey Oswald."

"Just shut the fuck up, will you!" But it was true. If Rochmann wanted to feel even worse, he could imagine rounding into peak condition only to have the Olympic rug jerked out from under him by this sanctimonious peanut farmer. He didn't want to think about it, but Chappell was relentless.

"This actually works to your advantage, you know, Rocko my boy. The '84 Olympics are going to be in Los Angeles, right? You know the Commies aren't going to turn the other cheek. They'll boycott us right back and," he shot his fist into the air in a triumphal salute, "it'll leave the medals available for mere mortals who weren't born in the Baltic."

"You don't know that."

"C'mon Rocky. You don't have to be Jeanne Dixon to know the Soviets aren't going to let this slide. Wouldn't it be great to actually

3

think about winning a medal instead of getting your ass kicked by a bunch of guys whose names look like a rack of Scrabble tiles?"

Rochmann had to smile despite his ill humor. "Bill, I can't even think about next week, much less 1984. I've dropped out of grad school twice now to train for Olympic trials. Maxed out my student loans. I don't know how I'm going to pay for this..." He waved his hand at the austere hospital room. "I might have to go out to Seattle and stay with my sister, get some shit job, I don't know, a waiter or something, 'til I pay off some debts."

"Yeah, you could take up bodybuilding. Be a cocktail waiter in a gay bar out there. Rake in the tips."

Rochmann glared at his tormenter but said nothing. The funny man seemed determined to have the last word.

Chappell poured some water from the metal pitcher on the bedside table into a paper cup, offered it to Rochmann, who shook his head, then drank it himself. "Rocko, look, I know you're bummed right now. But in the overall scheme of things, it's your lucky day. Arthroscopic surgery these days is miraculous; if you were a pro footballer you'd be in the game this Sunday."

"Football season's over."

"You know what I mean. We can start rehab right away. But take it slow, build up ligament and tendon strength. We know you can pile on muscle power when the time comes. I'll be starting my residency and will have access to any new anabolic steroid that comes down the pike. Who knows what we'll have in the next four years? Maybe we can even close the steroid gap with the Commies."

"Bill, you're not listening. It'll take all my stash to pay for this 'miracle surgery.' I'll need to get a job just to eat. Besides, I'm almost thirty; I think the old bod is saying it's had enough."

"Rocko. You're just a kid. Remember Schemansky. Forty years old, two back surgeries, and he takes bronze in Tokyo."

"Yeah, well, Schemansky was from the planet Krypton. Never be anyone like that again."

Chappell tapped his chest with his fist. "Ski had it here, Rock. And you do too. You want it, you can find a way to get it. You only took a leave of absence from grad school--they'll welcome you back with open arms. Do your dissertation; that's all you have left, right? Then get a cushy teaching job somewhere that'll leave time to train. You can always find more loans for tuition. I'll cover food and rent for a while. It'll work out fine."

\*\*\*

Two-and-a-half years after Carter's speech, the Soviets were bogged down in Afghanistan and the new actor-president's 'evil empire' rhetoric was bound to keep them in a surly mood. Los Angeles was certain to remain Commie-free.

Robert Rochmann, Ph.D., was in upstate New York, making his way around an outdoor buffet table at the reception for new faculty at Westerville State University. This ritual allowed the administration bigwigs to get together and look over the newbies, reminisce about the good old days, and offer sage advice.

Rochmann was uncomfortable at such affairs, people standing around talking about Reaganomics or liberation theology or the New York Rangers--as if he gave a damn. Besides, he had to cut his workout short in order to get there on time. It probably was only the first of many compromises, but after a year of penury, teaching part-time at a community college, this position paying a living wage was too good to pass up. Schemansky may have won medals in four Olympics but he had to work at some crummy jobs. Rochmann would settle for one Olympics and a good job with health benefits. Besides, there was loads of free food in front of him and he couldn't let it go to waste.

After his third trip to the buffet, Rochmann stood at the corner of the patio with the one person he'd met earlier, Susan Koenig, the other new assistant professor in the Psychology Department. She was going on and on about her research. Maybe she saw him as a competitor and wanted to impress him, or maybe she felt as uncomfortable as he did and reacted by talking about what she knew best--her dissertation. Rochmann felt like saying, hey, you got the job, this isn't an interview. Instead, he just nodded randomly and munched the tiny sandwiches piled on his paper plate. A cloying lemon scent hung in the air and he looked around for citronella candles so they could move away from them. It must be Susan's perfume he concluded; at least they were safe from mosquitoes.

His neck muscles tightened from tilting his head up to look Susan in the eye, or what could be seen of her eyes peering from behind thick lenses. She was a couple inches taller than him. Everyone was a couple of inches taller, or five or ten. Susan was maybe late-twenties, but her face foretold middle-age. She did have pretty lips, full, nicely shaped, but way too much lipstick, garish red, like the Soviet flag flapping in the breeze. He dropped his gaze to her breasts that heaved as she talked. Her white satin blouse was one of those big-shouldered, billowy things that camouflaged what lay beneath.

One of the things he missed most about parting company with Bill Chappell was the women. Tall, voluble, good-looking, Chappell's picture appeared in the dictionary under 'babe magnet.' And his girlfriends always had a friend for his pal, Rocky. Rochmann could hold his own after he met someone--women often were intrigued by his compact, muscular body--but he never had mastered that first hurdle. His year teaching at the community college had been lacking in more than just money.

His eyes continued downward. Susan's blouse was tucked in bunches at her waist, giving her a bulky appearance. She probably had a flabby butt and thighs under that long skirt. Probably never exercised, just sat at her desk, mailing out questionnaires.

"Do you ever do any kind of athletics?" he asked.

"What?" Her eyebrows shot up and the Soviet flag stopped in mid-wave.

"Athletics? Athletes," he said, suddenly aware of how strange this question sounded in the middle of her description of statistical significance.

"Why?" There was a wary look on her face.

Why indeed? He had to come up with something. "I think I read about a study that employed a survey similar to yours with female athletes."

She looked interested. "Oh really. Who did it?"

6

"I can't recall; it's not my area. It might have been in a review article in *Psych Bulletin*." He scrunched his face as though trying to recall the details.

"*Psych Bulletin*? Recently? I must have missed it. I'd love to know the reference if you come across it," she said with a note of respect.

"Of course," he said.

"Are you Robert Rochmann?" asked a low and breathy voice behind him.

He turned and looked straight into a pair of violet eyes, a color that should appear unnatural but fit somehow with the rest of the face. The woman's thick, black brows arched quizzically, producing slight creases in her forehead. It was a face of an older woman from which a younger beauty looked out. Most striking was her hair, white hair that rippled and cascaded down to her shoulders. She looked like an Eighteenth-Century French courtesan whose powdered wig had exploded, curls jutting out like sprung clockworks.

"Robert Rochmann?" she repeated.

"Uh, yes," he said. He turned toward her but made no follow-up inquiry of her name, no introduction to Susan, no question of how she knew his name. He just stood gawking at this extraordinary sight.

"I'm Nina Feiffer," she said, her smile broadening. She clasped his forearm and tugged gently, spilling the two olives that remained on his plate. She said to Susan, over his shoulder, "Do you mind if I steal him for a few minutes?" Susan just blinked behind her thick glasses, mouth open, and said nothing while Rochmann was led off by the arm, shuffling to avoid tripping on the woman's heels.

She dropped his arm and he walked beside her, wordless, still holding his empty plate. She smiled and greeted people in several conversational clumps; they smiled greetings in return. Rochmann nodded as if he knew them. She stopped when they had gone beyond the others, onto the green baize lawn next to a wall of closely trimmed hedges, like the bunker of a giant billiard table. A faint balsam fragrance swirled around her.

She said, with great cordiality, "I've been looking forward to meeting you, Robert."

7

He regained his voice. "Well, it's nice to meet you. Ms. Feiffer? Dr. Feiffer? Are you on the faculty?"

"Please, call me Nina. My husband is Dr. Feiffer, Marv Feiffer, Professor and Chairman of the Anthropology Department." She recited this as if giving name, rank and serial number. "I'm an artist," she continued with more verve. "That's why I wanted to meet you. I understand that you're a weightlifter. You certainly look solid." She stepped back and looked him up and down.

"Um, yes, I'm trying to get into competition shape. I've got a long ways to go." He wondered how she knew he was a weightlifter.

"You compete! That's fascinating! Do you know that fellow, what's his name, you know, sometimes they show weightlifters flexing their muscles on television? And he made that dreadful barbarian movie?"

Rochmann grimaced. "You must mean Arnie, Arnold Schwarzenegger. No, I'm not a physique--guy."

He almost said 'physique faggot,' an epithet used for his iron game cousins. If one thought about it, in the overall arc of the universe, hoisting two hundred kilos overhead was of no more intrinsic value than pumping up a twenty-inch bicep. But all that posing in front of a mirror, the dieting, the depilating, it was all just so girly.

He said, "I'm a weightlifter. I don't do the bodybuilding, posing stuff. That's something totally different."

"Really? What do you mean?" she asked. Her violet eyes fixed on his in a manner both unnerving and captivating.

"I do Olympic lifting. The kind they do in the Olympics, where you lift the weights overhead. I work for strength and speed, not size of muscles. Physique guys train completely different, pumping up each muscle for maximum bulk. All show and no go."

"But it must take a lot of muscle to lift those weights over your head," she said.

"Well, yes. But we don't do anything to build unnecessary bulk. Like biceps." He chuckled and flexed his arm in a mock pose. "You can always tell a weightlifter from a bodybuilder--no biceps. An

Olympic lifter looks like a tyrannosaurus rex, all legs and butt and little bitty arms."

"Frankly, I think some of those fellows you see on television are grotesque," she said, as if immediately converted to his point of view. "All brown and bulbous and shiny. Come to think of it, I think I have seen some Olympic lifting on television, too. They tend to be huge men, don't they, with barrel bellies, like sumo wrestlers? You don't look like that either." She looked at him cautiously, as if he might suddenly inflate.

"Yeah, when lifting's shown on TV, it's always the heavyweights. Vassily Alexyev weighs about 360. TV goes for the bizarre. We have all different weight classes, like boxing, from 56 kilos on up, though they never show us little guys. I'm in the 82-and-a-half kilo class, 181 pounds." He stopped, suddenly self-conscious, going on like this to a woman he'd just met. "I'm sorry, this must be really boring. What about you? You said you were an artist?"

"Oh no, it's not boring. I find it fascinating. I always like to learn new things." She laughed, shaking her white curls and flashing blue feather earrings that matched the eye of a peacock tail feather that was pinned to the breast of her coarse-knit black sweater. Full breasts. She stared over his shoulder for a moment, then spoke. "And, yes I'm an artist. Mostly painting. Some ceramics and sculpture when the muse and materials come together. Actually, that's what I wanted to talk to you about."

He probably knew as much about art as she knew about weightlifting, but at least he could emulate the same interest she had shown. "I don't think I've ever met a real artist," he said. "What kind do you do? I mean abstract, or pop art, or what?"

"Well, I call it 'emotional figurative.' It's not easy to explain. I'd like to show you my work and explain it in context. Could you come to my studio sometime, say, next Saturday, and I'll show you around?"

"Uh, I don't know," he replied. "I'm not an artist. I can't tell impressionism from expressionism."

"Or realism from surrealism," she said with a wide smile that revealed a slight gap between her front teeth. "Please come. I think you'll find it interesting, as a psychologist and an athlete. And I'm sure you can help my work. What would be a good time for you? How about early afternoon?"

He could not refuse such directness. "Well, I work out around noon on Saturday. So it'd have to be later. Sometime around five?"

"Perfect!" she said, again with that melodic laugh. "Let me tell you how to get there."

# Chapter 2: 'Roid Rage

E arlier that year, when Rochmann interviewed at Westerville, he had asked to see the recreation facility. His campus tour guide proudly showed him the Health & Fitness Center, the newest and most striking building on campus. A stark assemblage of glass and concrete, it loomed behind the white-pillared granite piles of the college quadrangle like a space ship visiting Stonehenge. Rochmann barely noticed the huge swimming pool, the martial arts and dance studios, the acres of hardwood floors for basketball and racquetball courts, focusing instead on the weight-training room. The large room was crammed with exercise machines but had a small area for free weights in the rear. Rochmann asked if he could build a lifting platform back there. Probably, the Assistant Director told him, but he'd have to get approval from an advisory committee.

After he was offered a faculty position, Rochmann made another trip to Westerville to make his pitch to build a platform. Around the conference table were seated five individuals: three men--one white, one black, and a Hispanic; and two women--one white and one black. Like most committees in academia, racial and gender balance was of key importance. This was a good thing for Rochmann, since the Director of the Center seemed to represent the white male idiot constituency. A tall, florid man, thirty years and a hundred pounds past his athletic glory days, the Director tried to dominate the group. When Rochmann said he would like to build a wooden platform, at his own expense, so there would be no damage to the concrete floor when weights were dropped, the Director said with a tone of finality, "You can't drop weights."

Rochmann took a deep, calming breath, then patiently explained that there was a very small margin for error in fixing a barbell overhead, particularly when working at one's limits, and sometimes gravity took control. In addition to the platform, he said he would supply his own weights, with rubber bumper plates, designed specifically to cushion the shock.

A trainer for the track team, a black male who knew something about Olympic lifting, came to the rescue. "It's like a high jumper. You can't clear the bar every time; you have to push the limits to get better." He added that he taught Olympic lifting movements to the track team, and it would be great if Rochmann could give them some pointers.

The Director changed his argument. "Well, it's just not safe. A barbell could fall on your head and cause serious injury. The Fitness Center simply cannot leave itself open to this liability."

Rochmann described how one simply moved away from a missed weight and let it fall harmlessly to the platform. "In fact," he said, "it's well documented that the most dangerous weight training exercise is the bench press, precisely because people can't get out from under the bar if they lose it."

This information diverted the Director into a discussion with the Assistant Director on whether bench pressing should be banned. The problem was resolved by a decision to post prominent signs in the weight room for bench pressers to use spotters, and attention again turned to Rochmann.

The Women's Athletic Director, a Dr. Beste, asked hii ' to describe Olympic lifting in more detail. Her dome of brown lacquered hair, resembling a football helmet, and square-jawed face without make-up, suggested she represented the middle-aged butch community.

"Well, there are two lifts, the snatch and the clean-and-jerk." As he said this, Rochmann noticed the Director nudge the Assistant Director, a sniggering smirk on his face. The nomenclature of the sport did not make his presentation any easier. The term 'snatch,' when introduced into the sporting lexicon early in the Twentieth Century, described the quick, abrupt nature of the performance. Like legerdemain by a magician, a barbell resting on the floor, suddenly, in the blink of an eye, appears overhead. But in later parlance, the sexual connotations of the word evoked giggles in the uninformed, that were only compounded when he described the technical variations of the 'squat snatch' and the 'split snatch.' The term 'clean-and-jerk' was not much better. Dr. Beste was ignoring the facial contortions of the Director and Rochmann directed his comments to her, sensing camaraderie with another ill-treated minority.

The fifth member of the committee, who was young, black, and female, a student athlete Rochmann guessed, asked how long he'd been doing it. Leave it to youth to bring up the age issue. But this was an opportunity to hype his experience. Self-promotion was not easy, since he usually focused on how far below the world's best he was rather than his actual accomplishments. But he enumerated some of his state and regional championships, including a second place in the Senior Nationals the previous spring. He omitted any reference to his knee injury and the Olympic boycotts, but emphasized the upcoming Los Angeles Games. In an unusual display of patriotic fervor, he talked about the possibility of a gold medal for America, and he could see he had them. Even the Director. All he lacked was a tape recording of *The Star Spangled Banner* to get them standing and cheering.

As soon as he'd gotten the go-ahead to build his platform, Rochmann celebrated by ordering an Eleiko barbell set. More than two thousand dollars, it was the most extravagant thing he'd ever purchased. "I know just how you feel," Chappell said when Rochmann excitedly phoned him the day the weights were delivered. Chappell had just taken delivery on a new BMW 323i. They were like little boys on Christmas morning, telling their best friend all the features of their new toys.

\*\*\*

Once fall quarter began, defending his turf and equipment required daily effort. Before each workout, Rochmann scouted the room to collect his bumper plates that had been dispersed in his absence. Brightly colored--red 25-kilo, blue 20-kilo, yellow 15-kilo, and green 10-kilo plates--they looked like circus train wheels scattered by a terrible derailment. It was hard to damage the bumper plates but his bar was another story. The bigger boys liked to leave a loaded bar, bowed with stacks of plates, on the bench-press or squat racks after they finished training, like Ozymandius proclaiming,

"Look what I have done and fear me!" Rochmann loathed these cretins and left his lovely Swedish-steel creation at home, making do with the cheap bars supplied by the Fitness Center. He brought in his precision chrome instrument perhaps once a month to try a maximum lift, carrying it into the weight room like Minnesota Fats walking into a pool hall with his ebony and inlaid-ivory cue stick. Nobody touched that bar but himself.

Control over the atmosphere of the weight room was another matter. Boomboxes blared rock music of the electric chainsaw genre, sometimes two at a time playing different tunes that reverberated through the room like aural shards of glass. Conversation between training partners was carried on by shouting over the music. The resulting racket would have inspired Dante to add another circle to Hell.

In the beginning, Rochmann tried to fight the noise, politely asking the owner of a boombox to turn it down, or sometimes just turning down the volume himself. But as soon as he returned to the platform, the volume would be cranked up again. Once, he just yanked the plug of the offensive device from the wall socket. The sudden silence caused everyone to turn and stare. The clanking of pulleys ceased and an audible murmur spread among the startled exercisers.

A large young man--clad in a tight, red, muscle-tee-shirt and billowy, camouflage-patterned parachute pants--got up from his apparatus and swaggered toward Rochmann. The gold chain around his neck glinted against the deep orange-brown of his skin; his biceps and triceps expanded like bowling balls; his lats spread his back into a broad vee; his chest thrust out and his pecs rippled; overall, a display worthy of a silverback gorilla. As he came closer, Rochmann could see the splatter of acne across the kid's face and shoulders, and his neck looked way too thick for such a youngster. He obviously was on the juice, and Rochmann thought of his own impulsiveness in pulling the plug.

"You got a problem?" the muscled kid sneered.

Rochmann looked up at the much taller figure with an icy stare, his competition face that took over when he approached the barbell in a major contest, the visage that Clint Eastwood assumed when confronting the bad guys on a movie set. "Keep--the--fucking--noise--down," Rochmann said quietly, but with explosive force behind each word.

The orange man's upper lip curled slightly and his right hand slowly clenched and unclenched, but he made no closer move, as though a glass barrier were between them, held in place by Rochmann's stare. They stood thus frozen for several seconds, the span of two or three slow breaths, though in re-telling the event, the time expanded to many minutes.

"Fuck you!" the young man suddenly bellowed. Still keeping his eyes fixed on Rochmann, he grabbed the boombox, then turned and stalked from the room.

A few minutes later, another guy came in with his tape player. As he was plugging it in, one of the spandex-clad coeds went over and said something to him. He looked back at the platform, where Rochmann was bending over the bar, and shrugged. For the remainder of that training session, the volume was kept to a level at which one could actually hear the clanking of weights and the murmur of voices.

But the next day, the music was loud as ever and Rochmann gave up. There were just too many of them and confrontation was risky. The ape-like threats distracted from his workouts. Actual violence was dangerous because the least injury could set his training back for weeks. So he ceded the auditory territory and began wearing foam earplugs that took the edge off the noise and allowed him to focus on the weights.

Visual distractions were another matter. Young women dressed like dancers from the movie, *All That Jazz*, contorted themselves on the various devices. Hoisting chunks of iron once had been the province of burly men at circuses and county fairs, where local yokels tested their manhood against itinerant Samsons. Charles Atlas, on the back cover of a million comic books, promised to turn 90-pound weaklings into musclemen who confronted sand-kicking bullies and aroused desire in bathing beauties. Now, those beauties no longer were mere admirers of macho muscularity; they had themselves become participants in the pursuit of physical perfection. Loosed from the shackles of the scullery, and spurred by ideals of personal fulfillment and gender equality, women strained to tone their glutes and abs on chromed contraptions of Rube Goldberg complexity. As with cigarettes, that had started as rough packets of tobacco, hand-rolled by cowboys and soldiers for brief moments of respite, but now were long and narrow, filter-tipped and menthol flavored, weightlifting had 'come a long way, baby.'

Between sets, Rochmann let his gaze rove over the brightly colored, undulating mounds of Lycra. Steroids were rumored to inhibit libido, but not nearly enough in his case. He could imagine activities forbidden by the Campus Conduct Code. It wasn't the Code, but his own awkwardness in initiating such activities, that held him in check. He tried to catch the eye of a girl doing leg extensions on the machine nearest the platform. Cute as a pixie, she was dressed, unlike the others, in plain black tee-shirt and shorts. Dark curly hair, olive skin, and great quads. He only wanted to smile at her, maybe get a smile in return, but she was like the opposite of those portraits you read about, where the eyes track you around the room. Even when she turned in his direction, she looked through, over, around him, like he was a ghost. He sighed and added plates to the bar for his next set. Thank goodness, at least, for his liaison with Nina.

# Chapter 3:  What the Doctor Ordered

The Saturday following the new faculty reception, Rochmann found himself, that first time, driving his old International Scout up the winding driveway through the trees to the Feiffers' house.  An Alpine chalet style, set into a steep hill, its dark timbers blended into the foliage and bare rocks.  A balcony stretched across the second story, behind which was a row of windows, shining with reflected sunlight.

Rochmann drove around to the back of the house, as instructed, where the driveway led to a three-car garage.  Chappell's new BMW would fit these surroundings.  His ten-year-old Scout, a rusty box on wheels, could be mistaken for the gardener's truck.  He went to the back door and pushed the doorbell button.  Not hearing a ring, he pushed it again and then raised his hand to knock.

The door opened at that moment and there was Nina, smiling her bright smile.  "I was upstairs in the studio," she said.  "Come in."  She had on a paint-spattered white tee shirt that hung loosely from her shoulders.  The bulge of her breasts and the points of her nipples were obvious beneath the thin cloth.  She wore black tights of a thick, nappy material, and was barefoot.  "Come up to the studio and I'll show you around," she said, leading him through the kitchen and down a hall to a large staircase at the front of the house.  Her white hair was drawn back into a long, frizzy ponytail that swung with her brisk pace.

Rochmann looked around as he followed her.  The room adjacent to the staircase was lit by the afternoon sun filtering obliquely between thick curtains, gilding dark polished wooden tables and bookcases.  Large tribal masks glowered from the far walls.  At the top of the stairs, Nina led him to a large open room that stretched across the front of the house.  It was very warm, smelling of turpentine and cedar.  Light streamed through the glass doors he'd observed as he drove up.

"My studio," Nina announced.  "It's a southern exposure, which is terrible light for painting, but at least there's plenty of it.  The north side is so dark, facing that hill, so I chose quantity over quality." She laughed her bright tinkling laugh.

"Why is that a problem? The view here is great." He walked to the expanse of glass and looked out at a valley of green-black conifers and hardwoods beginning their transformation to autumnal reds and yellows.

"The south light is so direct, it casts hard shadows that move as the sun moves across the sky. So if you're painting a model, every time you look, the light and shadow have changed. And the color changes too. North light is more stable, white and steady. Since I do mostly non-representational stuff, it's not a major problem." She laughed again. "Would you like some tea?" Her laughter seemed slightly forced, edgy.

"Sure," he answered. "This all your work?" He turned toward a wall where painted canvases were hung and stacked.

"Some recent things, and probably some old stuff too." She filled a teakettle at a small sink at the other end of the room where there was a cabinet, a hot plate, and a large loose-pillow sofa of creamy suede. Then she came over and stood next to him, her sandalwood fragrance blending sweetly with the air of the studio. "Take a look at them and tell me what you feel."

Most of the paintings contained a light-colored figure, raised almost in bas-relief, against a darker, multi-colored background, the paint applied in thick smears. The figures were humanoid in their proportions, but lacked defining detail other than conical outcroppings of paint in what might be the breast or crotch area, making some look like females and others males. Some were outstretched, some compacted, all were contorted. It looked as if the paintings could be placed in a certain order and riffled through so the figures would soar and leap in an animation sequence, like dancing starfish. Rochmann walked back and forth, examining some of the paintings more closely, squinting, trying to make sense of them.

"What do you feel?" she asked again.

"Well, I don't know much about art."

"I'm not asking for learned criticism." She chuckled with a reassuring tone. "What do you feel looking at them?"

"Well, they look lonely," he ventured.

"Yes, good. Go on."

"Like they're hemmed in by all the dark--stuff around them." He hesitated, trying not to sound completely stupid.

"And?"

It was like a Rorschach test, so what the hell, he just went with it. "Well, they're like scrambling around, trying to get loose. Sometimes they're totally beaten down, and sometimes they're, like, flying."

"That's marvelous! You're very perceptive!" she exclaimed, clapping her hands and laughing again.

Just then the teakettle whistled and she turned to attend to it.

"Saved by the bell," he muttered.

"Want anything in yours?" she called.

"Sugar, please."

She returned with two earthenware cups, squat and irregular, with white and blue splotches on them.

"You make these?" he asked.

"A long time ago. I was into vessels for a while. These are leftovers, actually serving a useful purpose. Quite unusual for an *objet d'art*. I imagine that's why they didn't sell.

"You sell these?" Realizing the incredulity in his voice, he began again. "I mean, how do you sell your work? There can't be much of a market around here in Westerville."

"Well I don't have my pictures hanging in the Hillside Inn, next to still-lifes of potted geraniums and snow-covered barns." She laughed with open mouth and bobbing ponytail at the incongruity of her work alongside that of earnest hobbyists, women who sought to fan a creative spark by taking painting classes at the community college and offering their greeting-card canvases for sale to people waiting for tables at the local pancake house. "I have arrangements with some galleries in the City. It brings in enough for materials and a tax write-off."

She faced him with her wide, open-mouthed smile and he tried not to stare at the gap between her front teeth, a little imperfection that was strangely attractive.

"But I don't want to talk about commercialism, I want to talk about creativity. I want you to pose for me. I want to paint you."

He looked at her quizzically. "A portrait?"

"I don't want to paint your face; I want your figure. I want to paint your body, the impact of your body."

"You use a model to paint these?" He waved his hand at the starfish paintings. "I mean, they're not directly pictures of people, are they?"

"They're pictures of people's feelings, mine, and others. You're right, I am trying to break out. And you can help me." She took his hand in hers, tracing the rough calluses on his palm with her fingertips and the thick veins on the back of his hand with her thumb. "You could really help."

"You want me to pose? You know I'm not a bodybuilder."

"Take off your shirt," she said in reply, stepping back and looking at him critically.

He was a little embarrassed and a little aroused at this request but the forcefulness of her command was intimidating. He pulled his sweater over his head.

"And your tee shirt."

Rochmann complied, tightening his abs. Only a few tendrils of hair curled around his nipples, with not much more in a small patch between his pecs. While a bodybuilder would envy the lack of chest hair--less to shave--he had always felt self-conscious about it.

"Come over in the light." She took his hand and led him in front of the windows where the slanting sun threw sharp shadows around his pectorals, abdominals, trapezius, latissimus, intercostals, deltoids, triceps, biceps. Though not 'ripped,' as the physique-ohs say, he knew his muscles were thick and well-defined.

"Yes, yes," her smoky voice murmured while she traced the shadows with a long, pink fingernail, her fingertips not actually touching his skin.

He stood warily, and watched her inspection circuit with his eyes, not moving his head.

"And now your trousers."

"Now wait a minute," he protested.  Mister Lucky was stirring and this could be embarrassing.  Rochmann couldn't decide if she was coming on to him or was just a wacko artist.  What if her husband came home?  What if someone drove up and saw him through the windows, practically naked?

"Well?"  She interrupted his silent soliloquy.  "Are you bashful?"

He laughed uneasily.  "Um, I guess so."

"Well, I'm an artist, a professional; just think of me as a doctor."

Maybe it was his consternation, or the calmness in her voice, but Mister Lucky subsided.  "Okay, doc," he said.

He removed his shoes and pants and stood there in his white sweat socks and jockey shorts, the sunlight warm on his legs.  He had a lot more hair on his legs, except for the front of his thighs where it had been rubbed away by repeated chafing of the barbell.  If there was one muscle he was proud of, it was his quads.  Each thigh was almost as big around as his waist and the muscles, in repose, hung over his knees like hams in a butcher shop.

She did not touch his quads or glutes as she had his upper body.  She just walked around him, twice, without saying anything.  Then, like a falcon diving from its aerie, her hands were inside the elastic of his shorts, pulling them down, and she was on her knees taking Mister Lucky full into her mouth.

"Hey!" he grunted, pulling away reflexively, almost stumbling on the shorts around his ankles.  She held on like a lioness on a wildebeest, digging her nails into his bare glutes, and glared fiercely up at him.  Resistance was futile.  "Ahh, do it," he whispered, as Mister Lucky came to life.  He grasped her white hair in both hands and thrust forward.

She was indeed a doctor--Doctor Deepthroat.  His vision whirled like flipping through TV channels:  the orange sunlight streaming in the windows, the odd-colored paintings along the walls, her white hair bobbing below his belly.  He closed his eyes and felt the flame of tension burn brighter and brighter, and then the fireball explosion.

\*\*\*

They were curled up together on the leather sofa, Rochmann naked, except for his socks, and Nina still fully clothed. It was like he'd fainted and regained consciousness with no idea of how long they'd been there. Blue shadows striped the room.

"That was--incredible," he said, breaking the silence that hung like mist. She kissed him, hard and probing with her tongue, and he could taste the sticky residue. He had never tasted--that--before; her kiss seemed depraved, wildly sensual. Mister Lucky twitched.

She looked into his eyes, only a little less fiercely than when she had first attacked him, and said in her lowest and breathiest tones, "I'll do anything you like. Whatever fantasy you've ever had. Anything."

He struggled to reply. His sex life for the past year had consisted of jerking off. Now it was like he had stepped into a *Penthouse* 'Forum,' except Nina was not your typical centerfold and his fantasies were limited to voyeuristic excursions in the weight room. Mister Lucky stirred some more.

"I'd like to see you naked," he said.

She smiled as if that were exactly the right answer, and quickly pulled her tee shirt over her head, revealing firm breasts, with large areola and protruding nipples like the tips of a child's fingers. She pulled her tights down over her hips, slowly, like a stripper; not a silly, exaggerated tease, just the right pace to build anticipation. She had a rounded belly and broad hips. As she wriggled to slip out of her tights, Rochmann watched with some unease as her pubic area emerged. Gray hair? No, black, like her eyebrows. And armpits.

She scooted back against the armrest of the sofa opposite him and, with her feline stare daring him to watch, put one foot on the floor and stretched her other leg along the back of the sofa. Then she reached down and, well, 'naked' did not describe her; more like inside-out. With her other hand, she pulled his face down between her legs and began to ride his tongue, sighing and whimpering and Oh Godding. Mister Lucky was now fully recovered and Rochmann climbed astride her. Nina shrieked as if injured, then wrapped her legs around him and commenced to buck and grind her pubic bone against his, flinging her arms back over the edge of the sofa.

Later, they reclined in an island of soft, colored light from a Tiffany lamp. Darkness from the windows filled the room as the sun had earlier.

Nina sat up and opened an enameled metal box on a low table beside the sofa. She withdrew a package of Zig-Zag rolling papers and a plastic baggie of marijuana, talking as she expertly rolled a joint, repeating her previous offer. "I'll do anything you like, whatever fantasy you have, anything." The tip of her tongue traced the edge of the rolling paper in a meaningful way. "But not any time."

She lit the joint with a cheap plastic lighter, inhaled deeply, and sat back contentedly, sinking into the buttery cushions. Exhaling noisily, she offered the cigarette to Rochmann. He declined with a slight shake of his head. Nina reacted only with a brief flicker of one black eyebrow, then took another hit. In between drags, she proceeded to lay out the ground rules with no pretense of, 'Will I see you again?'

"Marv travels a lot and when he's gone, you can visit here. You can spend the night if you want, but I won't sleep with you. I'm used to sleeping alone and I don't want to disrupt that habit. When Marv's home, well, arrangements can be made."

Rochmann wondered if she were sneaking behind Marv's back or if they had an agreement, like he'd heard about some married couples. The way she had hooked and reeled him in suggested she was experienced in this sort of thing. Did she take on a new guy every year? Did she have a stable of studs that he was joining? Despite their recent intimacy, it seemed impolite to ask. And thinking about other men was decidedly unpleasant.

Nina was still talking. "You can call here any time. Marv never answers the phone or even listens to the machine. He has a service for his professional calls and relies on me for anything else that might come up. Would it be okay for me to call you?"

"Of course," he said.

# Chapter 4: Honey, I'm Home

A light tapping sounded on Rochmann's half-open office door. "Come in," he called.

Susan Koenig entered, a tentative smile on her bright red lips. The room suddenly smelled as if it had been sprayed with citrus air-freshener. She and Rochmann had not spoken much since the faculty reception a few weeks earlier. The chair beside his desk was filled with stacks of student papers so he pointed at the Victorian-style, red velvet fainting couch against the wall and nodded for her to sit down.

He had inherited the office from old Professor Hirtz, a Freudian who had used the couch for research on free-association. Rochmann was a behaviorist and had no use for it, but liked its antique shape. The Psychology Department employed a zoological strategy in selecting faculty, hiring individuals of various psychologist species. A half-century after the hey-day of psychoanalysis, Herr Professor Hirtz had finally retired, making room for someone from the modern era. Rochmann taught courses in learning and behavior analysis. Susan was the specimen for survey research and statistics. She sat primly on the edge of the couch, her knees pressed together under the canvas tent that was her skirt.

Rochmann put on a congenial expression. "How're you doing?"

"Fine, thank you," she said. "I wanted to talk about Psych 101. I thought since we each teach a section of Intro, it might be a good idea to get together and compare notes."

As junior faculty, it was their lot to teach the introductory course. Rochmann had served time as a teaching assistant in grad school, and had taught Intro in the community college, so this course was a breeze. Susan, he knew, had been a researcher and had less classroom experience.

"Sure," he said. He opened the bottom drawer of his desk and pulled out a thick folder. "Be glad to show you what I'm doing. I've divided the course into units..."

"Ah, just a minute," Susan interrupted. "I don't mean right this second. I just thought, you know, maybe sometime after work we could, ah, talk about classes and things."

"Hmm," he replied, and looked at his watch thoughtfully, as if it controlled his time allocation. "Usually don't have a lot of time after I get done here. I'm pretty heavily scheduled, trying to fit everything in."

For a moment she looked disappointed. "I know how it is. I'm real busy too, writing up my dissertation for publication, trying to find research grant money. I just thought it'd be a good idea to, you know, see how our sections are coming along. I, ah, also was wondering what research you're doing. You know, just kind of see how things are going, in general. How you're adjusting to life in this little town."

Research--the only research he was doing was how to lift more weight. Westerville University was little more than a liberal arts college with a few Master's degree programs tacked on. The absence of publish or perish pressure left him time to train. But her 'life in this little town' remark suggested she had more than academics in mind.

"Yeah. That's a good idea. Um, it's just that right now, with all these new course preps..." His voice trailed off.

"Come on, Robert. You could use a break from course preps. I need a break, too. How about coffee or a drink after work on Friday?"

No ambiguity there. He looked at her closely. On the binary Fuckability Meter, the needle was dead center: if he were deprived enough, it might tick over to the 'yes' side of the scale. But at the moment, thanks to Nina, Susan was definitely a 'no.'

"Susan, it's not only classes. I don't know if you know this, but I'm training for the Olympics next year and have a very heavy workout schedule--after classes every day and on weekends too. I'd be happy to talk about Intro over lunch sometime, but I really don't have time otherwise."

She stood. Her expression was hard to read. "Well, I admire your dedication," she said. "I'll check my schedule and see about lunch. Good luck with your training."

The lemony cloud remained after she left. Susan was a perfectly nice woman his own age with whom he could have, perhaps, a sensible relationship. But no, he had to sneak around with a married woman, a former flower child who made peace and love her life work.  Even if Nina had him on this intermittent schedule, it was worth the wait.  Nina went to the City a lot of the time, doing the art scene and God knew what else.  Probably the Yankees.  With her, it was feast or famine.  But Lord, those feasts.

***

That evening, after workout, Rochmann noticed how short the autumn days had become.  It was not yet seven o'clock but seemed as dark and still as midnight.  He unlocked the back door to the small house he was renting in the student ghetto and snapped on the kitchen light.  Its radiance stopped abruptly at the living room entryway that loomed like a black rectangle, the darkness beyond almost palpable.  The house felt empty.  Of course it was empty; he lived alone.  But the feeling of emptiness was unusual.  "Honey, I'm home," he called.  His mocking voice echoed from the bare walls.  When he had roomed with Chappell, they'd been the perfect odd couple; he was Felix to Bill's Oscar.  Without Chappell to leave stuff lying around, the place was sterile.  Usually he took comfort in order and cleanliness, but tonight he would have welcomed someone's shoes under the kitchen table.  Perhaps he should get a cat.  Or a houseplant.

He took one of the dinners he'd previously prepared from the freezer compartment of the refrigerator, a square-foot pan of spinach lasagna, put it in the oven and turned on the timer.  He flipped on the lights in the rest of the house, banishing the darkness at least as far as the windowpanes.  In the bathroom, he dug his dank sweat clothes out of his workout bag and hung them over the shower rod to dry, oblivious to the odor of salt and ammonia.  In the spare bedroom that served as his study, he switched on his Apple IIe computer.  Selecting a floppy disk that contained the program he'd written to keep track of his progress, he clicked it into one of the drives and inserted a data disk into the other one.  While supper was heating, he entered the numbers that summed up his day:  sets, weights, reps for each exercise.  He called up the graphs and noted his progress--jagged amber lines on a dark screen.  He typed in the dosages of drugs he'd consumed: four aspirin and a Coca Cola before workout, thirty milligrams of Dianabol in three ten-milligram doses during the day.

'Feelings?' the screen prompted, the word blinking like a light atop a distant radio tower. Why had he added that to the program? His feelings always tracked his training: when his lifts improved, his mood was up; when lifts were down, so was he. A feeling of emptiness returned, an existential moment. He thought of Susan in his office that afternoon. Perhaps she had experienced an existential moment too, and tried to do something about it. It took guts to ask him out. Had he handled it badly? Why did he always think of sex? Well, it was only natural: he's a male, she's a female, the basic imperative of the species is sex. But they were homo *sapiens*; humans had an intellectual side in addition to the old grunt-and-grope. He and Susan could have a civilized, intellectual relationship. Ah, but the intellect is in the service of the grunt-and-grope; Freud and the sociobiologists were right on that score. What if Susan wanted to fuck? He was no stud but maybe offbeat women found him attractive. If Nina wanted his body, why not Susan? No, he'd made the right decision. He didn't need Susan to complicate his life.

He thought of Nina in her big house on the hillside and wondered if she and Marv still did it. She said she slept alone, so probably not. Or maybe they had one of those kinky relationships where they aroused each other with tales of their extramarital adventures. He could ask and Nina would tell him; she was amazingly candid about sex. Alarmingly so. Her suggestions of new activities and asking about his fantasies were sometimes intimidating. He could not tell her his fantasy--one of those nubile coeds in the weight room. Or someone to eat dinner with tonight, ask how his day had gone, listen to a jazz album, cuddle up with him in bed.

'Feelings?' the cursor still blinked. He typed in '0,' a tidy way to summarize his existential twinge, and it corresponded to the plateau in his training. Perhaps, like Susan, he needed a change in routine. He decided to print out the graphs and mail them to Chappell. Maybe Bill had come across some secret Bulgarian training method or a new twist in anabolics that could boost his progress. Rochmann was due for a check-up anyway. The lab would examine his bodily fluids and send the results to Bill to see if his liver was rotting or his balls shriveling or whatever other side effects the steroids might have.

The oven timer dinged. He waited while the dot-matrix printer clicked and buzzed, the tractor-feed churning out the trend lines of his life. He ejected the disks and put them into their case, shut off the computer, turned off the lights, and headed toward the yellow glow from the kitchen. If there was an emptiness inside, lasagna would have to fill it.

# PART II

# SEX

# Chapter 5: No Sex

A description of Soviet training methods in a weightlifting article that Chappell sent him, told how lifters got a massage after every workout. Rochmann looked up 'massage' in the Westerville yellow pages and found a single listing for the Oriental Massage Parlor. A phone call yielded only a recording, stating the hours it was open, so he drove out to take a look. The address was in a run-down strip mall on the edge of town. He parked in front of a laundromat, some distance from the parlor, on the remote chance that someone from the university might recognize his old Scout. Through the window he could see people waiting while the machines churned their clothes. He strolled up the covered walkway, glancing into shop windows as though to hide his intentions from anyone watching him. The few passersby seemed totally disinterested.

*Oriental Massage Parlor* in red neon script shone in the slit of a window set in a cinderblock façade, painted glossy red. Rochmann hesitated. What if he met someone from the university in the waiting room? Chuckling at the thought--it would be like two Baptists encountering each other in a bar--he pushed open the door. Three black vinyl armchairs sat empty on a floor of black and white tiles in a checkerboard pattern. The walls were painted red below and white above, with several framed drawings of tiny people cavorting in a landscape of conical mountains and flowering trees--nothing explicitly pornographic but you could tell what they were up to.

He walked up to a chest-high bamboo counter that stood along the back wall, behind which was a doorway hung with strands of red beads that formed a curtain. Within a few seconds, a girlish-looking Asian woman emerged. She was barely five feet tall, slender, clad in a short red silk robe tied with a sash. Her legs were bare and she shuffled in flip-flops much too large for her tiny feet. She had a round face with a small button nose and bright black eyes, framed by long, black hair that hung to her shoulders. She smiled brightly and said, "You like massage?"

"Ah, yeah. Can I get a back massage? How much does it cost?" He emphasized the word, 'back.'

She pointed to a hand-lettered sign taped to the countertop that stated:  WARM  OIL--$20,  TOTAL  BODY--$30,  SHOWER--$40, TWO  GIRL--$50,  CASH  ONLY  NO  CHECK  NO  CARD.  She looked up in a very friendly way. "I only work today. No two girl."

"Look," he said, "do you do regular massage, for the muscles? No sex.  Can I just get a massage, for my back?  I don't need any touching of my, ah, private parts."

The smile left her face.  She looked at him curiously, a slight wrinkle between her painted eyebrows. "I be right back," she said.

The beaded strands of the curtain swayed and clicked as she disappeared, and the muffled rise and fall of two women talking rapidly in an exotic language could be heard.  Then an older woman, dressed in a long-sleeved white blouse and black trousers, bustled through the beads.  She was even shorter than the first, heavier, her gray-streaked hair pulled back in a tight bun, but with the same round face.  The girl stood behind her.

"What you want?" she demanded.  Her tone was accusing, as if he'd asked to corn-hole her daughter.

"Uh, a back massage.  For sore muscles," he stammered, patting his shoulder. "I'm an athlete.  Very sore muscles." He flexed his arm and pointed to the biceps. "My back and shoulders are very tired." He rubbed his lower back with both hands, then held them up and made wiggling motions with his fingers.

"Ahh, athlete," the older woman said.  Her face relaxed. "You want muscle rub.  I do that.  Girls not know how.  I can fix muscle good."

"Good," he said. "How much do you charge?"

"Total body."  She pointed to the chart. "Thirty dollar, total body.  You feel good."

"That's a lot of money," he replied. "I don't need any, ah, you know, sexual touching."

The older woman pursed her lips, but her eyes remained soft. "Okay, twenty dollar," she said. "You let girl watch.  I teach her."

"Alright," he said, "it's a deal."

"You pay first. Twenty dollar."

She locked the money in a drawer beneath the counter and said, "You come through here."

Behind the beaded curtain was a hallway lined with cheap paneling and four plain wooden doors. The woman led the way to the last door, the girl's flip-flops flapping behind him. She entered the room and turned on a table lamp, its shade draped with a red gauzy cloth. "You take off clothes and lie down on stomach. Leave underwear on," she said, then turned and brushed past him.

The cubicle was paneled in the same wood grain as the hall and was furnished with an old medical examining table draped in a white sheet. A small metal table stood in the corner, on top of which was the lamp, and on a shelf below were many bottles containing oily liquids. There was a four-legged stool and a metal folding-chair with some white towels stacked neatly on its seat. A large No Smoking sign hung on the wall, along with several brass hooks. He took off his clothes and hung them on the hooks, taking care to place his wallet in the toe of one shoe and stuff the remaining space with a sock. He placed his keys in the other shoe and filled it with the other sock. Then he lay face down on the table and waited.

The older woman proved expert in working into quiescence the sinews, joints, and muscles of his back, arms, and legs. She seemed to enjoy the activity as well, exclaiming over the thick slabs of muscle, sometimes in English, sometimes in her own language. In that language she instructed the younger woman, whose softer, more delicate touch was not as effective. Rochmann would tell her, "Harder," and she stood on tiptoes, attempting to bear down with all her slight weight.

He visited about once a week. A daily massage, like the Soviet lifters enjoyed, did not fit his tight budget and limited time schedule. But with these regular visits, the staff became quite congenial. The older woman was called Mrs. Ang, the girl he met the first day was Mai, and a second girl was introduced, incongruously, as Julie. Perhaps her parents had been impressed by the star of *The Sound of Music*, or perhaps it was really Zhu-Li. She was taller than the other two women, with a more oval face and aquiline nose. He introduced himself as 'Rocky.' Both girls became quite proficient at the 'muscle rub' but he preferred the ministrations of Mrs. Ang. The girls in their silken, loosely-tied robes, with their silken, shapely legs, distracted him from becoming as deeply relaxed as he could with the older woman. They dutifully kept their hands where Mrs. Ang had taught them, but still their touch was sensual and he could imagine what other performances they were skilled at. His liaison with Nina saved him from compromising their 'muscle rub' relationship, and he was comforted by the thought that he did not have to pay for sex.

As fall quarter drew to a close, Rochmann had settled into a comfortable routine. Training was going well, classes were under control, Nina provided excellent diversion, and weekly massages were icing on the cake. Except for occasional lonely feelings, who could ask for more?

# Chapter 6:  Married, With Children

Rochmann spent Christmas holidays with Bill Chappell in New York City, doing little except eat and work out.  It was nice being with his old friend and he returned to Westerville with some reluctance.

The first day of winter quarter, he descended into the dimly lit stacks of the library in search of material for one of his courses.  Looking for a book on the topmost shelf, he shuffled backward on tiptoes, squinting to make out catalog numbers.  He stumbled over something, lurching backward into the opposite shelves and knocking several books to the floor.  A woman sat on the floor at his feet, mini-skirt hiked up across her thighs.  She must have been crouching down, looking for something on the bottom shelf.

"Whoa, I'm sorry!"  He extended his hand to help her up but pulled with too much force.  They staggered like drunks on an icy street and both burst out laughing.  He quieted abruptly as her face and form came into focus.

Her eyes were iceberg blue; that was obvious even through the muted light and the round, red-framed glasses perched on the tip of her elegant nose.  "I'm okay," she said.  Her hair was the color of Chardonnay, pale gold gleaming in a crystal goblet on a white linen tablecloth.  It was pulled back tightly into a chignon, like a ballerina, pushing the features of her face into the foreground, with glinting gold hoop earrings setting off her pale skin.  She was saying something.  "Damn library!  I can never find anything here.  You wouldn't have any idea where the *Journal of Child Psychopathology* is, would you?"

"What?"  His eyes reluctantly deferred to his ears.

"The *Journal of Child Psychopathology*.  Would you know where they keep it?  I can't find it anywhere."

"I don't think the library carries it.  Are you on the faculty?  You can put in a request.  Not that you'll get it, but they like to document faculty needs."

"I'm a grad student.  In Speech Pathology.  I need to find this article for my thesis."

"Grad students don't count," he said with a chuckle. "But you know, I bet Sam Golding has that one."

"Who?"

She looked like a fashion model, tall and willowy. Her severe hairdo and glasses seemed like a disguise. He could imagine her in a movie, Marian the Librarian, pulling off her glasses and shaking loose her long, golden tresses.

"Who did you say?" she repeated.

"Ah--Sam Golding. Dr. Golding. He's professor of child psych. In the Psych Department. I'm on the faculty there, too. This library is so lousy we have to subscribe to most of the specialty journals ourselves. I'm pretty sure Golding gets that one." He smiled, looking up at her, and she smiled down at him. Usually he was content with his short stature--less distance to move the weight--but at that moment he would have given a million dollars to be a foot taller.

Her name was Gretchen Norstrand. Rochmann said he'd check with his colleague to see if he had the journal issue she needed and she agreed to call his office in the morning. When she left, the stacks seemed even darker. Unable to recall what he'd been looking for, Rochmann headed for the gym.

\*\*\*

That evening, he called Sam Golding at home. Golding was also an assistant professor, only a couple years older than Rochmann, but he seemed much farther down the turnpike of time: balding, paunchy, and worried about tenure. He had three kids and his wife was a graduate student in political science or something at SUNY-Albany. She had delayed her studies to work while he completed his Ph.D. and now it was his turn to support her.

Golding's wife answered the phone with a harried tone, sounds of a child crying in the background. Rochmann had met her a few times, Hannah somebody, not Golding. Sam once had confided that they'd gotten into a big argument before their wedding when he had refused to hyphenate his last name with hers. If her mother had not threatened suicide, Hannah would have called the whole thing off.

Finally, they agreed to each keep their own last names and to hyphenate the children's names--'something-Golding.' Rochmann asked what if their kids married people who also had hyphenated names and they did the same with their kids: 'something-something-something-Golding.' And then the next generation, his great-grandkids, would never make it out of first grade because they couldn't learn to write their names. In a few generations, their offspring would have to carry stacks of computer printouts with them just to keep track of their last names. After a few beers, the observation had seemed hilarious.

Sam came on the line and Rochmann asked if he subscribed to the *Journal of Child Psychopathology.*

"Yeah, I get it. You taking up a new area or conducting a poll?"

"No, I met this grad student who was looking for it in the library. A Viking goddess, Sam, gorgeous! I told her there was this incredibly sexy, knowledgeable guy who would be happy to help her out in any way possible. Are you going to be in tomorrow afternoon? She really wants to meet you."

"Christ, I have to take Sarah to the doctor. We've got keys to each other's office, remember? Whyn't you just get it for her yourself?"

Between classes and kids, Golding was hard-pressed to have any life of his own. He sometimes invited Rochmann over to watch 'the game' on television when Hannah was out of town and he was babysitting. Rochmann visited more out of pity than any affinity for sports involving sticks or balls. They talked guy stuff--cars, politics, hot-looking girls in their classes. Golding was a classic classroom lecher, going on and on about the way some coed crossed her legs with a panty flash or another brushed her tit against him in a crowded hallway. He fantasized about sex with a campus cutie, despite the Conduct Code. The forbidden fruit aspect seemed to inflame him and Rochmann liked to tease him by pointing out lovely specimens. Gretchen provided an opportunity to be especially cruel.

"I don't think you want to miss this one, Sam. Six feet tall. Blonde. This could be the one that ruins your life."

"Just a minute." Rochmann heard a muffled conversation. "Okay. Hannah can take the kid to the doctor. I can meet her at four but no later because I have to pick up Noah and Leah from daycare. This better be good."

\*\*\*

Gretchen called the next morning and Rochmann passed along the information on Golding's schedule. The following morning, he was grading quizzes when there was a quiet knock at his office door. He said, "Come in," and when he looked up was surprised to see Gretchen. Before he could speak, she placed a journal on his desk.

"Could you give this to Dr. Golding for me, please. I xeroxed the article I needed and wrote a little note thanking him."

"Sure thing. Glad to help. Will you need any more?"

"Well..." She spoke slowly, glanced over her shoulder, took a step closer and placed her hands on his desk, looking down, it seemed, from a great height. She wore black-rimmed glasses that matched her black and white ensemble. "I could use some more articles from that journal, but quite frankly, I don't feel comfortable asking Dr. Golding."

"Really? Golding's a pretty helpful guy. I'm sure he'd be glad to lend them to you."

"It's not that. It's, I don't know, like he just kind of kept staring at me. It was creepy."

The poor bastard's fantasies must have gotten out of hand. Rochmann had to hear more. "Really?" he said again, with a concerned tone, squaring up the stack of papers on his desktop to emphasize that he was not staring. "Golding's kind of an intense guy, always looks right at you."

"I guess so," she replied. "But he wasn't staring me in the eye, if you know what I mean. He said he'd like to talk with me about my project. Over lunch or after class sometime. I can't get the time of day from my major professor. Why'd he want to talk to someone who's not even in his department? I felt like he was coming on to me." She stopped suddenly and looked startled, as if surprised by her own words. "I shouldn't be saying this to you. Like you're his friend and all."

"No, that's quite all right." This was great. He could hardly wait to rub Golding's nose in it. Rochmann gave her a reassuring nod. "Do you want me to say something to him? If Golding is," he paused, searching for the right word, "*intimidating* students, he should correct that, both for the students' sake and his own," another pause, "professional standing. You know there's rules against harassment in the Campus Conduct Code. Did he say or do anything that was, you know, inappropriate?"

"Oh no, nothing like that. It was just his look. It's hard to explain. It's no big thing. I'd just prefer not to deal with him. But he does seem to be the only one on campus who subscribes to that journal and I might need to use some more of them. What do you think? Am I being silly?"

"No, I think you're right to trust your feelings," he replied, repeating some psych-speak from a course in counseling he'd once taken. "Look, how about if you need any more articles, you let me know and I'll borrow them for you. Sam and I borrow journals back and forth all the time."

"That'd be great." She turned up the wattage of her big, bright smile. "If it's not too much trouble."

"How could it be trouble?" He smiled back. "Just give me a call or drop a note in campus mail."

"Thanks so much." And she was gone.

At noon, Rochmann ran into Golding in the hall. "Man, what'd you do to Miss Norstrand, you icky man?" He gave a big leering grin.

"What? Did you see her? What do you mean?"

"She stopped by to return your journal. Said you assaulted her with your eyes."

"What? That's, that's ridiculous! C'mon, you're joking!" There was a guilty note in Golding's voice.

"Yeah, I'm kidding, you old fart." Rochmann laughed. "Though apparently, you did slip in your own drool. She said she was 'uncomfortable' at how you stared at her. And asking her out on a date."

"That's not what happened," Golding protested. "What else did she say?"

Rochmann said, "We can't stand here yakking. I'm going to lunch. Come along and I'll fill you in."

"I just got here. Well, okay. I got to hear about this."

They walked out of the building and across the quadrangle to the faculty parking lot. The sky was overcast with thick clouds and a cold wind blew vortices of brown leaves and scraps of paper in the dry and silent fountain at the center of the Quad. Rochmann led the way to his Scout; its horizontal surfaces shone a pale, shiny green, the color of lima beans, but its flanks were scarred with blisters of red-brown rust.

"Nice car," Golding said.

"Gets me where I'm going. Get in; door's not locked."

"Where we going?"

"My house. Lunch is cheap there." Rochmann backed out of the space and entered the stream of traffic.

"So, what'd this bitch say?" Golding started right in. "I mean I make this special effort to do her a favor and she complains about me? I waited and waited, was late picking up the kids, too. Are you serious? She actually said I stared at her. Well, Christ, what's she expect? She looks like a goddamn *Cosmo* model--she should be used to being stared at. Not that I stared. I mean I looked at her, you got to look at people when you talk to them, right? And she's wearing these bright red tights, these long, long legs, and a little black skirt. Bright red stockings, and those big bazoombas, and you're not supposed to look? Gimme a break."

Rochmann let him ramble on without interrupting. He drove up his steep driveway and led the way through the back porch into the kitchen.

Golding was still talking. "I mean I tried to be nice, tried to take an interest in what she's doing, be helpful. Shit, they complain about professors not taking an interest in students. I didn't have to lend her anything, didn't have to talk to her, didn't have to consider her in any way."

Rochmann pulled out a chair from the kitchen table and said, "Take a load off. I'm making sandwiches, grilled cheese and onion. Want one or two?"

"Just one. No onions. Makes my breath smell."

"Now, isn't that considerate?" Rochmann said in a teasing voice. "Here's a professor who's so concerned about his students that he avoids onions so he won't offend them--when he sticks his tongue down their throat! Cheddar or muenster?"

"I don't care. Cheddar. You're a prick, Rochmann. You know I never touched her, never even came near her. God, looking at people the wrong way--the Vision Police will be after me. Orwell was right. Well it is almost 1984. Yeah, give me some onions."

"That's the spirit. Fuck the Olfactory Police! Live dangerously." Rochmann laughed. He put four cheddar and onion on rye bread sandwiches in a large cast-iron frying pan sizzling on the stove, set a bowl of apples on the table, grabbed one, rubbed it on his sleeve, and spoke between bites. "You know, Sam, think about her history for a minute. Here's this beautiful girl who's probably been looked at, stared at, all her life."

"Yeah, and she loves every minute of it, except if I do it."

"Sometimes she does, no doubt, sometimes she probably really gets off on it. Pretty girls use their looks to control guys, hell, to control women too. It's how they make their way in the world. But sometimes things might get out of control. You don't know, maybe you look like her funny Uncle Louie who used to grab her at the family picnic. Maybe her English professor pawed her when she was a freshman. You just don't know. It wasn't you, Sam, it was the situation--and her history." He turned the sandwiches over in the frying pan.

"Jesus, Rochmann, what're you, a psychologist? No, you're probably right. I certainly didn't do anything," he paused, "wrong. You know, I said that she could come talk to me about autism--that's what her paper's on. But I didn't stare at her tits or anything. Christ, they like reach out and grab you. I just tried to, ah, talk to her, like a helpful professor."

"Yeah, you and I both know you're a married, shot-your-wad, has-been who wouldn't hurt a fly, much less unzip yours. But the point is, she's scared of you. Probably senses your testosterone level. Us short guys are less threatening. If it's okay with you, I'll be a go-between for her and your journals. I'm sure she'll be friendlier with a little more time. You want some orange juice?" He set a plate with one sandwich in front of Golding and placed the frying pan with the other three on a trivet across the table from him.

Golding said, "Yeah, you're all heart, Rochmann. Sure, she can borrow my journals. Just let her know what a generous, good-hearted guy I am. Shorty," he added. "Only three sandwiches? That's a light lunch, you muscle-bound eunuch. Yeah I'll have a glass of ojay."

# Chapter 7: Just a Geek

G retchen telephoned to ask about another article and Rochmann told her he'd leave the journal she wanted with the Psych Department secretary to pick up when she got the chance. It would be nice to see her but he didn't want to seem like another slobbering schmuck. A classic approach-avoidance conflict: like a rat in a maze, hanging on the periphery of desire.

He retrieved the volume from Golding's office and noticed the article she requested was a review of psychoanalytic theories of autism. He jotted a note, 'What do you want to read this voodoo for?' and paper-clipped it to the cover. On his way to lunch, he stopped by the secretary's desk.

"Sydney, this journal is for a grad student in speech path. She'll be by this afternoon to pick it up."

"I'll see that she gets it." Sydney stood buttoning a long gray coat and pulling on matching leather gloves. She was a well-groomed woman in her fifties, with tightly curled salt-and-pepper hair, and eyeglass frames a little on the ornate side of fashionable. Her desk was the web of all activity that transpired in the Psychology Department and she the quietly competent spider at the center.

He noticed Susan, waiting for Sydney to get her things together. "How're you doing, Susan?" he asked in a friendly tone.

"Just fine, thank you," she said with all the warmth of a tax assessor.

\*\*\*

The next morning, Gretchen phoned again. "What do you mean by voodoo?" By the end of their conversation, she asked if she could borrow Rochmann's journals that had articles on the behavioral treatment of autism.

She arrived at his office late in the afternoon as he was putting his weekend homework in his briefcase. He picked up a stapled sheaf of purple-inked mimeographed paper and handed it to her. "Here's a reading list on language learning that I dug out of my files. It's from my prelims, so it's a few years out of date, but most of the classic work of Lovaas' treatment of autism treatment is listed."

"This is really nice of you," she said. "I'm lucky to catch you in. Not many professors are around on Friday afternoons."

He wavered. It was true. Except for Sydney, everyone had gone. He could stand close as they looked for the volumes on his shelves, their hands could touch as they examined the contents of a journal. He could be a little late for workout. He even could skip it for once. He thought of Golding.

"Ah, well, to be honest, I was just leaving. I've got an appointment. But tell you what. My journals are on these shelves over here." He waved a hand in their direction. "You pick out what you need and leave a list of what you take on my desk. I'll tell Sydney that you're here and she can lock up when you're done." If Golding's eagerness affronted her, he could be cool. He would call Nina to see if she was back in town.

***

On Monday, Gretchen popped into Rochmann's office just before noon. There had been a light snow over the weekend and the day was bright and clear, but very cold. She knocked lightly, walked in, and seemed surprised to see him with his jacket on. She wore a bright, multi-colored ski jacket and white, fur-topped boots. "Hi. I always catch you leaving. Just wanted to return these." She held up her briefcase. "Better bundle up good; it's really frigid out there." She did a foot-warming stomp for emphasis.

"Yeah. I'm on a pretty tight schedule. Should've brought my lunch today, but I didn't so I have to go out to eat." He paused a beat. "Wanna come with? Talk about what you read? Student Union cafeteria?" He certainly wasn't going to invite her to his house.

"Uh, okay. I did want to ask you about some of this stuff. Would that be okay? I don't want to ruin your lunch."

Ruin his lunch? This would make his day. Walking down the hall, she launched into an animated description of one of the procedures she had read about. On the stairs, they passed Golding.

Engrossed in her talk, she seemed not to notice him. But Rochmann grinned and winked.

Going down the outside steps, Gretchen slipped on a small patch of ice and he quickly grabbed her arm to steady her. "Oops! Thanks," she said. "We seem to do a lot of falling."

He released her arm. "Yeah." He struggled to think of something more to say. "What'd one autistic kid say to the other autistic kid?" His voice hung in frosty clouds.

"Huh?"

"What'd one autistic kid say to the other autistic kid?"

"What d'you mean? I don't know." She looked at him as though he'd asked her an exam question.

"Nothing. They don't communicate." He gave a weak chuckle.

"Nothing? Oh, it's a joke. Nothing. Oh, that's awful."

"There's worse. Knock knock."

"Oh God. Who's there?"

"Autistic."

"Autistic who?"

"Autistic who?" he repeated.

"Autistic who?" she said slowly.

"Autistic who?" he mimicked her.

"Oh God. I get it. Echolalia. You're terrible." She swatted at him playfully with her briefcase. "Where'd you hear those? D'you know any more?"

"Just made 'em up." He pushed open the door of the Union and held it for her.

"I just want some coffee," she said. Rochmann led the way to the sandwich shop and ordered a large Philly cheese steak, a slice of chocolate cheesecake, a bottle of celery soda, and coffee. They found a booth in a back corner. "Ooh, that cheesecake looks good," she said as he placed the tray on the table.

"Help yourself." He pushed it toward her.

"Oh no. I can't eat that," she protested. "Well, maybe just a little bite, with my coffee." She cut off a corner of the cake with a plastic spoon.

"Well, I guess you have some questions about Lovaas," he said, taking a bite of sandwich. "Fire away." He ended up giving a mini-lecture about learning principles and how they are related to teaching language to autistic children.

"I guess I should've taken your class," she said as Rochmann finished the cheesecake. "I had an undergraduate psych course on learning. Rats and stuff, but I didn't see how it was related to people, especially autistic children. The way you describe it, it makes sense. I guess I need to do more reading on it."

"I can recommend some books. Loan you some in fact--on human learning and special populations. Come back to the office after lunch and I'll load you up."

\*\*\*

That night, around ten, Rochmann's phone rang. It was, of course, Golding. "You putz! I saw you two. Where'd you go? A little private tutorial? And she's in your office like she owns it. Some go-between you are. I know what you're going between."

"Hey, hey, you dirty old man. Calm down. You had your chance and you blew it. This is strictly professional."

Golding got in a few more jabs but Rochmann only half-listened. He really should thank Golding for showing what not to do. He'd just be Not-Sam and see what developed. Not that he had a plan for developing anything. The game with Golding was fun, as was imagining Gretchen's body beneath her stylish clothes. She was enjoyable to talk with, so attentive and appreciative. But the next step, the possibility of there being a next step, was a void.

\*\*\*

That same evening, Gretchen was discussing Rochmann with her apartment-mate, Latasha Williams, also a graduate student in speech pathology. A vivacious, dark-skinned African-American, from a working-class family in New Jersey, Latasha seemed an unlikely comrade for the blond, willowy debutante from Westchester County.

Yet they had become quite close while rooming together over the past two years.

"This Dr. Rochmann is really nice," Gretchen told her.

"Yeah, I know who you mean," Latasha replied. "I took a psych course from him last quarter, remember? He loaded all these assignments on us, this due on a particular date and that due on another date and so many points if you get it in on time. Always adding up these points to make your grade. Couldn't let anything slide. But it was fair, you knew what you had to do. Yeah, he was all right. Made these dumb jokes that nobody understood."

"I know," Gretchen said with a chuckle, recalling the autism gags. "He seems, I don't know, pretty mellow. I mean he's real busy and stuff, but not frantic about it. Like Dr. Schmidlap, my thesis chairman. She's always rushing around, no time for anything, blowing off appointments."

"Yeah, I'm glad I don't have to deal with her any more." Latasha had finished her thesis and was preparing to graduate at the end of winter quarter. "So this Rochmann, he's a real short dude, right. And he wears these funky clothes."

"Yeah, but he's kinda cute. He's sort of stocky, like a miniature football player."

"I remember he had this huge butt. He's got a black man's ass." Latasha broke up giggling.

"Really? I'll have to check it out next time I see him." Gretchen joined the giggling.

A week later, after another lunch with Rochmann at the Student Union, Gretchen reported back. "You're right about his butt; it sticks out like a shelf. He always seems in a hurry to leave. I wonder where he rushes off to on Fridays. You think he has a girlfriend?"

Latasha was getting dressed to go out with her boyfriend, an English major named LaShawn. There were no male graduate students in Speech Pathology. "Poor girl. You're in a bad way, thinking about some shorty professor's butt. What're you going to do this evening?"

"Oh, the usual. Popcorn and a video. I'll give Carl a call and see how he's doing." Gretchen had been dating Carl since they were sophomores at SUNY-Albany. Tall and handsome, he now was a law student at Columbia. She occasionally went down to the City to spend a weekend with him, but he was inordinately occupied and even when she was there he spent most of his time studying. He was, like her, from a good family, knew about wine and the theater, played tennis and golf. Once he got out from under his studies he would probably make a good husband, though they had no specific plans.

Gretchen fixed a salad and was plopped down in front of the TV, wrapped in a large flannel robe and big fluffy slippers, when Latasha emerged from her bedroom.

"You're throwin' your life away, girl," Latasha said, putting on her coat and gloves. "You think Carl's sitting home every Friday night, eating popcorn? You know how men are. You should get that shorty professor to take you out. Well, don't wait up. See you tomorrow."

\*\*\*

Rochmann had arranged to meet Nina on Sunday, his day off from training. She often visited the antique and craft shops that dotted the surrounding countryside. When Marv was in town, this provided a convenient way to get together. Rochmann would rent a cabin in one of the little rundown motels on the edge of some village and they'd rendezvous at a prearranged shop. The clandestine arrangements and seedy rooms made their couplings even more exciting. When they got together that Sunday afternoon, Rochmann could imagine Gretchen's long legs and large breasts; it probably added extra vigor to his performance.

They languished on the hard-sprung bed, pillows and blankets strewn about. The musk of sweaty sex hung in the air. "You're an animal," Nina said--perhaps a compliment, perhaps a subtle reminder that she was ready for more.

"Well, I had a good workout yesterday. Workouts always make me horny." He rolled over onto his stomach and stretched his arms above his head. "Give me a massage, would you please?"

"Yes sir!" she laughed. "Anything to promote good workouts." She straddled his buttocks, her pubic hair tickling his glutes, and pulled the blankets up over her shoulders to shield their naked bodies from the coolness of the room, making a pyramid of warmth while she pressed and plied the muscles of his shoulders and back.

"Wake up," she said gently. "It's getting late and I should get going soon."

"Huh? Was I sleeping?"

"Like a baby."

Late-afternoon sunshine filtered through the moisture condensed on the inside of the windows. He rolled to his back and sighed. "Wait a minute." Grabbing her hair, he thrust her face into his groin. She took Mister Lucky into her mouth and began her wonderful work. He stretched and sighed again, deeply inhaling the cool air. Squinting, the white hair undulating between his legs appeared blond in the golden light.

*** 

Friday lunches at the Union had become a regular meeting for Gretchen and Rochmann. She told him she had given a draft of her literature review chapter to her advisor but had no idea how long it would take to get a response from her. He offered to take a look at it but she demurred. "Maybe the next draft, after I've worked over Dr. Schmidlap's comments."

"Sure, whenever." He gazed dreamily at her hair, recalling Nina's head in his lap.

"What're you looking at?" She sat back abruptly and patted the top of her head. "Do I have something in my hair?"

"Uh, no. Was I staring? I'm sorry. My mind must've wandered off."

"Oh. What were you thinking?"

"Well, ah, just all the stuff I've got to do this weekend. Got a, you know, busy weekend."

"Oh really. What's happening? What keeps you so busy, anyway?" A personal question, uncharacteristically bold.

"Um, papers to grade and class preps. And workout. I have a big training day on Saturday. Household stuff--shopping, laundry. And my car. I have an old car that I work on and I need to change the oil. You know, there's always a zillion things."

"Yes, I know. A zillion things. Me too." She got up and began putting on her jacket. "We'd better get going on them." She walked out of the lunchroom with her arm in one sleeve of her jacket, struggling with the other sleeve.

***

"What a jerk!" she told Latasha that afternoon. "Here I am, talking about, you know, the weekend. Like, what's he doing? And he's thinking about his car! Change his oil! He might as well have said he had to wash his hair. He's either not saying anything because he has a girlfriend, or he's really a first-class geek."

"Maybe he's gay," Latasha observed. "You know a lot of those weightlifter guys are queer."

"What d'you mean? You mean he's one of those muscle-bound guys? He did say he works out."

"I was talking with LaShawn about him; he's got this friend that works out at the Health Center and he says Dr. Rochmann is in the weight room all the time. Shawn said he acts like he owns the place, like a wild man, crashing and throwing weights around. Some of the guys think he's a real asshole, like he's some big shot Mr. America or somebody. Shawn said a lot of the muscle guys are really, you know, fairies. His friend's not, but he knows some guys that are."

"That is too weird." Gretchen's voice was quiet, reflective "D'you really think he's gay? He doesn't look like a Mr. America. I guess he could have muscles under those baggy clothes, but he certainly doesn't show off. I thought he was just, you know, chunky. He's pretty laid back, not effeminate really, just, I don't know. No, he dresses way too sloppy to be gay. Gay guys are always, you know, really sharp. Latest fashion. No, I think he's just a geek."

"Whatever. All I know's that I'm going out. You should too, girl."

"Well, hell," Gretchen sighed. "I could drive down to the City and see Carl. The roads are clear. That's what I'll do, just drop in and surprise him. See you Monday."

# Chapter 8:  Rebel Without Effect

T wo weeks passed and Rochmann had not heard from Gretchen.  There was a knock on his office door and he looked up, expectantly.  Sam Golding walked in.  "Where's your friend?  I haven't seen the blonde goddess around lately," he said with a smug look.

"Golding, she's a student.  She turned in a draft and is waiting for feedback from Schmidlap.  She'll be around when she has more to talk about."

"Sure she will.  She picked your brain, gave you a cheap thrill, and checked out."

"Well, at least I had a brain to pick, and got a thrill.  That's more than I can say for you."

"Okay, Mr. Hot Stuff, tell you what.  I'll bet you a six-pack of imported beer that you don't score with her."

"Sam, I don't want to score with her.  She's a grad student and I only have a professional relationship with her."

Golding gave him a look like a traffic cop who's been told, 'Honestly, officer, I was just doing the speed limit.'  "Yeah, and I'm joining the Jesuits."  He stabbed a hairy forefinger at Rochmann.  "Listen, numb nuts, you date her one time and the six-pack's yours."

"Gosh, for a prize like that, I guess I'll have to go for it," Rochmann said in a mocking tone.

Golding waggled his eyebrows like Groucho Marx.  "Imported beer, any kind you want."  He turned and left the room.

It would be nice to shut Golding up.  It would be nice to run his hands over those long, shapely legs.  And it would surprise the hell out of Chappell, to come up with a girlfriend hotter than any of the chickies he dated.  And with brains to match.  Gretchen would contact him again, he was sure of it, even though she'd acted rather odd the last time they had lunch together.  But when he did see her again, he'd ask her.  Ask her what?  He hadn't asked a girl out, one-on-one, since high school.  His face warmed at the recollection, not of any specific incident but the general feeling of insecurity, of intruding where he wasn't welcome.  College had been another story, especially after he met Chappell: pairing off at parties, getting fixed up, women actually pursuing him. But to single one out from the herd, pursue her and take her down--that was new territory.

***

Walking across campus between classes, Rochmann caught sight of a familiar, brightly colored ski jacket, topped by long golden hair and a white furry cap. He maneuvered through the throng of students and caught up with her.

"Gretchen!" he called. She paused, turned, and gave a half smile, her eyes the color and temperature of an iceberg shadow.

"How've you been? Haven't seen you in a while." He smiled in his most engaging manner.

"Dr. Rochmann. Nice to see you." Her tone did not match her words. Her expression remained fixed and she resumed walking at a brisk pace.

He almost had to jog to keep up. "Gretchen, is something the matter? You seem upset. Did I do something wrong?"

She stopped and faced him. "No, you haven't done anything. Thanks for your concern but I really can't talk right now." Almost as an afterthought she added, "I've got an appointment with my advisor." She turned and strode rapidly away.

Back at his office, he typed a note on his computer: 'Dear Ms. Norstrand, I hope things went well on your thesis and that you did not run into difficulty concerning learning approaches to autism. I enjoyed working with you and would be glad to provide any further assistance. Sincerely yours.' He read it on the monitor, deleted the 'enjoyed working with you' phrase, then added it back, and printed it on the dot matrix printer. He tore off the perforated paper and signed, 'Robert' at the bottom, read it again, added 'Rochmann, Ph.D.' to the signature, and placed it in a campus mail envelope.

A couple days later, his office phone rang. "Hi, Dr. Rochmann, this is Gretchen." Her voice sounded its usual cheery tone. "Got your note. Sorry I was, uh, short with you the other day. Lots of stuff

53

going on. Dr. Schmidlap's not real happy with my first chapter but that's okay. I can deal with it."

"It's good to hear from you. I was concerned that I might've got you in trouble with the Lovaas stuff. I'd like to help, unless you think it'd get you in deeper. Want to have lunch Friday?"

\*\*\*

She arrived at the Union a half hour late, in a flurry of haste. She brought her draft chapter, bleeding red ink from Dr. Schmidlap's comments. After they'd finished eating, they spent a long time going over it. She concluded, "I think what I'll do is set up a list of specific points to compare the learning with the other approaches to autism," she concluded. "It's twice as much work as just handing her what she wants to hear, but I like that. I like shaking 'em up a little bit. It makes it more my own project."

"A bit of a rebel, eh?" He smiled at her. "Just don't be a rebel without effect."

"What? A rebel without a what?" Her forehead wrinkled above the blue glasses frames that matched her blue angora sweater.

"A rebel without effect. You've heard of a rebel without a cause? I've always considered myself a rebel without effect." He grinned at her puzzled look. "It's just a play on words. It's no big existential statement. I just like the way it sounds."

"Rebel without effect," she repeated. Her face was solemn. "Yeah, I like that. Are you a rebel?"

"Well, I'm certainly not a comedian if you take my jokes so seriously." He laughed, uncomfortable with her serious expression. "No, I don't think I'm a rebel. I just sort of march to a different drummer. How about you? Are you a rebel in other ways than your thesis?"

"No, I'm pretty conventional. I've always kind of gone along with the crowd. Only here, there's not much crowd to go along with. Grad school's a lot different than being an undergrad."

"Just wait. It only gets worse. Once you get out, there's no time for anything." This reminded Rochmann it was time to get to the weights. "Well," he said, in a getting-back-to-business tone, "you seem to have your thesis direction well under control. Was that what you were upset about the other day?"

She looked directly into his eyes. "No, not entirely. It's, there was, um, some personal stuff." She stopped.

"I'm sorry. Anything I can do? D'you want to talk about it? After all, I am a professional psychologist." He smiled to indicate irony.

She continued her steady gaze, her irises seeming to turn a deeper blue. "Well, maybe you can tell me why men are such jerks." She was not smiling.

"All men, or any one in particular?"

"All of 'em that I know, anyway." She pursed her lips and looked away. "Oh what the hell," she said, more to herself than to him. "I went down to visit my boyfriend a couple weeks ago. At Columbia. Surprise him. Well I surprised him alright. He had another woman in his apartment. Living there, practically. I mean, we weren't exactly engaged, but I thought we had an understanding. What a creep! I mean, are all men like that? Gotta have sex all the time? I mean I can understand, maybe, a one-night-stand, but she had, like, moved in. Closet full of clothes and everything. He must've had to clean out the place when he knew I was coming. Jesus! What a jerk!"

"Yeah, I can see that would be pretty upsetting." Rochmann could imagine Marv busting in on him and Nina.

"It's bad enough I don't have anyone to go out with here. Now I don't even have week-ends in the City to look forward to." She bit her lip and turned her face away, blinking back tears."

"I'm sorry," he said. "Being alone can be a bummer. I know."

They sat without speaking for a full minute. The lunchroom was almost empty; there was only an occasional clink of spoons in cups. Now's the time, you fool. He could see Golding's eyebrows waggling at him.

He said, "Look, Gretchen, I don't know how appropriate this is, but I've been wanting to ask you out for a long time." Once these words were out, more tumbled forth. "I just didn't want you to feel like I was exploiting the situation. You know, there are these rules about professors dating students. It's not the rules so much as what they're supposed to cover, you know, a student feeling she has to go out with a professor in order to get his attention. I'm enough of a rebel not to give a damn about the rules themselves, but, ah, they do point to a possible problem. I mean, I'm really glad to help you on your thesis and will continue to, if you want, even if you don't want to go out with me. There's no contingency there at all. But if you would like to have dinner some evening, or see a movie, or play Scrabble, whatever, I would like to do that with you. Maybe now is not a good time, you're upset about your boyfriend and all. But, well, there I've said it."

She smiled at him, not her big, toothpaste ad smile, but a small, pensive one. "That's really nice, Dr. Rochmann."

"Robert," he said. "Call me Robert." 'Rocky' was too intimate; Chappell called him that, and Nina. Maybe Gretchen would get to know 'Rocky,' but 'Robert' was enough for now.

"Robert," she repeated. "No, I don't feel like you're exploiting me. And I think now would be a good time to go out. I don't want to sit home this weekend and think about that creep and his roommate. So, if you won't get in trouble with the rules, yes, I'd like to go out with you."

"Great! How about dinner tomorrow evening? What's a good time for you? I'll pick you up, say, eight o'clock? Is that okay? What's your address? Do you like seafood? Or Chinese?"

She chuckled at his eagerness. "Sure, eight is fine. You pick the place. I just don't eat red meat. Here, I'll write down my address and home phone." She wrote on a corner of the legal pad on which she had been taking notes during their discussion, tore it off and handed it to him. "Well," she said, nodding with finality. "I've kept you long enough with my problems. Thanks for your help. See you tomorrow, then, Robert."

***

"Well, how was the date with the professor?" Latasha returned to the apartment on Sunday afternoon, full of questions. She had stayed around Saturday evening, like a concerned mother, to answer the door and talk with Rochmann while Gretchen was getting ready. "He's sure a short little dude. Don't you feel weird next to him?"

"Not really. Being tall used to bother me in high school but I guess I've grown up. Robert didn't seem to mind."

"So, what happened?" Latasha insisted.

"So, he's driving this clunky car. Like a little truck or jeep, really. The heater hardly works and my feet are like, freezing. But he's real proud of it. Two hundred thousand miles and it runs better than new, he says. I guess he works on it himself."

"Well, that matches his clothes. He dresses like a dork."

"Yeah, he told me about that. He is a weightlifter, like you said, and it's real hard to find clothes that fit. Like he can't wear a sport coat because to get one that fits his shoulders, it's too big around the middle. And pants, to get pants that fit around his legs--he didn't say anything about his butt--the waist is way too large. So he just wears sweaters and 'fat man's pants' he calls them." She giggled.

"So, I guess he's not queer. Otherwise, he'd get his clothes tailored to fit." Latasha joined the giggle.

"No, I'm sure he's not gay. He told me about weightlifters and 'physique-ohs' he calls them; they're not actually weightlifters. See, there's three different kinds. There's Olympic weightlifting--the overhead lifting like they do in the Olympics--that's what he does. Then there's 'powerlifting,' you know, like bench presses and stuff. And then there's bodybuilding, or physique-ohs; he doesn't like them at all. I told him how I was on the track team in high school and he said Olympic lifting is like the pole vault; it takes lots of strength and timing to move your body around the bar at just the right moment. And powerlifting is like the dash, pow, straight ahead. And bodybuilding, I asked him what that was like on the track team and he said that was like people standing around on their tippy toes showing off their calf muscles. It was so funny!" Gretchen laughed aloud at the recollection.

"That's funny?" Latasha did not seem impressed.

"Well, we'd had a bottle of wine. It was pretty funny at the time," Gretchen admitted.

"So you guys hit it off pretty good. You do the 'pole vault' with him?"

"You're awful!" Gretchen threw a couch cushion at her roommate." He was a perfect gentleman. Held my hand, gave me a sweet goodnight kiss. I don't know about the 'pole vault.' We'll see how it goes."

***

Mrs. Ang usually chatted with Rochmann while she plied and pounded his overworked flesh, asking what happened to produce a strain or spasm that he complained about.

"You not married?" she inquired one day.

"No, I'm not married," he replied. "Why?"

"You not like girls? You don't think my girls are pretty? Maybe you lift too much weights." She apparently had been thinking quite a bit about her unusual client.

"I like girls," he said. "I, um, have a girlfriend."

"You marry her soon?" Mrs. Ang asked.

"Uh, no. She's already married."

"You have girlfriend married lady? That not good." Her tone was scornful. Rochmann suppressed a smile at this moral judgment from a woman who ran, apparently, a small-scale brothel.

"It works for us," he replied.

"Not good," she repeated. "You should find pretty girl and get married."

Was she taking a maternal concern for his welfare? Or was she trying to make an arrangement for one of her wards? "I'll work on it," he said. One more reason not to dally with the girls; mama-san might be a matchmaker. Still, it was hit or miss with Nina's schedule. One dinner with Gretchen did not make her a 'girlfriend.' But maybe it would be nice to have a woman he could think of as his, someone he did not have to share.

# Chapter 9: Clean and Jerk

Rochmann was pleased to discover that Gretchen liked Woody Allen movies, ethnic restaurants, and physical fitness. Even better, she asked him to show her some exercises in the weight room; he agreed, on condition that she come to his house for dinner afterwards. They arranged to meet about an hour before his regular workout time on Saturday. Gretchen showed up, dressed in black tights and a *Hard Rock Cafe--New York* tee shirt knotted at the midriff. Her hair was done in braids twisted atop her head, emphasizing her elegant neck. Rochmann wore his usual baggy, faded sweatpants and a stained sweatshirt with sleeves cut off at the elbows. There were only a few other people in the room, and, miraculously, no boombox, so they could talk in normal tones.

"I need some exercises to firm up my bustline," Gretchen said with a trace of shyness. "I run and ski, and that's good for the legs, but I don't do anything for my upper body, and I'd like to have more, uh, support than just a running bra."

"Well, the breast, as you know, is made up of fatty and glandular tissue," Rochmann said in his lecture voice. "But you can build up the muscles under the breast--the pectoralis, or pecs." He looked in her eyes as he spoke, trying not to stare at the *Hard Rock Cafe*. "Building up muscle could decrease some of the fatty tissue as well as provide structural support."

"That's for me," she said, laughing. "So how do you build up the pecs?"

"Well, one basic exercise is called 'flys.' I'll show you." He demonstrated the motion and she followed suit, lying supine on a padded bench, her chest thrusting upward and her legs splayed apart. Her tee shirt tightened over the two large mounds that flattened as she lowered her arms on either side and grasped a small plate in each hand. "That's good," he said. "Bend your elbows just a little more. Bring the weights up, exhale, then inhale deeply as you lower the weights." He offered hints and counted as she repeated the motion, watching her with professional detachment, just as Nina had observed him that afternoon in her studio.

She did several sets of flys and other exercises as well: wide-grip benches and behind-the-neck pull-downs. In between her sets, he did his stretching routine. Time passed quickly. Embarrassment in referring to her 'bustline' disappeared as they talked about their bodies as things apart from themselves, a means to an end. Jock talk.

"Well, I think that about does it for you," he said. "Don't want to overdo it. You'll probably be a little sore tomorrow. I'd better get started with my stuff."

"What are you going to do?"

"I'll start with clean-and-jerks. Work up to a heavy double, maybe a single. After that, some auxiliary exercises." He ended lamely, realizing this probably made no sense to her.

" I'd really like to see what you do. If you don't mind me watching?"

"No, that'd be great. I just won't be able to talk to you much between sets; I have to really concentrate. It'll take a little while to warm up, so if you want to go run or ride a stationary bike or something. I'll be on the platform back there." He pointed to his domain, beyond the jungle of machines.

She left. Rochmann gathered his bumper plates together in the back of the room, inserted his earplugs--even though boomboxes were absent, earplugs had become part of his routine--and placed his Eleiko bar in the center of the platform. It was time to get serious.

He'd worked up to 110 kilos for three reps when he saw Gretchen standing across the room. He waved to her and pulled up a bench where she could sit, close to the platform but off to the side, out of his direct line of vision. Between sets, he sat on another bench to the rear of the platform where he closed his eyes and tried not to think of his audience.

He increased the barbell to 130 kilos, and made 15-kilo increments after that. As he walked up to the barbell at 160 kilos, he glanced in Gretchen's direction; she was not there. With a flash of disappointment, he unbuckled his belt and looked around the room, but she was nowhere to be seen. He stretched, rebuckled his belt, chalked his hands again, and gripped the bar. As he pulled the weight past his thighs it seemed slightly out of position, and when he squatted under it, he rocked forward and struggled to regain his balance. He stood easily, but the jerk went slightly to the front and he had to take a couple steps to recover it. He held the bar briefly, then let it fall with a clang. "Damn!" He had planned on two jerks with this weight. His schedule called for 170 and here he was struggling with 160. He cursed himself for altering his routine for some stupid woman. Well, when the going gets tough... He loaded 170 kilos on the bar, draped a towel around his traps to keep warm, sat down on his bench and closed his eyes to meditate, rehearsing the kinesthetic sequence of the lift.

He stood, letting the towel fall from his shoulders, buckled his belt, chalked his hands, and walked toward the barbell. He was determined not to look for Gretchen but spotted her out of the corner of his eye, sitting on the bench. She smiled and gave a small wave of her hand. He nodded acknowledgment but did not change his routine. The weight went up easily. Very easily. After he put it down he double-checked to make sure he'd loaded it correctly. Only then did he look right at her with a big grin and a thumbs up. She responded in kind.

He walked over to her. "Got time for one more?" She nodded and smiled with enthusiasm. He loaded the bar to 180 kilos, then, after a moment's hesitation, added the little one-and-a-quarter plates for 182.5 kilos, the metric equivalent of 400 pounds.

The *zone*. Athletes, musicians, performers of all kinds know about the zone, where every synapse synchronizes with the vibrations of the universe and a difficult feat is accomplished as smoothly and naturally as sunrise. Some never get there, some achieve it many times, but no one has the key. Practice of course, endless rehearsal, honing technique, building strength, readying oneself. And then sometimes, mysteriously, an extra element is added, a catalyst that transmutes sweat into gold. The magic ingredient has many names-- Lady Luck, alignment of the planets, biorhythm, desire--but answers to none. For Rochmann, that afternoon, in the weight room of the Westerville Health & Fitness Center, it might have been the watchful presence of a tall, blonde, graduate student in speech pathology.

The barbell seemed a living thing, the steel shaft flexing in his hands as he pulled it from the floor, the plates hesitating before beginning their ascent. The bar bowed downward on his clavicles as he squatted under it, then recoiled upward, almost pulling him to a standing position. One breath, two; he bent his knees and drove it aloft, skipped one foot forward, the other back, and dropped under it. He stood and held it overhead, the barbell quivering, his arms and back and legs as straight and still as sequoias.

The barbell hit the platform with a great crash and he rebounded upward, as though released from gravity. He was flying. "Yes!" he exulted. He vaulted to where Gretchen stood and gave her a big, sweaty hug. "That ties my personal record, the most since knee surgery! Man!" Words failed him. He took both her soft hands in his hard, chalky ones and squeezed. "Thank you, Gretchen. Los Angeles here I come!"

***

Afterwards, Rochmann skipped his usual visit to the massage parlor in order to get dinner started. He set to work, chopping vegetables and chicken breasts into bite-size pieces. He placed a large kettle of water on the stove to boil for rice, real rice, not the 'minute' variety, for its superior texture and nutrition. As an undergrad, he had begun cooking in order to cram in as much protein and vitamins as he could on a limited budget. He and Chappell ate cheaply and well. As a graduate student, he'd progressed to an interest in spices and flavors and the discovery that a tasty meal was a potent lure for women to visit their lair. Young women were sometimes likely to reward a male-cooked meal with sexual favors.

At the appointed time, seven o'clock, Gretchen had not arrived. Annoyed, he placed the bowls of chopped comestibles in the refrigerator, went into his study, turned on his Apple IIe, and entered his workout data. A half-hour passed quickly and the reminder of his personal record sent a wave of exhilaration over him. There was a knock at the front door and, when he opened it, Gretchen's appearance only heightened his mood. Dressed in her usual miniskirt and tights, her multi-color ski parka and fuzzy white tam, she beamed a radiant smile.

"I brought some wine," she said, handing him a bottle of Chardonnay, *Chatelain-Desjacques*, not the local New York stuff.

She watched with interest while he stir-fried the vegetables and chicken in the wok, adding them in sequence to cook them to just the right texture. He prepared a ginger-garlic sauce and she exclaimed over the aroma. The rice was sticky and soft, overcooked he explained, but she seemed not to notice the connection to her tardiness. German chocolate cake, not as good as his mother's, but pretty good for store-bought, topped off the meal. Rochmann was ravenous, eating twice the amount that she did, but still not feeling full. It was as if every sense had been amplified. The food was exceptionally tasty. Gretchen was magnificently beautiful. Vanilla-scented candles blended sublimely with her faint, sweet fragrance.

He talked expansively while they ate, about his training goals leading up to the first contest of the season later that spring. He was sure to do at least 185, maybe 190, and a 140 snatch. That would put him right on schedule for even more at the Olympic trials.

Rochmann rinsed and stacked the dirty dishes in the kitchen sink while she watched. After drying his hands, he took one of hers and led her into the living room. "Do you like jazz? I've got a lot of classics: Miles Davis, Weather Report, Stanley Turrentine..." He leafed through a shelf filled with LP albums.

"You pick," she replied, not indicating if any of these were agreeable or even familiar.

He selected a Stanley Clarke album and put it on the turntable. Clarke's pumping bass and adventuresome solos fit his mood. He turned up the volume; his amplifier and speakers were old but of good quality, inherited when Chappell moved on.

He opened another bottle of wine, having consumed most of the first one himself. It calmed him, slowed his speech. He gazed at Gretchen, seated on the sofa, smiling up at him, long legs tightly crossed. Everything seemed perfect: the lights, the music, her loose blonde hair cascading over her shoulders. He topped off her wine glass on the coffee table and sat down next to her, their hips touching.

"You sore from the workout?" he asked.

"No. Maybe a little," she replied, rubbing the area above her breast.

"You know, massage is good for sore muscles." He reached over awkwardly and rubbed her shoulder.

"You'd like to massage my pecs, I'm sure," she said with a 'valley girl' inflection.

Taken aback, he removed his hand. "Uh no. I mean, that's not what I meant."

"Well, what did you mean?" she teased.

"Well, maybe," he replied. He gently massaged the back of her neck, turned her face toward his and kissed her.

They kissed for a long time, deeply. He gently nibbled her lips, her ears, her neck. He massaged the muscles of her shoulders. He moved his hand down slowly and slid his fingers under the fabric of her blouse, touching the warm skin beneath, like an adolescent, inching toward 'second base.' He caressed her breasts, hefting their fullness, gently massaging them through her brassiere, but when he started to slide his fingers inside the silken material she sat up suddenly, taking his hand in hers and turning it palm up, rubbing her fingertips across the callused ridges. "You have such strong hands," she said.

Was this a compliment? A complaint? His fingers were thick and short. Calluses marked each joint and rose like tiny mountain ranges along deep valleys in his palms.

"Did I scratch you?"

Nina exalted in his rough hands, the ridges on his thumb, which she liked to suck and hump between her legs like the penis of a barnyard animal. Gretchen seemed too civilized for such wild abandon.

"Oh no, they just, you know, felt hard." She smiled, stretched, and rose from the sofa. "Where's the bathroom?"

When she left the room, Rochmann stood up and adjusted Mister Lucky. His hands weren't the only hard thing. Her going to the bathroom was a hopeful sign. Emptying her bladder, maybe inserting a sponge or diaphragm, there were many reasons a woman retired to the bathroom before allowing access to her treasure. He turned the record over--it had ended some time ago--and started the second side. He stretched his back and shoulders; they were beginning to tighten from that afternoon. He felt his palms for any sharp edges that might scratch her delicate skin or catch on silken underwear.

Gretchen returned. A faint smile played on her lips but her eyes seemed serious. She nodded at the speakers. "That's nice; who is it?"

"Stanley Clarke, one of my favorites."

She picked up her wine glass and took a sip, then draped an arm over his shoulder and bent so that her forehead touched his. Her breath smelled sweetly of wine.

"Robert, I really like you," she began.

This was not a hopeful premise. The conclusion, 'Let's get naked and have wild and crazy sex,' did not usually follow from such a statement.

Anticipating, he said, "But..."

"Well, I'm really not ready to, uh, go any farther. It's me, not anything you've done. It's been a long time and I'm just not ready right now."

The break-up speech--'It's not you, it's me'--and they hadn't even been together yet.

"Yeah, it's been a long time for me, too." He tried to sound deprived but hopeful. It was true, in a way. It had been a long time since he had pursued anybody--Nina required only scheduling. What tack should he take now? Be more insistent? Girls had to say no; nice girls like Gretchen always said no; it was part of the game. "There's no rush." He meant to sound tender and understanding, yet disappointed. "Let's just listen to some music, have some more wine, talk, it's okay."

They listened to a couple more albums. She chattered about skiing and tennis and sailing in the summer with her family. He listened politely but said little. She left around eleven after a warm, if not passionate, kiss.

"Goddammit!" he cursed the door as it closed behind her. "Damn, damn, damn, dammit! They always have to call the shots. Control the situation." Like Lucy with the football in the *Peanuts* comic strip, enticing Charley Brown. Here it is, go for it. Come on, come on, and then jerking it away at the last second. "Augh!" says Charley Brown, lying on his back. "Ah, shit!" Rochmann said. He had clean-and-jerked more than 400 pounds that afternoon. World-class lifting. He deserved to get laid.

\*\*\*

A thin layer of snow covered the lawns and roads. A warm, moist front had moved in with a gray fog that muted sounds and hinted at heavier snow to come. His breath added to the swirls of mist, and steam poured from the tailpipe of the Scout as he took off, tires sliding. There were a couple cars parked in front of the massage parlor; he hesitated and drove past. He turned around at the next intersection and drove back, resolutely parking next to the other cars. The neon sign in the window shimmered in the foggy air and the red enameled walls glistened with moisture.

There were two men in the waiting area, an older man in work clothes and a younger one who looked like a college student. Neither looked up as Rochmann entered. He stood at the counter and waited. Mai gave a look of surprised recognition as she came through the beaded curtain. "You want muscle rub, now?"

"I'd like something different." He looked at the chart taped on the counter top. "I'd like this, with you." He pointed to the 'shower' listed on the menu.

She smiled. "That be forty dollar. You wait a little bit, okay?"

He paid, selected a magazine to occupy his gaze, and waited his turn. He could not help looking up as the girls entered to lead each customer through the curtain. The girls gave him a friendly smile. Mrs. Ang was nowhere to be seen.

When it was his turn, Mai took him through one of the doors into a small room almost filled by a fiberglass shower stall. "You take clothes off and start water," she instructed. "Read rules here." She pointed to a plastic-laminated sign taped to the outside wall. "I be right back."

The sign said: 'SHOWER RULES. 1. NO TOUCHING GIRL WITH HANDS. 2. NO KISSING GIRL. 3. NO SEX INTERCOURSE. 4. NO EXEPTIONS.' He noticed the misspelled word.

Mai reappeared, her long black hair fixed tightly in a knot atop her head. She carried two white towels, a sponge and a bar of soap. She slipped off the short terry-cloth robe that she had exchanged for her silk one. Her tan body glistened with oil and dark nipples stood out on her small breasts. She wore only a thong bikini bottom and over-sized flip-flops that clopped on the floor as she got into the shower with him. She pulled the curtain shut and smiled shyly.

She held up the sponge and soap. "These very clean," she said, as if reading his mind. "Not used before."

Mister Lucky was fully erect before she had soaped Rochmann's chest and she did not object when he grasped her slippery buttocks, in violation of rule number one. He pressed her tightly against himself as she completed her ministrations with hand and sponge.

Afterwards, he sat on a low stool while she dried him off, his erection slowly subsiding.

"You okay now?" she asked, patting Mister Lucky solicitously with the towel.

"Yeah, I'm okay."

"You come back soon," she said. "We make you pretty happy."

The 400 had made him happy. Now, he just felt tired, deflated. Alone.

# PART III

# DRUGS

# Chapter 10:  Coke Virgin

T he following Saturday, Gretchen invited Rochmann to her place for dinner.  Cooking was not Gretchen's forte:  she dressed up a frozen pizza with extra mozzarella and mushrooms, but it was accompanied by salad and a nice Chianti.  Gretchen did know wines.

Even better was her announcement after they'd eaten.  They were seated on the sofa and she said, "Robert, I know you were kind of disappointed last week when I put you off."

"Well, yeah.  But you said you weren't ready and I've got to respect that."

"I didn't totally explain.  What I meant was that I'd started on birth control pills and hadn't completed a full cycle.  I have now." She removed her glasses and placed them on the coffee table, next to a second bottle of wine, and gave him a meaningful look.

It took several seconds to process this.  Women were so rational about sex.  "I was going to ask if you wanted to go see *Tootsie*."  He smiled and extended a hand to her neck; it was hot to the touch and he could feel the slight throb of an artery.  "But I suppose we could find something better to do than watch Dustin Hoffman in drag."

A kiss was a good place to start.  A full frontal kiss.  She broke off intermittently to flavor her tongue with Chianti.

Rather than her usual miniskirt, Gretchen was wearing a long, flowing skirt with, conveniently, no tights beneath.   His fingers explored the temperature gradient of her bare leg.  Her kneecap was cool to the touch, her outer thigh a little warmer, and her inner thigh warmer still.  Degree by degree, he followed the pathway to the edge of her bikini underwear.  She parted her legs slightly and his fingers wriggled under the elastic to the center of warmth beneath.

They shed their clothes quickly, but before continuing, Gretchen said she needed a break.  She walked, naked in the lamplight, to the bathroom.   Rochmann marveled at her narrow waist, the perfect spheres of her buttocks, her long, runner's legs, her slender ankles. She was the most beautiful woman he'd ever seen, prettier than any of Chappell's girlfriends.

She was gone for several minutes. Mister Lucky began to fade but was resurrected by her return. She pushed Rochmann back on the couch and straddled him. The pupils of her eyes were large and black and shining. Slowly, she pressed herself onto him, one leg folded on the couch and the other providing traction for her thrusts. He'd had enough wine to dull his urgency and just lay back, watching her breasts heave and her pale, golden hair fall over her face. She leaned over to reach the bottle of wine and Mister Lucky slipped out. She sat on the floor and took a long drink, then passed the bottle to him. "Gotta go again," she said, and again the undulating globes of her buttocks disappeared from the circle of light.

More than hour must have passed this way, Gretchen taking breaks to go into the bathroom and returning to find a new position. Her tongue had a faint metallic taste and there were some white flecks under her nose, but with everything that was happening, such details were quickly lost. Finally, Rochmann got on top, with her legs over his shoulders, and pressed down so that her knees almost touched her ears, plunging deep. He pounded as hard as he could while she clutched his buttocks. They achieved simultaneous convulsions and he collapsed heavily atop her.

They lay entwined as their breathing slowed, kissing and nuzzling each other's salty-wet neck and forehead. Rochmann rolled off and slumped to the floor. Gretchen sat up and drained the last of the wine. "Want more?" she asked, holding up the empty bottle.

"Some water would be good."

"Yeah, water, ice water would be great!" She went into the kitchen and returned, wearing a pink chenille robe, carrying two large plastic cups of ice water. "I'm cold," she said as she handed him a cup. "You want a towel?"

"Nah, I'm okay." He retrieved his tee shirt from under the couch, wiped the sweat off his face and chest with it, and put it on.

She sat on the floor beside him and snuggled close. "Damn!" she said. "Rocky, Rocky, Rocky."

\*\*\*

For the remainder of the term, they spent every weekend, and some weeknights, together. While the intensity of that first time was not repeated, the promise of comfort and consistency was appealing. When Latasha graduated at the end of the winter quarter, rather than look for another roommate, it made sense for Gretchen to move in with Rochmann.

"It's not necessarily a long-term thing," he explained to Golding. "We'll just play it by ear while she finishes her degree and looks for a job."

"I hope your dick falls off," Golding replied.

Chappell, on the telephone, offered congratulations but warned, "Be careful, buddy boy. Make sure she doesn't interfere with your lifting."

With some discomfort, Rochmann phoned Nina to tell her that he had a girlfriend moving in with him. She did not seem surprised or distressed at the news, but rather congratulatory, as though he had won a prize. "I won't call you at home any more," she'd said in a matter-of-fact way. Neither said anything about him calling her.

\*\*\*

One Saturday evening, Gretchen looked at him seductively, with half-closed eyes and pouty lips. She said, teasingly, "You wanna try something with me?"

"I'll try anything with you, babe." Rochmann gently nipped her ear lobe.

"Be right back." She went into the bedroom and returned with a gold brocade make-up case. She placed it on the coffee table, unzipped it and removed a small brown glass bottle about the size of her thumb, a small mirror, and a single-edged razor blade.

"Like to do some coke?" she asked, with a beguiling look.

"Don't know. Never tried it."

"You've never done coke? What kind of old fuddy-duddy am I living with?" She said this jokingly but with genuine incredulity.

"Well, nobody ever offered me any, you know, in the weight room or the faculty lounge." He chuckled, defensively, at his naivte.

"C'mon, half the faculty get ripped," she said with a laugh. "How'd you get through grad school? Mmm-hmm, a coke virgin. You're in for a treat."

She poured a small hillock of white crystalline powder from the bottle onto the center of the mirror and began to chop with the razor blade, making quick ticking noises. After several passes she separated the pile into several smaller mounds and scraped these into parallel lines with the edge of the blade. She sat back contentedly and carefully wiped the residue from the razor blade with her fingertip and rubbed it on her gums under her upper lip. "Got a dollar bill?" she asked.

Rochmann fished his wallet from his back pocket. "A new one," she said, "nice and crisp."

She rolled the bill into a tight tube. Holding it lightly between thumb and forefinger, with her pinky extended like a debutante at afternoon tea, she brushed the hair back from her face and bent toward the mirror. She sniffed up half a line with each nostril, wiped a fingertip over the end of the dollar-tube and rubbed it on her gums. With a big smile and sigh of satisfaction, she handed it to Rochmann.

"Your turn," she said, Eve offering Adam the apple.

"What if I sneeze? Remember that scene in *Annie Hall*, where Woody Allen blows the pile of coke all over the room?"

"Rocky, c'mon."

"All right." He exaggerated reluctance as a way to hide his misgivings.

Following her example, he snorted half a line in his right nostril and the other half in his left. Sitting back, he examined the sensations. There was a metallic taste in the back of his throat. The air seemed colder in his nostrils as he inhaled, and he could feel his pulse pounding. The speedy feeling was like the time he and Chappell had experimented with amphetamine; it made the weights feel lighter but screwed up his timing.

"Okay!" Gretchen exclaimed, breaking into his reverie. She was pulling her sweater over her head. "C'mon big boy, let's play."

He fumbled with belt and zipper and she pulled down his trousers and jockey shorts. She licked her fingertip and pressed it to a line of cocaine, then wiped it around the edge of Mister Lucky's mushroom cap. Rochmann leaned back on the couch and watched, his hands intertwining her golden hair. She licked the residue from her fingertip, then greedily took Mister Lucky into her mouth. She did not deep-throat him, as Nina had done, but seemed intent on sucking off every molecule of coke. The drug had a slight anesthetic effect, sustaining him at the edge of high excitement but not pushing him over.

"Now your turn," she said. Her voice seemed to have changed into Nina's throaty huskiness. She loaded her sticky fingertip with coke and sat back, spreading her legs and pulling her nether lips apart, she daubed the pasty stuff on her swollen clitoris. She rubbed her gummy finger on Rochmann's tongue and pulled his head down between her legs. Pulling one knee up to her chest, she pushed the coffee table away with her other foot to give him room.

The primary tastes of sweet and sour, bitter and salty, combined with the textures of smooth and wet, exploded in his mouth. Gretchen almost pushed his tongue through his lower teeth as she pressed against him, but soon her cries and gasps signaled release for both of them.

Snorting and sucking, licking and rubbing, they worked their way through the lines on the mirror. When he finally entered her, Mister Lucky was like a pencil, hard but strangely thin. Gretchen locked her ankles and pressed her thighs together for the tightest possible fit, bucked and squeezed with abandon, and soon was shuddering with yet another orgasm. Her excitement triggered his reaction and he finally achieved a tepid ejaculation, an anti-climactic climax. She clasped her arms tightly around his sweaty torso, as though trying to increase the weight that lay atop her, kissing his face and neck and making animal noises in her throat. Exhausted, but restive, he rolled off and lay beside her, breathing heavily. She snuggled close, murmuring, as she had that first time, "Rocky, Rocky, Rocky."

A hot shower had only a slight calming effect and Rochmann slept fitfully, unable to find a comfortable position.  When at last dawn gave hue to the dim objects in the bedroom, he got up with gritty eyes and aching joints and limped to the bathroom.  A second hot shower was more relaxing than the earlier one, and he almost dozed while standing in the tub.  A cold blast, when the water heater depleted its contents, doused his half-dreams.  Wrapping a towel around himself, he meandered into the kitchen.  The pitcher of orange juice seemed to weigh five kilos as he lifted it to his lips.  He flopped heavily on the living room couch and stared at the stripes of light that streamed through the slits of the venetian blinds onto the opposite wall, marking the slow trajectory of the sun.

The sounds of Gretchen busily clattering in the kitchen awakened him.  The smell of coffee teased his nose.  He got up stiffly and tottered into the kitchen, surprised to see her setting out utensils. "You want some pancakes?" she asked.

"Sure."  His vocal chords responded reluctantly to their first use of the day.  He opened the refrigerator and poked among the contents. "No orange juice," he rasped.

"Somebody drank it."  She was smiling  "I think there's some frozen."

"I'll have coffee," he said, daunted at the prospect of preparing frozen juice.  He got a large mug from the cabinet and filled it, adding generous amounts of sugar and milk.

"How many pancakes?" Gretchen asked, pouring mix into a large bowl.  She was wearing a short white terry cloth robe that revealed her long, slender legs.  It was tied loosely and her large breasts swung as she stirred the batter.  She was amazingly beautiful and acting very friendly, but Mister Lucky did not stir.

"Whatever," he said.  "You cook 'em and I'll eat 'em."

# Chapter 11: Pavlovian Conditioning

"God damn!" Rochmann slammed the door and stomped through the kitchen like a tantruming child. "God damn, damn, damn!" He threw his workout bag on the floor, then picked it up and stormed into the study. It was obvious that Gretchen was home--the door was unlocked and the lights were on--but he did not look for her.

He was sitting in front of the computer, impatiently tapping a floppy disk on the edge of the desk while the IIe booted up, when Gretchen came into the room. "Rough workout?" she asked, putting her hands softly on his shoulders and her lips close to his ear.

"Goddamn cocaine!" he said through clenched teeth. "Hate to see what percent decrease this cost me." He jammed the disk into the drive, clicked it shut, and drummed his fingers while it whirred into action.

Gretchen inhaled sharply but did not remove her hands. She gently massaged his shoulders, the tips of her breasts brushing the back of his head. "You've had bad days before," she said quietly. "Ups and downs."

"Not like this!" He opened his log book and began transcribing numbers into the computer. "I was ten, twenty kilos down. Couldn't finish my final sets. It was all I could do to keep from just walking out." He took a deep breath and patted her hand. "At least I didn't pull anything," he said a little more calmly.

A graph appeared on the screen, showing a wavy line that trended slightly upward, with a sharp dip at the end. "Look at that," he said sitting back, shoulders drooping. "Set me back over a month."

"Maybe it was the sex," she said, kissing his ear.

He leaned back into her and sighed. "No, sex just gives me a one-day plateau, at most a couple-percent decrease. Nothing like this."

"You keep track of sex?" She dropped her hands and stepped back.

"I keep track of everything: sex, caffeine, alcohol, colds, sleep..." His voice trailed off. He did not say 'steroids,' though he had more data on this factor than any other. "God, I wonder how long it'll take to recover?" He said this more to himself than to her.

"Sometimes I notice coke makes me a little tired when I go running, you know, after doing it, and it probably slows me down a little. But I'm fine in a couple days," Gretchen said in a hopeful voice.

"That's aerobic exercise, and you're not pushing your limits. Even if I recover fully in a week, that's a week that I'm supposed to be making gains, so I'm still behind."

"I guess this means you won't do coke with me again?" Her tone was somewhere between plaintive and resigned.

"Damn right!"

There was a long silence while he typed some more numbers and comments into the computer. She again placed her hands on his traps and gently massaged them.

"I guess I should say I'm sorry," she said quietly. "I didn't mean to hurt your training." She paused. He stopped typing but said nothing. "I thought it would be fun," she continued. "I, I really like doing it on coke." Another pause. "Rocky, I, it's like I need coke to get off, to, you know, have an orgasm." She squeezed his shoulders hard with this admission, then let go and stepped away.

He swiveled the chair around to face her. The room had grown dark and the glow from the computer screen revealed a glint of moisture in her eyes. He reached out and took her hands. The chair creaked and tilted dangerously as she sat clumsily in his lap.

"Oh baby," he said softly, nuzzling her hair with his lips, "it's okay. I don't, I mean, you can do whatever it takes. It's fine with me. I mean, I like it when you get all horny and crazy." He spoke haltingly but his tone seemed to reassure her and she relaxed. Her talking about sex, and the warmth of her buttocks in his lap, provoked a slight tumescence. He squeezed her and nibbled her neck. In some Hollywood version of life, this scene would end with their sinking to the floor, engaging in tender sex, and her experiencing glorious orgasm without the need for cocaine. In the real world, she stiffened slightly and tilted her head away. He asked, "So, how did you find out that coke, uh, did this for you?"

Gretchen cleared her throat and paused, then in a barely audible voice she said, "I, for a long time, I never had, I didn't have, you know, orgasms. I, uh, read books and tried, you know, their recommendations. I even went to a shrink a couple of times, but that was just too weird."

He hugged her gently but said nothing.

"When I was a junior in college I, um, went to a fraternity party. That's where I met Carl, and he had some, you know, coke. Well, we went to his room and did it. The coke, I mean. And it was just so wild. And then we were doing it, you know, screwing on the bed. And I came. It just happened, without even trying. So after that, I could usually come when I'm doing coke. I mean, I don't do it that much. It's not like I'm a coke whore. You know, just with Carl when we were going together. And now, I'd like to do it with you, but I didn't know it, you know, affects your weightlifting so bad."

"Hmm," he muttered. "Pavlovian conditioning. That's neat."

"What?" Gretchen sat up.

"The coke," he said. "It's like a conditioned stimulus. It's been paired with orgasm and now you need it to get off. What a neat conditioning experiment that would be."

She stood up. "An experiment? I tell you the most intimate thing in my life and you think of an experiment?" Her voice was shrill, accusing.

Now he was on the defensive. How had that happened? One minute he was the injured party, righteously angry because his life-long goal had been placed in jeopardy by this blasted drug. And now he was the bad guy because he'd said the wrong thing?

"Gretchen," he said, reaching for her hand, "I'm just trying to understand. You know, understand what's going on."

She jerked her hand away. She would not be mollified. She was off the hook. "Well you don't understand!" She stalked from the room.

It was an occasion for a second effort. He should have followed her, held her gently, told her, "I'm sorry, please help me understand." But he sat there, looking at the dip in the graph. "Fucking bitch!" he said to the computer screen.

***

Rochmann phoned Bill Chappell to see if he had any data on cocaine effects. He left a message with Bill's answering service in the City and waited for a call back.

In less than an hour, the phone rang and Rochmann spilled his woeful tale. "Let me get this straight," Chappell said. "This incredibly beautiful woman wants to get high on drugs and have wild monkey sex, but you'd rather lift hunks of iron over your head."

"Well, that's not exactly how I'd put it. But yeah, that's sort of what's going on."

"That's my man," Chappell said. "Look, I'm pretty sure you'll bounce back quickly. I'll check my files and ask around. But you should get over a one-time fling like this in a few days. Don't push it, and don't beat yourself up about it. Or her either, what's her name, Gretchen? You'll be fine."

***

Despite Chappell's reassurance, the estrangement went on for over a week while Rochmann's lifts slowly recovered to their former level. Finally, on a day that his squat increased by 2.5 kilos over his 'pre-coke' level, he approached Gretchen. She was sitting on the couch watching television.

"Look, Gretchen," he began, "we have to get over this. I'm not mad at you, and I'm not sure why you're mad at me." He sat next to her and she turned off the television. "I don't care if you use coke, you know, if that's you, fine. I just can't do it. That's me. We've got to let each other be who we are. Okay?"

Her lips formed a small, sad smile. "You're right, Rocky," she said at last. "I'm sorry, I, it's just that I hate feeling I'm, you know, different."

"You're different all right," he replied, putting his arm around her. "You're different in a way that I like. Vive la difference." He pulled her closer and began kissing her. "Getchyer coke, if ya' want it baby, 'cause Rocky wants some of that difference."

It made no sense but seemed to express the right feeling. She did not get her brocade case, and she did not have an orgasm, but she seemed content with his desire and his efforts.

# Chapter 12:  Steroid Addiction

O n Sunday, Gretchen said she was going shopping for curtain material and some items to fix up the place a little. Rochmann was a fastidious housekeeper but his sole effort at decorating had been to tape a few pictures of Vassily Alexeyev, cut from an old *Sports Illustrated*, on the wall above his computer.  She said she might check out some of the craft and antique shops that she'd heard about.  Rochmann thought of his last rendezvous with Nina, not that many weeks ago, and declined her invitation to go along.  He told her Golding was on child-care duty for the weekend and he'd promised to keep him company while his wife was away, watch a basketball game on TV or something.  She frowned at Golding's name but said nothing further.

Sam's living room was cluttered with toys and children's clothing.  Rochmann sat on a sagging couch in front of a twenty-seven-inch color television, his host's prized possession, although stacks of Disney and educational video cassettes indicated Golding had to negotiate his viewing time.  The two younger children were napping, and the oldest was at a friend's house, so the child psychologist appeared to be in a good mood.

"How's married life?" Golding asked in a teasing tone.  His round face was stubbly, his lank hair uncombed.  He wore pajama bottoms, slippers, and a wrinkled *New York Jets* sweatshirt.  He lit a cigar and exhaled a long stream of foul smoke, its odor overwhelming the faint, sour smell of diapers.

"Wonderful, as you well know," Rochmann said with a grin.  He sipped the beer Golding had pressed on him, but refrained from the chips and salsa, laden with salt and other unhealthy substances, that lay amid sections of the Sunday *New York Times* strewn on the coffee table.

Golding shot him a baleful look, then sat up in his recliner and turned his attention to the TV screen.  A commercial for deodorant had ended and some talking heads began a discussion of steroid use by athletes.  Rochmann took another sip of beer and, to show his disinterest, reached for a chip.

"What's the deal on steroids? Don't weightlifters use that stuff?" Golding asked.

Rochmann took care to sound nonchalant. "The International Olympic Committee banned them in '76. It's against the rules for Olympic sports. They're not illegal and I don't think there's any rules against it in the pros, you know, like football. I'm sure those guys are juiced to the max. Don't think it'd help much in basketball or baseball, but you never know."

"I don't get it," Golding went on, nodding at the television screen. "Here's this guy saying that steroids don't actually help athletic performance; it's just a placebo." He listened to more of the discussion. "And this other guy says they're supposed to have all these life-threatening dangers. It doesn't make sense. Why would guys making millions of dollars from sports risk their health for no good reason? I mean it's not addictive, is it?"

"Nah, I don't think it's addictive, not like heroin or alcohol." Rochmann held up his can of beer and grinned.

What *was* addictive were the performance gains. Steroids were decidedly more than placebos. Chappell had once done an experiment, giving him a supply of pills that looked just like the real ones but without the active ingredient. Within a week, the weights he'd handled easily began to get heavier and he'd complained bitterly about his slump. Only weeks later did Chappell tell him about the switch. Rochmann understood his friend's interest in science, but still had been pissed at the needless decline in his progress. He recalled his outrage at the cocaine episode with Gretchen. It was the weights that were addictive, not the pills.

"Yeah, but are they life-threatening?" Golding asked. Rochmann's short answers only seemed to make him more insistent.

"I think the threats are way overblown. It's like *Reefer Madness*, you know, that film from the '30s about the evils of marijuana?"

Golding laughed. "Yeah, we used to show it at frat parties. Watch it while we were stoned. What a riot."

"Yeah, when you use scare tactics, the effect just boomerangs. When people see all those terrible warnings are bogus, they figure there's no bad effects at all. Even though there are some health risks, they're totally ignored. Actually, the medical use of anabolic steroids is pretty benign. I mean it's used for burn victims and geriatric patients, you know, for wasting diseases. So it can't be too dangerous."

"Like medical marijuana? You know, for cancer patients?" Golding asked.

"Sort of. Only anabolics do more than stimulate the appetite. They actually promote muscle growth. Not that it's a magic pill; it doesn't just make muscles pop out. What steroids do is let you train harder, recover faster. Fucking Russians train six, eight hours a day, six days a week. No way you can do that without help." To suggest his own purity, Rochmann added, "I train maybe three, four hours a day, and I'm totally wrecked."

Another commercial came on and Golding turned down the sound. "So if it works so good, why doesn't everybody just get on the bandwagon?" he asked. "Why try to stop it?"

"A big part is political," Rochmann said. "Steroids were like a secret weapon discovered by the East Germans and Soviets, about twenty-five years ago. So they're breaking world records right and left, and the official U.S. reaction is, this is a Commie plot that has to be stopped. You know, old goody-two-shoes Carter and then the 'evil empire' rhetoric that got Bonzo's buddy elected. But the unofficial response, by the athletes, was, where can I get this shit? So you've got this split between the government, trying to stop the Communist menace, and the athletes, who want to fight fire with fire.

"So it's just political? There's really no bad effects?"

Rochmann knew Bill Chappell had wanted to answer that question, to specialize in sports medicine and do research on steroids, but politics made it impossible. Nothing on the subject was taught in medical school and Chappell had to track down the sparse scientific literature on his own. Certain doctors, whose names were circulated quietly in locker rooms, found a good source of revenue by providing steroid prescriptions. But so far as Rochmann knew, he was Chappell's only client, and Bill did a good job keeping track of his health.

"Well, like any drug, there's side effects," Rochmann said. The real problem is, it's been forced to go underground, so there's no medical supervision at all. People get stuff on the black market; it may be good or it may be shit. Guys figure if one pill's good, ten will be that much better. Bodybuilders inject the stuff by the gallon. Supposedly, at super high doses, your balls and liver can shrivel up. Women grow beards. Men grow tits. People have hair-trigger tempers. But no one monitors side effects or dosage levels. That's where the harm is. At therapeutic levels, it seems pretty safe."

"I don't know," Golding said. "If there's a possibility of side effects, why take the risk at all?"

"Well, athletes are risk-takers. People have this myth that athletes are a bunch of super healthy people, but to compete at the highest level, they have to push their bodies past their limits. Athletes are not in it for their health. You've got little 12-year-old gymnasts with stress fractures, runners ripping their hamstrings. The National Football League busts up more guys than the U.S. Marines. But athletes choose to take the risk to compete for," he paused, "money, glory, whatever they're in it for. And if there's something that might give them an edge, well, what's one more risk?"

The game resumed on television. Golding turned the audio up and pushed back in his recliner. He said, "Well, I'll just take my risks with beer and potato chips."

What Rochmann was taking risks for fell into the 'whatever' category. In other countries, weightlifters were superstars. A national champion was like a Heisman Trophy winner. But there was no money or glory, or even acknowledgment, in the U.S. He did weightlifting for its own sake, like an addiction, and if steroids helped him do it better, like coke helped Gretchen get off, so be it. But he was after more than a good feeling, more than the buzz of a perfect clean-and-jerk, great as that was. The Olympic Games were a quest he'd been on for half his life. Reaching them, even the watered-down Los Angeles variety, would validate that quest. And it would also release him, allow him to put the addiction behind him and see what else life had to offer, though he rarely thought of life after Los Angeles.

Golding's questions aroused another concern that Rochmann tried not to think about. More worrisome than the side effects of steroids was the problem of the urine tests at national competitions. Rochmann knew that winners at the Senior Nationals that spring, and at the Olympic trials the following year, would be tested for steroids. Chappell assured him that water-soluble pills, and using diuretics a couple weeks before the contest, all traces would be washed out of his system. That certainly had worked when he was tested in the past, but there was talk of more sophisticated testing procedures. Chappell said everything would be fine. Rochmann wanted to believe him, but it was his ass on the line, not Bill's.

Golding's voice intruded. "Hey, I said do you want another beer while I'm up?"

"Huh, what?"

"Another beer? What'r'ya, asleep with your eyes open?"

Rochmann blinked. "Yeah, I guess I was. No more beer for me, thanks. Must be time for my Sunday afternoon nap."

"One beer and you're ready for a nap." Golding's voice was full of mock scorn. "You jocks are a bunch of pussies."

# Chapter 13:  Set 'Em Up, Joe

L ate one afternoon, Sam Golding looked up from the paper he was correcting when Rochmann walked into his office. Golding said, "If it isn't Lover Boy.  What's happening?"

"Just wondered if you want to go for a beer?  I'll buy."

Surprised, Golding asked, "What, no workout today?"

"I'm taking it easy before a contest coming up real soon.  Just wondered if you want to get a beer or something."

Golding looked at his watch and grimaced.  "Have to pick up the kids in about an hour."

"Just a quickie, Sam."  There was a plaintive note in his voice.

"Okay, lemme wrap up a couple of things.  Where do you want to go?"

Rochmann suggested they meet at the bar of one of Westerville's nicer restaurants.  Golding arrived to find Rochmann staring at his refracted image in the crackled mirror behind rows of liquor bottles glistening in multicolored spotlights.  The place was quiet and the bartender moved with practiced efficiency, setting up for the cocktail and dinner hours.

Golding perched on a stool and pointed to the pilsner glass in front of Rochmann when the bartender stopped by, indicating he'd have the same.  "How come you're not running home to your Swedish sweetie?"

"Well, funny you should ask."  Rochmann took a long pull of his beer and wiped his lips with a forefinger.  "You've been married a long time.  How do you do it?  I've been living with this woman for a few weeks and it's driving me up the wall."

"Ahhh," Golding exhaled with a note of satisfaction.  Ever since he'd found out his colleague was stupping the stunning graduate student, jealousy had been itching like a bad rash.  "Life with an angel is not paradise?" he asked.  Maybe God was not so unfair after all.

"Nothing terrible, just annoying stuff that gets to you every once in a while.  I know a relationship is a series of adjustments.  Like, I don't hang up my sweat clothes to dry on the shower rod any more. Before she moved in, not a word; now it smells like cat pee, she says.

No big deal. I got a trashcan with a tight lid and put it on the back porch; drop off my sweats before I come in the house. Of course they're frozen stiff as a board when I take them out to do laundry, but I can compromise."

"So, what's the problem?"

"Well, the Olympic trials are next year, right? She knew that when she moved in. I thought she'd be supportive, but instead it's like she's resentful. She was all pissed I wouldn't take off on spring break with her. She couldn't understand that I can't just go to some health club and work out on the machines. You know, I've got to be super organized to fit in training and classes. And she's just, I don't know, just this chaotic person. Sometimes it seems like she tries to sabotage what I'm doing."

"Like what?" asked Golding. "How's she sabotage you?"

"Well, not sabotage exactly, but she's really disruptive. Sometimes it seems deliberate, though mostly it's just that she doesn't consider anybody else. She has her own agenda and just assumes that everybody else should fall in line."

"Hmm, she's inconsiderate of your needs," Golding reflected. He was enjoying playing counselor.

"Well it's not like I need much from her. What I need is time: time to work out, time to recover, time for class preps. And she wants me to, I don't know, go shopping with her. Paint the bedroom, go to the hardware and look at paint chips. I mean if she wants to paint the place, fine, I'm happy for her to do it, but I don't have time for that sort of stuff. Decorating the bedroom is really low on my list of priorities. But it's like we've got to do it together."

"Nest building," said Golding. "It's a female instinct thing. Get the mate involved in building the nest."

"I'm not a goddamn bird. I'm not even a mate, at least in any kind of permanent sense. I mean we've never talked about any long-range kind of thing. And the house is only a rental, but she's got to fix it up. Matching curtains and bedspread and walls. And she gets really snippy if I don't join in. I mean I keep the place clean--and she's really messy, too, just drops stuff on the floor, doesn't even close the cupboard when she gets a glass--and then makes jokes about me being a neat freak if I say anything. You know, if I like things kept neat, it's silly, but Lord help me if I don't want to discuss color schemes."

The two men attended to their beers, then Rochmann went on. "Another thing that bugs me is, when you try to do something with her at a particular time, she's always late. She runs on Gretchen mean time."

"Gretchen mean time?"

"Yeah, what Gretchen means by time is different than what the rest of the world runs on." Golding groaned at the pun and Rochmann continued. "Take this evening. We planned to meet here at six. I know she's not going to be here at six but I don't know how late she'll be; it could be six-fifteen, it could be seven-fifteen. So, I'm stuck waiting."

Golding drained his glass and waved to the bartender for refills. He patted Rochmann's arm in a gesture of understanding, but said, "Well, pal, to be honest, I don't have a lot of sympathy for you. A lot of guys would be glad to wait fifteen minutes, or two hours, if a hot babe like Gretchen showed up at the end of it."

Rochmann half turned on the stool to face him. "Yeah, I think that's her attitude, too. Guys've always been willing to put up with it, just as long as she would give 'em that big smile. Like, 'you're lucky to be with me.' But it makes it difficult to live with her on a daily basis. That's why I'm talking to an old married man. You're saying, just deal with it? Things don't change?"

"Oh, things change alright, just not for the better. Just wait'll you have kids. Then you go from number two in the relationship to number three, four, five."

Fresh beers arrived and Golding took a sip, then spoke to Rochmann's reflection in the mirror across from them. "You know, when I was a kid my father was king. Mom was like a buffer between him and us kids, making sure he wasn't disturbed. 'Go outside and play, your father's resting,' she'd say." He took another swig of beer and gestured with his glass at the silent television screen flickering above the bar. "Television. We watched what Papa wanted on TV--Milton Berle, he loved Uncle Miltie, but we couldn't watch Ed Sullivan. Sid Caesar yes, Ernie Kovacs no. Even if he wasn't home, 'turn that off,' Mom would say, 'your father doesn't want you watching that.' She cooked what he liked and we ate it or nothing. I never had seafood until I was in college--Papa didn't like fish. But these days. Now the kids are in charge and moms are there to make sure their interests are served. Do we ever have snow crab? No, the kids won't eat it. Fish-sticks they like; we have fish-sticks. Talk about schedules, I'm scheduled up the whazoo--the kids have soccer practice, music lessons, Hebrew lessons, orthodontist appointments. After they're in bed we tape PBS documentaries and animal shows for them; God forbid I should watch Miami Vice. I talk to other guys at soccer practice and it's the same for them. A whole generation, we were good boys, did what our mothers wanted, obeyed our fathers. Now it's our turn to be king and whoops, moms have allied with the children against us. No more, 'be quiet, your daddy's resting.' Now it's, 'your night to fix dinner and put the kids to bed; I'm going to class.'"

Golding stared into his half-empty glass. "Tell you what, Rochmann, I'll stay here drinking beer and wait for your girl friend. You pick up my kids at day-care, feed 'em dinner, go over their teachers' reports, put 'em to bed, write checks for the doctor bills, and, for a really good time, stay up and watch Johnny Carson until my wife gets home from the library."

He did not say, 'my wife with sagging breasts and dimples on her butt,' but that's what he meant. "I'll trade you, Rock my boy, my wife and kids, who are all very punctual by the way, for a night with your time-impaired, blonde sex-goddess."

Rochmann started to reply, but stopped. He looked pensive, inhaling several times as if searching for the right words. Finally, he said, "Well, all I can say is that living with a woman who looks like a sex goddess can be frustrating." He emphasized the words, 'looks like.'

"Like how?"

Again Rochmann paused to search for an answer. "Here's an example. She goes around the house in her underwear, tee shirt and panties, just gorgeous. Every man's dream, right? So I like, go for it, and she goes, 'Are you crazy? How dare you touch me? I'm trying to study.' Now to me, a woman wearing only a tee shirt and panties is an S-D for sex, but for her, it's only being comfortable."

"S-D, what's an S-D?" broke in Golding.

"S-D, discriminative stimulus. You've never had a course in learning? It's a signal that reinforcers are available."

"Got it. You behaviorists," Golding moaned.

"Anyway, I think those Iranians have it right. Keep the women wrapped up in, what's that thing called, you know, that long black robe and veil? No mistaking it, an S-delta, no reinforcement available. Then when they're unwrapped, it's clearly time for fun. But when women run around half-naked all the time, the signals are all mixed up. You have to learn to ignore it, repress any arousal. You know what I've discovered? You can use the 'Mother-in-law effect' to make a good-looking woman unattractive."

"What the hell is the 'Mother-in-law effect?'"

"You know, in every introductory psych text, in the perception section, there're these optical illusions? The 'Mother-in-law or the wife' is the one where there's this beautiful young woman, her face turned away, or depending on how you look at it, it's an old crone with a big nose. You stare at it and it switches back and forth from one to the other."

"Oh yeah, I know the one you mean," said Golding.

"So what I've found, is that you can do that with actual women. You can look at even the most beautiful woman, a supermodel or movie star, and if you look at her a certain way, you can make her appear ugly. Focus on a certain feature, imagine her very fat or skinny, I don't know, just change the gestalt, and all of a sudden she's no longer attractive. You know they say, 'beauty is in the eye of the beholder?' Well, 'ugly' is too. It works with all these hot coeds running around campus. And I use it on Gretchen in her underwear around the house. Otherwise I'd be in a sexual frenzy all the time."

Golding looked at his watch and stood up. "The Mother-in-law-effect. You poor bastard. You better go lift some weights, or take a cold shower. I'm late; I gotta go."

As he was leaving, he heard Rochmann ordering another beer and asking the bartender, "You married?"

# PART IV

# ROCK AND ROLL

# Chapter 14:  David Berger Memorial

Rochmann woke at his usual six a.m.  Gretchen lay beside him, gently snoring.  He snuggled up to her and tried not to think about the plans for the day.  They were going to drive to New York City, check into a hotel, eat, maybe see a movie, and retire early.  Tomorrow was the big day, his first contest since moving to Westerville.  It would be a major test before the Nationals, later that spring.

When he could lie still no longer, he rose and weighed himself on the bathroom scale, satisfied to find he was a half-pound under the class limit.  He dressed in the dim light that seeped through the bedroom curtains Gretchen had bought, not deliberately making noise but not being stealthy, either.  Gretchen snored on.  He went into the kitchen and started the coffee maker.  This was for her; he had stopped drinking coffee and cola for the past month in order to reduce his caffeine tolerance.  By clearing caffeine from his system, he felt he'd get a bigger boost when he dosed himself with it just before lifting.  Anything to improve performance.

He poured a bowl of cereal and tried to watch a morning television news show.  Reports of the U.S. supplying weapons to the Afghan freedom fighters assured continuing Soviet antagonism toward competing in the L.A. Olympics.  After an overweight, over-grinning weatherman promised a clear but chilly day, Rochmann switched off the TV and went into the bedroom.

"C'mon babe, it's time to rock and roll," Rochmann whispered, prodding the sleeping woman.  She grunted and moved slightly.  He opened the curtains, letting in the morning sun.  "Looks like it's going to be a nice day," he added in an encouraging tone.

Gretchen groaned.  She was not, as she frequently reminded him, a morning person.  But she did get up, performing her morning toilette like a slow-motion zombie.  There was, in actuality, no real hurry, so long as they got to the City before traffic congealed in the afternoon rush.  But having set the process in motion, he was anxious to complete it.

"Coffee's ready," he called through the bathroom door, trying to sound merely informative. There was no reply. "You want some toast?" Receiving no answer, he once again checked his equipment bag: lifting suit, jock strap, lifting shoes, sweat socks, two short-sleeve sweatshirts, long-sleeve sweatshirt, sweat pants, lifting belt, bath towel, roll of adhesive tape, a box of No-Doz, ibuprofen, tube of Deep Heat, small bottle of Nu-Skin, two cans of Jolt cola, two Hershey dark chocolate bars, three bananas, honey in a small plastic bottle shaped like a bear, and a combination lock. There was nothing he'd forgotten and nothing had disappeared since he had packed and checked it the previous evening. Nothing would disappear on the trip to the City either, but he would check it again when they got to the hotel, and again the next morning before leaving for the venue. He zipped the bag and carried it into the living room, setting it next to their two wheeled airline cases by the front door.

Hearing the bathroom door open, he called again, "You want some toast?

"I'll take care of it," Gretchen called back, a peevish edge to her voice.

"I'll load the car then." He carried the bags out to the driveway where Gretchen's Honda Accord was parked. He had filled it with gas and checked the tire pressure and fluid levels the previous evening. His old Scout, though capable of the trip, was not competitive at interstate speeds, besides having no cassette player. Gretchen had volunteered to drive her car, giving him the added bonus of relaxing for the three-hour journey. A gift from her parents when she had finished her bachelor's degree, the Honda had seen little use since she'd stopped commuting to New York to visit Carl. It promised to be a good trip if he could only get her started.

When he came in, she was sitting at the kitchen table stirring a cup of coffee, still in her oversize pink chenille bathrobe, her hair wrapped in a towel. At least she was up and moving. "Oh god," she sighed. "What time is it, anyway?"

"About eight," he said, nodding at the kitchen clock on the wall behind her. When Gretchen had moved in, she'd set all the clocks in the house from five to fifteen minutes ahead. She'd explained that when she looked at a clock, she would think it was later, so she would hurry and thus be more likely to be on time. He pointed out that when she looked at a clock she would figure that she had more time and would be more likely to be late. It was his first exposure to Gretchen mean time and a discussion they'd had only once. He made sure his wristwatch was accurate.

***

Almost an hour later, Gretchen backed the Honda down the driveway and into the street. They set off with a slight swerve as she buckled her seat belt. There were more swerves as she moved her seat rearward and adjusted the mirrors. Rochmann reclined his seatback and closed his eyes.

On the highway, the car veered again as Gretchen undid her seatbelt and reached under her sweatshirt, behind her back, to undo the clasp of her brassiere. Rochmann opened his eyes a slit and, without turning his head, watched as she went through Houdini-like contortions while steadying the steering wheel with the tops of her thighs. She finally withdrew her brassiere from her sleeve, heightening the impression of a magic trick. The first time he had witnessed this performance, he had been amazed and somewhat aroused. He had attempted to touch her breast and had learned, abruptly, that she was not performing a striptease for his benefit, but was only getting comfortable while she drove.

On the interstate, Gretchen set the cruise control for 74 mph and clicked a *Hall & Oates* cassette into the player. She pushed her seat further back and placed her right foot, sans shoe, on the dashboard. She was wearing tight-fitting sweatpants and her long leg rested invitingly near his hands. Rochmann kept his hands folded and stared through the windshield. The early spring sky was bright and colorless, a high thin cloud layer diffusing the sunlight across shadowless fields. An immense flock of tiny black birds rose into the air and coalesced into a single organism that wheeled across the expanse like an animated spray of coarse pepper on a linen tablecloth.

***

A screech of tires and loud honking jolted him awake. "Fucking idiot!" Gretchen yelled.

"Are we there yet?" Rochmann asked with a grin.

"We're on Queens Boulevard. Where are we going again?"

"Lost Battalion Hall. Look for a red brick building on your left. I need to stop in and check my weight."

"How much could your weight change since yesterday? You're worse than a high-school girl at prom time." She had been teasing him about his obsession with weight the past month, noting his frequent trips to the bathroom scale.

"I want to check out the official scale that'll be used for weigh-in. And I need to gauge how much I can eat and drink." Rochmann generally weighed a little above the class limit of 82.5 kilos and could easily lose the excess the week before a contest. However, he did not want to lose too much for fear it would weaken him. And he did not want to weigh even a few grams heavy, requiring him to sweat it out in the steam room in the hour prior to competition, running the risk of dehydration and muscle cramps. So the natural balance of bodyweight fluctuations was replaced by anxious monitoring of food intake and continuous trips to the scale.

***

"No problem," he said, rejoining her in the sparsely furnished lobby where she'd waited while he went to the men's locker room. "Let's check into the hotel and then get something to eat."

"So who's David Berger?" she asked, pointing to the sign thumb-tacked to the bulletin board, announcing the 'David Berger Memorial Weightlifting Contest.'

"He was one of the Israeli athletes killed at the Olympics ten years ago. You know, in Munich, when the Palestinian terrorists took them hostage. He used to live in New York so they hold this meet in his honor every year."

They walked down the wide concrete steps. A cool breeze, carrying a hundred smells of the city, was refreshing compared to the musty, sweaty, liniment and faint urine odors that saturated the locker room. March in New York was no April in Paris, but after a winter in Westerville, the atmosphere thrummed with possibility.

They got in the car and Rochmann gave directions to the nearby hotel. "It's not the Ritz," he said as they pulled up and stopped.

"I'll say." Gretchen's tone suggested she was used to staying at the Ritz.

But their room was clean and neat, if not luxurious, and she said nothing more. Rochmann suggested they eat at a Chinese restaurant within walking distance and Gretchen agreed.

As they walked, Gretchen asked, "So, did you know this guy, David Berger?"

"No, I was just starting out. Saw his results in the lifting magazines. I was a middleweight then, 75 kilos, same as him, so I always looked to see what other guys in my weight class were doing. He was pretty good, but we had a couple world-class middleweights back then. Russ Knipp had the world record in the press, and Freddie Lowe was close to it in the jerk. So the only way Berger could make an Olympic team was to lift for Israel. I think he had dual citizenship, you know, with Israel."

"God, that's awful," Gretchen said. "To go to all that effort and then just get shot down. If he'd stayed here, he'd still be alive."

"You never know. He could have been run over by a cab. At least he got close to his dream." They stopped at a cross walk and Rochmann looked at the people hurrying by in the afternoon shadows, yellow cabs swerving, truck horns honking. "I wonder if he knew what was coming, if he still would've gone."

"How can you say that?" Gretchen frowned. "Of course people don't go somewhere if they know they're going to die."

"I'm not so sure," he said. "There's good old Dr. Faustus."

"Who?"

"Never mind. This is getting morbid."

They entered the Moon Palace and were seated in a booth near the door. They placed their order and Rochmann looked around. The midday rush had ebbed and only a few customers lingered over tea and fortune cookies.

In an effort to lighten the somber mood the discussion of Munich had brought on, he said, "Not enough people to do the Schachter test."

"What's that?"

"A few years ago, this psychologist, Stanley Schachter, noticed that obese people in Chinese restaurants used chopsticks less often than normal weight ones. He proposed that chopsticks take longer to get food to your mouth and obese people can't stand the delay." Rochmann liked to throw out little bits of knowledge. The teacher role was comfortable, reminiscent of his first days with her. Words seemed to add inches to his stature.

"Ever since I read that," he went on, "I look for people using chopsticks. Not many people use them anyway, but I've never seen a fat person do it. Like me." He smiled, sticking out his belly and patting it. "I've tried 'em a few times, but it's just too frustrating. I want to get that food in there *now*."

"Me too," she said. "It just seems, I don't know, fake or something to try to eat with them. And I bet the waiters get a big laugh, too, watching clumsy white people try it."

After eating, they emerged from the restaurant into the brisk air. Gretchen seemed invigorated. "I'm glad I came. I really love the City. " She added, "Being here with you." She hugged his arm affectionately and leaned down to press her cheek to his. He picked up the vibe; they could go back to the hotel and spend a delicious time in bed. But like a Spartan warrior, he had a pre-contest celibacy rule. He stepped to the curb and waved his arm for a taxi.

"We're not walking back to the hotel?" Gretchen asked in a surprised tone as a yellow cab swerved to the curb.

"C'mon, let's go uptown and pay someone a visit," Rochmann said, opening the taxi door for her.

# Chapter 15:  Doctor Jock

G retchen got in the cab.  "Visit who?" she asked as Rochmann slid in beside her.

He gave an address to the driver, then said, "Bill Chappell, Doctor Jock, an old friend of mine.  He's a real letch--I'm sure he wants to meet you."  Rochmann put his arm around her shoulder and hugged her, playfully.

"Now why would I want to meet a letch?  I already live with one."

"Well, he's tall-dark-and-handsome.  And well off.  He's a real doctor, not a poor college professor like some people."

"You trying to get rid of me?"  She kissed his cheek.

"Well actually, yes.  Tomorrow afternoon, anyway.  While I'm lifting, I'd like Bill to keep you company, explain what's going on."

"And afterwards?"

"Then you're mine, baby, all mine."  He gave her thigh a squeeze.

They got out at a brownstone façade in the middle of a block of prosperous apartments near Central Park.  The lobby had shining black marble floors and potted palms; a woman at the information desk, chatting with a security guard, looked up.  "Dr. Chappell," Rochmann said.  The two nodded and went back to their conversation.  Rochmann and Gretchen took the elevator, emerging into a wide hallway lined with frosted glass doors.  He led the way to one on which the names of a half-dozen doctors were painted; at the bottom was 'William R. Chappell III, M.D., Internal Medicine.'  The door opened on a corner suite with windows on two sides and framed posters of MOMA exhibitions on the other walls.  Well-dressed patients reading magazines were seated at equal intervals around the room.  Rochmann approached the semi-circular counter that surrounded the business portion of the office.

"Can I help you?" the receptionist asked.

In an official tone, he said, "Would you please tell Dr. Chappell that Dr. Rock is here to consult with him about a case of hypertrophic gluteus."

"What?" She looked uncertainly from him to Gretchen and back again. "Do you have an appointment?"

"This is a consultation. Hypertrophic gluteus," he enunciated slowly. "Dr. Rock. Please tell Dr. Chappell. He'll know what it's about."

The puzzled woman left the desk and went through a door to the rear.

A couple minutes later, a tall, smiling man strode through the door. His crisp, white lab jacket was tailored to fit his broad shoulders and flat stomach; the obligatory stethoscope dangled from a jacket pocket and a blue plastic nametag showed this was indeed 'DR. WM. CHAPPELL III.' Chrome aviator-style glasses with grey-tinted lenses masked his close-set brown eyes, crinkled at the corners in laugh lines. His chestnut hair was stylishly cut, with just a touch of gray at the temples.

"Dr. Rock!" He enthusiastically pumped Rochmann's right hand while squeezing his left shoulder. "Hypertrophic gluteus, eh? Turn around and bend over and let me check 'em out." To Gretchen, he said, "It's okay. I'm a real doctor."

"And this is Gretchen," Rochmann said.

Chappell shook her hand more gently and looked her up and down with an exaggerated leer. "She's not nearly as ugly as you told me, Rocko."

The people in the waiting room looked up furtively from their magazines.

Taking Rochmann by the shoulders and turning him around, Chappell said, "Both of you, c'mon in the back, we'll talk and I'll do a quick check-up." He guided them to an empty examining room and said, "Take off your clothes, both of you. I'll be back in a couple of minutes." Gretchen sat down in one of the chairs. Rochmann removed his jacket and shirt and leaned against the examining table.

"What's with him?" Her voice was halfway between amusement and irritation.

"That's just Doctor Jock. More bark than bite."

"Well, he could certainly work on his people skills. And what's with this 'real doctor' thing?"

"After college, when he went to med school and I started a Ph.D. program, he joked that he was going to be the 'real doctor.' Just a way of dissing me – a guy thing."

"Men," she said with feigned disgust.

A nurse entered and wound a blood-pressure cuff around Rochmann's thick upper arm, took one reading, frowned, and repeated the process. She wrote on her clipboard, then gave him a professional smile. "Now, some blood?" She drew two small vials and said, "Doctor will be in soon." She repeated her smile and soundlessly closed the door.

A few minutes later, Chappell came in, carrying a small black vinyl case that he placed on the desk. "You guys look great! Some greater than others." A smile and wink at Gretchen. "You're in speech pathology?"

She nodded.

"Good field. You do important work. You want to work in a hospital, let me know. I might know some people." To Rochmann, he said, "You ready for the Berger Memorial? How you feeling?"

"Pretty good, pretty good. No major injuries. Must have a good doctor."

"Well, I'd like to take a little closer look if I could." He turned to Gretchen. "If you'd, um, take a seat in the waiting room for a couple of minutes."

When the door closed behind her, Chappell said, "Now, take off your tee shirt and sit up here." Seated on the examining table, Rochmann was eye level with him. "Hmm, amazing traps." He squeezed the thick muscles on the top of Rochmann's shoulders. "Breathe deeply," he said, placing the stethoscope several places on his chest and back. "Pump sounds alright." He then took two blood pressure readings, as the nurse had done. "Blood pressure's a little high."

"Meet tomorrow. I'm pretty hyped."

"Well, more than a little high. You've always been borderline but this is up quite a bit. You been doubling up on the 'roids?"

"No way. I always follow doctor's orders."

"Well, you'll be taking a drug holiday after this meet, right? Let's see what happens then."

"Can't," Rochmann said. "This is just a tune-up, remember? Nationals coming up in six, seven weeks. Have to stay juiced for that."

"Hmm. That soon? Well, we can still take a week or so off. Keep our eye on it. Here, I want you to take this home with you." He indicated the vinyl case on the desk. "A sphygmomanometer. You know how to use it. Take your blood pressure every morning when you get up. Keep track of the data. Add it to your computer program. I know you'll love that. And send me the readings. Okay?"

Rochmann nodded, his lips in a tight line.

"Everything else looks fine," Chappell said. "Your skin's clear, no unusual hair loss, we'll see how the liver tests come out. Any aggressive rages? Punch out the dean lately?"

Rochmann smiled and shook his head. "Thought of it a couple times."

"How's your pecker working? A normal man would be on top of that Gretchen two, three times a day. You're complaining she wants to do sex and drugs? I'd sell my soul to Satan for a deal like that."

"Well, like I told you, coke tore the hell out of my training."

"Yeah, and cocaine is definitely a no-no with hypertension. You two are getting along okay? Without the coke?"

"Yeah." This was not the time or place for details.

"She really likes you, I can tell. Hey, you going to lift some big weights tomorrow?"

"You're coming, right? Like we planned? You can talk Gretchen through the contest. She won't know what the hell's going on."

"You don't want me to coach you?"

"I can coach myself. I'd feel better if Gretchen wasn't left alone. Hey, you still seeing that stewardess? We could all have supper together after the meet."

"She's out of town, San Francisco or Seattle or someplace. I have this exchange student that I'm working on, an art student from France. I'll see if she's available. What time's the meet start?"

"My group weighs in at eleven, lifting starts at one, so any time around then."

"You'll do great, Rock. See you tomorrow." They clasped hands and gave each other a brief hug. "Don't forget your cuff," Chappell reminded him.

As they left the office, Gretchen asked, "What's that?"

"A blood pressure cuff. Something else to keep track of."

"You have high blood pressure?"

"Comes with the territory." He tried to sound nonchalant.

On the elevator down to the first floor, Gretchen said brightly, "Let's go shopping. I never get to the City any more."

"Gretchen, I have a meet tomorrow. I need to rest up at the hotel."

"Rocky, I drive all the way down here with you, sit around a smelly gym, meet your weird doctor friend, the least you can do is go to a couple stores with me. You can rest while I look around."

He sighed. The elevator opened and they walked, without speaking, to the front doors of the building. When they were outside, she turned to him. "Fine, you just go back to the hotel. I can go shopping by myself."

"No, no, you're right. I'll come with you."

He'd been shopping with her before and knew the drill. There were chairs where package-laden men could sit while their women ranged among the racks, searching, holding garments up, murmuring their interest or disgust, disappearing for a while, only to emerge suddenly with the rhetorical question, "How does this look?" Even in the eyes-averted atmosphere of New York City, camaraderie could develop between men as they exchanged knowing glances about the absurdity of their situation. In fact it could be enjoyable if other men were present. Having this amazingly beautiful woman seeking his approval marked him clearly as an alpha male.

His tone brightened as a cab that Gretchen hailed lurched to a stop. "Hey, you can model some sexy lingerie for me."

"You have a meet tomorrow, remember," she said curtly as he opened the door for her.

"Yes, but afterwards I'll need some calming down." He stroked her thigh as the cab swung into traffic.

"We'll see," she said in the tone a mother uses with a child who has asked to stay up late for a television special.

\*\*\*

Rochmann walked up the steps to the looming brick building. He'd gone to lunch and had about an hour before he would need to start warming up. As he entered, he heard his name called over the loudspeaker: "Robert Rochmann, first attempt snatch, 140 kilos."

The food congealed in his stomach. How could this be? He had at least two hours before he was scheduled to lift.

Someone rushed up to him. "Where have you been? Your session started an hour ago."

His name came over the speaker again. "You have two minutes to appear on the platform."

His heart raced. How could this be? He couldn't even get his lifting suit on in two minutes. Should he pass on his first attempt? Ask for another five kilos so he'd have time to get dressed? But there was no way he could lift that amount of weight with no warm-up.

"Wait!" he called." "Something's wrong here! Wait!"

"Wake up! Wake up!" Gretchen shook his shoulder roughly. "You're yelling in your sleep."

He sat up groggily. "Mmmph," he grunted. "I was dreaming." He took a deep breath. "Thank God, it just was that dream. Damn recurring nightmare."

"What? What dream?"

"Hmm," he sighed. "Let's just go back to sleep."

"Rocky, you woke me up. Tell me what you were yelling about."

He snuggled against Gretchen's warm body and told her about his panic at being late for the start of competition.

"Poor baby," she said, tenderly stroking his shoulder. "Do you have this dream before every contest?"

106

"No. Just sometimes. Haven't kept track if it's a bad sign or not."

He hefted his thick leg over her thighs, draped his arm across her breasts, and nuzzled his nose into her neck. She shifted her hips, pressing into his groin, perhaps aroused by this display of vulnerability. But he determinedly ignored Mister Lucky and soon was snoring softly.

# Chapter 16: A Gift of God

Chappell gently nudged the reclining figure with his foot. "What'd you weigh?"

Rochmann slowly sat up. Weights clanked and crashed on the other side of heavy, gray canvas curtains that separated the competition from the warm-up area in the basement of the Lost Battalion Hall. A voice on a static-filled public address system announced names and numbers. "Sounds like the morning session is about done," Rochmann said. "What time is it?"

"Almost one. How was weigh-in?"

"No problem. Weighed 82 even."

"You eat? Want me to get you something? Who's in your class?"

"Just local guys. Nobody to push me. That's okay; I know what I have to do. Had some bananas and honey. I'm fine." Rochmann stood slowly and bent side to side. "Have to start stretching soon."

"Gretchen here?" Chappell asked. "Didn't see her out front."

"Still asleep at the hotel. Or shopping again. No telling when she'll show up. Just keep an eye out for her, okay?"

Shortly after one o'clock, twenty-five men in five weight classes, between 82.5 kilos and heavyweight, marched out to stand in a line around the lifting platform, a motley group that varied greatly in height and width. Some were dressed in shiny nylon warm-up suits adorned with swoops and stripes; others, like Rochmann, wore baggy, sweat-stained sweatpants and shirts. The announcer called their names and each stepped forward to a smattering of applause and encouraging shouts. Friends and family made up the audience; they sat on folding chairs arranged in jumbled rows, chattering amiably among themselves. Children clambered on a boxing ring off to one side.

Chappell watched the competition and checked a couple times to see how Rochmann's warm-ups were going. He appeared to be totally focused on lifting and Chappell said nothing about Gretchen, who still had not shown up. Finally, Chappell saw her in the doorway at the side of the room. She wore tight black slacks that emphasized the length of her legs, and a downy white angora sweater that emphasized the fullness of her breasts. She carried a black woolen jacket, a black shoulder bag, and a black Saks Fifth Avenue shopping bag. Her pink-flushed face and golden hair added a note of color. All eyes in the audience turned toward her and the murmuring declined a few decibels. Chappell shook his head. This woman seemed totally wrong for his old friend--obviously expensive tastes, and that cocaine thing. But Rocky seemed to genuinely like her. Maybe she'd be good for him.

Chappell stood and waved. Gretchen beamed an electric smile and made her way toward him. She startled as a loud thud resounded. A voice on the crackly p.a. announced, "That's a good lift for Clark." Heads swiveled back to the lifting platform.

"Have I missed him?" she asked in a breathy whisper. "Hard time finding a cab. I came right here," she indicated the shopping bag which rustled as she settled in to a chair next to Chappell.

"No, Rock hasn't started yet. Should be soon. It's good to see you."

The announcer said, "130 kilos on the bar, 286 pounds. This will be the final attempt for Clark. Zielinsky on deck for the increase."

"This lift is called the snatch," he told her. "The guy has to pull the barbell from the floor and catch it at arms' length overhead in one motion."

Gretchen watched without displaying much curiosity as a big man contended with the barbell. Chappell offered no more explanation. She looked up when the loudspeaker crackled, "Loaders, increase the bar to 135 kilos, 297 pounds, first attempt for Robert Rochmann. Peters on deck." Rochmann appeared from behind the curtain and stood chalking his hands while the loaders adjusted the bar.

"Look at his legs," Gretchen exclaimed, as though she'd never seen them before.

"Yeah, he's pumped," said Chappell.

Even in repose, Rochmann's thighs flared amazingly, like a clown's pantaloons, quadriceps hanging over his knees, then coming alive, quivering with each step as he walked toward the platform, waddling like a fat man, swinging each leg out and around the other. He wore a wrestler's tunic, royal blue with white stripes banding the leg openings and shoulder straps; a touch of white chalk marked the bulge between his thighs. The dark blue shirt beneath his suit was almost black with sweat.

Rochmann stood over the bar for a few seconds, eyes closed, inhaling deeply, then bent and grasped it in the wide snatch grip. The barbell rose from the floor slowly, then accelerated in a blur and Rochmann was under it in a deep squat. He stood easily, though his reddened face indicated exertion. A buzzer sounded for the down signal and he let the barbell fall heavily to the platform.

A table to the side of the platform held a wooden box with a row of three white light bulbs protruding from the front, and a row of three red bulbs beneath them. Rochmann turned and walked back to the warm-up area without acknowledging the clapping audience or the three white lights that indicated the referees' approval.

"That's an easy opener for Rochmann," said the announcer. "That puts him ahead of everyone in the 181 class. Same weight, first attempt for Peters."

"Very strong," said Chappell. "Looks like a good day."

"This guy's a lot bigger." Gretchen nodded at the man standing at the chalk box while the loaders tightened the outer collars that secured the plates on the bar.

"He's in the 100 kilo class, or maybe 110," replied Chappell.

"So they're not competing against each other?"

"No. Rock's got his class sewed up."

Peters was a muscular black man, about six feet tall. He wore no shirt and his upper body seemed made of cannon balls, black spheres forming his shaved head, immense deltoids and biceps, his trapezius and latissimus bulging from under the thin straps of his bright red tunic.

"He looks really strong," said Gretchen.

"Looks don't count that much in this sport," Chappell replied.

The man in red marched up to the bar, grasped it with hands against the inside collars, and gave a mighty heave. He caught it in a half squat, the bar tilted to his left; he stood and took a couple steps forward before stopping for the down signal. He let the bar drop to the platform, turned, and shook his fist angrily at the three red lights.

"No lift," said the announcer. "I'm sure he'll take that weight again. Sabatini will also take 135 for his first attempt."

"Why'd they turn it down?" asked Gretchen. "For walking with it?"

"No," replied Chappell. "Press out. His arms were bent when he got the weight overhead and he had to lock it out. You have to catch it with your arms straight. You can walk all over as long as you stop and get it under control."

"Seems silly. I mean he lifted it."

"Rules are rules. Gotta have a net to play tennis."

"You play tennis?" she asked.

"Some. I play a little of everything, tennis, basketball, racquetball, golf. I'm not focused like Rocky."

"Tell me about it," she sighed. "That man would be in the gym twenty-four hours a day if he could."

"That's my boy. You play? Tennis?"

Used to. Before I met Rocky." She gazed off at the large man approaching the barbell.

Sabatini was definitely a heavyweight. His arms and legs were thick cylinders that barely tapered at wrists and ankles, and his stomach protruded so much that it looked difficult for him to bend over and grasp the bar. But once attached to the barbell, he seemed like a spring-loaded mechanism. The bar rose easily and he jumped under it with surprising agility. The audience yelled and clapped at the spectacle.

"Strong," remarked Chappell.

What a man!" Gretchen laughed and Chappell grinned at her apparent enjoyment.

Peters repeated his earlier performance, to the same effect. There was a two-minute wait before he tried again. The announcer stood and stretched, talking with the others at the scorer's table. People walked out to go to the concession booth upstairs. There was continuous chattering and occasional bursts of laughter. Chappell looked at his watch. Gretchen rolled her eyes.

"Borrring," she said with a sigh.

"Yeah, when a lifter follows himself it really drags," Chappell agreed. "They should have cheerleaders or something."

As if in response to this observation, the announcer clicked on the microphone. "Peters really needs this lift to stay in the competition," he urged. "How about some encouragement, ladies and gentlemen?" There was a smattering of applause and his friends called out, "C'mon, Damon! You can do it! You the man!"

Peters wore an angry scowl, as though the barbell had insulted his mother. He tore the weight from the floor, barely squatting under it, and ran forward to steady it, stopping just before reaching the edge of the platform. The head referee ducked to one side before yelling, "Down!" The audience laughed. Peters stepped back to the middle of the platform, let the weight fall, and turned to face the lights. Two whites and a red lit up. He pumped his fist in exaltation and turned to grin broadly and wave to his friends, who yelled and clapped. The rest of the audience joined in.

"He still pressed it out," Chappell said. "Just did it quicker. The judges probably don't want him to bomb out if it was close."

"Well I'm glad he made it," said Gretchen. "I think he did it the first time."

"Yeah, I wish he would've," Chappell said in a worried tone. "This long wait's not doing Rock any good."

Another heavyweight, who looked muscular and athletic like a professional football player, missed 137.5, using a technique similar to that of Peters. After another two-minute wait, he made it on his second attempt.

Finally, 140 kilos was placed on the bar for Rochmann's second attempt. The lift appeared to go like his first one, except the bar remained suspended above his head for just a fraction of a second before crashing down in front of him. He remained squatting, hands still gripping the bar, head bowed, for a couple of seconds.

"I was afraid of that," said Chappell. "Got cold waiting. I'm going to talk to him." He hurriedly left his seat and went behind the curtains.

Rochmann was standing with a towel across his shoulders, head down and lips pressed together. "Plenty high, Rock, just a little in front," Chappell said. Rochmann nodded. "And relax your hips in the squat; you have to get all the way under it."

Rochmann nodded vigorously and looked up with a tight smile. "Yup, no problem." He rolled his shoulders and jumped up and down in place a couple times.

"C'mon Rock!" Chappell yelled and slapped him on the back. "Do it!" He stood behind the scorer's table while Rochmann strode purposefully to the chalk box.

"Quiet please," said the announcer, and the chatter in the auditorium died down.

This time the bar remained fixed overhead and Rochmann's face broke into a smile as he rose from the squat and faced the referee.

Chappell gave him a big hug when he walked off the platform. Rochmann gathered up his towel and sweat clothes and walked with Chappell to where Gretchen was sitting. Other lifters stopped him to shake hands and pat his shoulder in congratulation. As he sat down, the people seated nearby leaned over to say, "Way to go," "Awesome, man," "Great lifting."

Gretchen turned on her megawatt smile and kissed him gently on the cheek. "Very good," she said, giving his sweaty shoulders a hug.

"Well, I wanted more," he said. "Not today, I guess."

"That's your best, isn't it?" asked Chappell.

"Ties my best. Did it at the Nationals last year. Want to get 150 at the Trials. I think the pull is there, just have to get under it quicker. Better timing."

Rochmann pulled on his sweatshirt and pants, and sat back to watch the heavyweights finish their snatches, his arm around Gretchen. "How do you like the contest?" he asked.

"I like watching you. And some of the other guys. But there's a lot of time with nothing happening. And even when they're lifting, it's like up and down, so fast. And sometimes they turn down a lift for some dumb reason."

"I know. It's not a very good spectator sport unless you really know what to look for and watch closely. And there's a lot of down time between attempts."

"I think they need cheerleaders," said Chappell.

Gretchen rolled her eyes. Rochmann said, "*You* wouldn't even need the lifters if there were cheerleaders."

One-hundred forty-five kilos was loaded on the bar and Sabitini, the big heavyweight, made it easily. The guy who looked like a football player also tried this weight for his third attempt but pulled it only to his waist before dropping it disgustedly. One-hundred fifty kilos brought out the last lifter, a man slightly taller than Rochmann, with longer arms and even thicker thighs and shoulders, but with less muscular definition and a slight paunch. He had pale brown skin and close-cropped, curly black hair. His black eyes stared intently beneath half-closed eyelids at the bar.

"This guy's good," Rochmann said, sitting up. "World-class. He's from Cuba. Got bronze in the World Champs a while back. If he can get U.S. citizenship he'll be our 90 or 100-kilo national champ and have a good shot at an Olympic medal."

Gretchen asked, "Guys do that a lot? Move to other countries to lift on their Olympic teams? Like Berger went to Israel?"

"Not that much. The International Olympic Committee frowns on it. Besides, there's no money in lifting. If this guy played baseball, he'd be a millionaire. I think he just wanted to get away from Cuba. Athletes there are supported well. The Cubans kick our butt in the Pan Americans. Soviet coaches. I guess he just got tired of the control. He didn't even do it the usual way, defecting at some international competition. He just disappeared and a year or so later, somebody finds him driving a cab in New York, just trying to make a living for his family. He wasn't training at all, put on a lot of weight. Word is, a bunch of rich Miami Cubans, who like to rub Castro's nose in it, got together to support his training. The guy's amazing, getting close to his best lifts already, but he has to lose some weight."

"Carlos Varza, lifting in the hundred kilo class, first attempt," the p.a. system sputtered.

Gretchen looked up suddenly at the name 'Carlos,' but it may have been only a startle response to the sudden shouts of encouragement. A couple seated behind them chattered excitedly, their staccato Spanish like pebbles shaken in a cigar box. Most Latinos in the audience were Puerto Ricans, but all united to cheer on their brother. Varza did not disappoint them, diving under the barbell with blazing speed and catching it in a low squat position, his buttocks resting on his heels. His arms and shoulders quivered as he stood with the weight, but he held it successfully for the down signal. Loud whoops and yells followed the three white lights and the announcer had to call for silence as Sabatini stood ready for his third attempt at the same weight.

Rochmann said, "He is *so* quick. *Lodarok boga*, a gift of God, as the Russians say. I'd give anything to have his fast-twitch fibers."

Sabatini narrowly missed the 150, dropping it in front of him. Varza missed 155, getting under it but failing to fix it overhead. He passed his third attempt.

"There will be a ten-minute intermission before we begin the clean-and-jerks," said the announcer. Rochmann gave Gretchen a kiss on the cheek and clapped Chappell on the shoulder before making his way into the warm-up area.

# Chapter 17:  Best Lifter

G retchen watched Rochmann walk away with that strange, rolling gait of his.  She gave a big sigh.

"Want to get a snack, stretch your legs?" asked Chappell.

"Sure," she said, and they joined the jostling group on the floor of the auditorium heading for the exit.

Clean-and-jerks, by virtue of the two motions involved, take longer than snatches.  And the dead time between attempts as the bar was loaded and adjusted, or two-minute rest periods imposed for a lifter who followed himself, increased the perception of time in slow motion.  Gretchen fidgeted distractedly as the afternoon wore on.  Chappell tried to explain the technical aspects of various lifters, and she listened courteously, but the trajectory of the bar or the position of a lifter's elbows were as meaningful to her as a golf commentator's analysis of backswing to a Martian.

"Where's Rocky?" she said impatiently.

"Hey, the later he starts the better.  Clean and jerk's his best lift.  Wouldn't it be great if he beat all these big guys?"

Finally, only three men remained:  Sabatini the heavyweight, Varza the Cuban, and Rochmann.

"One-hundred seventy-five kilos, 385 pounds," intoned the announcer.  "First attempt for Robert Rochmann.  If he makes this, he'll win the 181-pound class."

"Good," remarked Gretchen, "then we can go."  Nevertheless, she sat up and watched attentively as Rochmann cinched in his wide leather belt and stalked to the center of the platform.

"Man, look at that bar bend," exclaimed Chappell as Rochmann squatted under it, the plates at either end sagging downward.  He caught the bar slightly forward and had to pause to gain control, forcing him to remain in the squat position a fraction of a second too long to catch the upward rebound of the plates.  But he stood easily and rammed the barbell solidly overhead.  This drama in six seconds was obvious to the practiced eye of Chappell but meant only the end of a long afternoon to Gretchen.  Disappointingly, Rochmann disappeared behind the canvas curtain instead of walking over to join them.

Sabatini made the same weight with no trouble, his girth making the barbell appear to shrink in size when he grasped it. Varza displayed his amazing quickness in squatting under the barbell but his legs trembled slightly as he stood with it. He jerked it overhead easily, to a chorus of Spanish accolades. The sight of these three men of disparate size lifting the same huge weight brought the audience to life. Rochmann acquired a vocal following that yelled for *el nino*, the little one.

The enthusiasm was catching and Gretchen forgot about leaving. "C'mon Rocky!" she shouted when he appeared for his second attempt at 180 kilos. This weight appeared to go easier than the previous one, and he smiled at the cheering audience after letting the barbell crash to the floor. Sabatini chose to take a higher weight. Varza stood at the rear of the platform and fixed his smoldering, half-lidded gaze on the barbell, as if he could levitate it by sight alone. He had more difficulty standing with this weight, requiring a couple of bounces from the squat position before coming erect with it. He split under it quickly but his shoulders and arms shook as he held it overhead. The crowd yelled and whistled approval.

"Loaders, 185 kilos, 407 pounds, for Sabatini's second attempt," the announcer broke in. "Rochmann, on deck."

"Damn, Rock's hanging with the big boys!" exclaimed Chappell.

"He'll get it," said Gretchen, recalling that time in the weight room when he'd done four hundred pounds.

Sabatini struggled, his purple face showing strain as he stood from the squat. He took several breaths before driving the bar up for the jerk, and walked forward a couple steps with the bar overhead before steadying it for the down signal. Again, the audience loudly approved this display of immense exertion.

It was Rochmann's turn. The barbell seemed to move in the same precise fashion as before, just a tick more slowly. He lagged slightly in squatting under it, catching it so low that his buttocks nearly touched the platform. He caught the bounce of the plates and stood deliberately, hydraulically, and paused to breathe, once, twice, three times, his stomach expanding and contracting over his belt. He bent his legs, extended them, the barbell seemed suspended as he split under it, locked his elbows and held it aloft. Almost done. He dragged his right foot forward, stepped back with his left foot so they were evenly aligned, and stood before the head referee with the visage of a conquering gladiator. As if to savor his victory, he held the barbell overhead for a moment after the down signal, then lowered it to his chest, bounced it from his thighs, and replaced it gently on the platform, grasping it for yet another second, as if unwilling to relinquish control. Finally he stood, smiled broadly and waved to the cheering, stomping, whistling crowd.

Then the chant became, "Car-los! Car-los!" as the barbell was adjusted for the Cuban's third attempt. Rochmann stood behind the scorer's table and watched respectfully while Varza turned on his levitating stare. But it did not work this time; the barbell bounced off his chest as he tried to squat under it. Sabatini did the same with 190 kilos, and it was over.

"Way to go, Rocky! Just great! That last lift was just super! I'm sure you beat Varza for Best Lifter!" exalted Chappell when Rochmann finally made his way through the crowd of well-wishers.

"Thanks," he said, giving Chappell a hug, and Gretchen a bigger hug and a kiss. "I'm happy. Five of six, personal record jerk and total. I'm on my way."

"What's 'Best Lifter?'" asked Gretchen.

"It's an award based on a formula to compare guys across weight classes, to see who's best overall," replied Chappell.

"Well, congratulations again," she said, and gave Rochmann another kiss.

"Where do you want to eat?" he asked Chappell. "You're coming, right? You got a date?"

"Darn right, I'm taking you guys out. My treat. Don't know about my date though. I'm sure Gretchen won't mind going out with two good-looking guys."

"My dream come true," she laughed.

***

Gretchen dined with two men that evening, or perhaps three. Carl, her faithless former boyfriend, joined them at the periphery, never in focus: a ghostly presence in the name 'Carlos,' chanted by the crowd that afternoon; the figure of the tall, dark-haired, well-dressed man at the far table; the shrimp cocktail he always ordered, being devoured at that moment by Dr. William Chappell, III.

The haunting was precipitated by a telephone call she had made while out shopping that morning. She called from a phone booth-- perhaps because it was convenient, perhaps so the call would not appear on the hotel bill. Was it a spur of the moment impulse, triggered by being in New York, a city where she and Carl had spent so much time together? Or by a desire to find out how an old friend was doing? Or something else?

Carl had seemed so distraught last winter when she had told him she never wanted to see him again. He could understand her being upset, he'd told her. But it was only a dalliance, the woman in his apartment meant nothing to him, he'd assured her. Was that true, or were they still happily living together? Carl had tried to contact her after her ultimatum, but Latasha had screened his calls and Gretchen returned his letters, unopened. After she moved out of her old place and in with Rochmann, his efforts ceased. Now, with hints of spring in the air, much of her fury and anguish over his betrayal had subsided. Had this other woman really been a passing affair? Or had she stayed with him? Or had Carl moved on to yet another? There was an open-endedness that kept the matter alive. Besides, it would be fitting to let him know how well she was doing, finishing up her master's degree and living in a committed relationship with a professor and Olympic athlete.

Committed. Well, Rocky seemed committed when it came to other women. But she knew she would always be number two to this strange sport, this obscure pastime that was not carried out in the crisp, clean atmosphere of a golf or tennis club, or grassy ballparks filled with thousands of cheering fans. No, it was done in smelly, low-rent basements, by men of odd shapes and sizes, performing the same repetitive act over and over in a Sysiphean battle with gravity.

She had hesitated for some time before going through with the call. It would be easiest if his answering machine picked up; she could just leave a cheery message and walk away, relieved at avoiding a brush with complication. She rehearsed what to say if a woman, the other woman, answered. She would ask to speak to 'Henry,' she would be apologetic for dialing a wrong number, and she would know for certain how things stood. But Carl himself had answered, his familiar voice producing an unexpected intake of breath, an unwanted pause before stating her practiced greeting.

"Hi, Carl. This is Gretchen. I was in town and just wondered how things are going for you."

He sounded surprised and pleased to hear from her. Could they meet?

"No, no I can't see you. I'm real busy. I'm in town with my boyfriend on, uh, business." Describing Rochmann's status as a college professor, an aspiring Olympian, seemed somehow out of place. "I have to meet him shortly. I just wanted to say hello. How is law school going?"

He was studying for the bar exam and had interviews scheduled with several prestigious law firms. The woman in his apartment had moved on and he was much too busy to get involved with another. He was happy she was doing so well. Did she plan on staying in Westerville after graduation?

With a lawyer's instinct for the kill, he had gone straight to the heart of her relationship with Rochmann. This was the unanswered, indeed, the unasked question. Rocky had been so focused on preparing for his contests, and she so busy completing her thesis, it was easy to put the next step of their relationship on the shelf. It was difficult to imagine a long-term future with him, yet she would be disappointed if he did not want her to stay. Rochmann's horizon seemed to extend only to the Olympics next year. She presumed she was welcome to stick around as long as she didn't interfere with his training. After that, perhaps she would become the center of his attention. But was that what she wanted? She assumed she would have a career working with children. Maybe have a child herself. But with Rocky? These questions were much too difficult.

"I haven't decided," she told Carl. It was getting late. She had to go. No, she would not meet him. She did not want him to call. She would think about staying in touch and would contact him if she decided to do so.

Now, at the restaurant, she looked at Bill and Rocky sitting in animated conversation, reviewing the nuances of each lift and its portent for the future. Despite his obsession, Rocky was a sweetie, gentle and witty, even good-looking in his own short-statured way.

He would expect to have sex that night as was due the Best Lifter. Indeed, he had asked her to shower with him at the hotel before going out. She'd refused, saying it would make her too tired to stay awake during dinner, and he had not pressed the matter. Carl had always been more urgent, less deferential about sex. That might have been due to their living at a great distance and seeing each other only sporadically. But Carl's taking up with another woman during her absences indicated that he, perhaps, had a greater need than Rochmann did. And, of course, there was the cocaine that fueled their intensity. There would be no cocaine this night. She did not like to travel with it; there was always the possibility, however remote, of some brush with the law that could make life difficult, even for an upper-class white woman like herself. Besides, her stash was dwindling and she had no contacts to get more. Carl had always supplied their needs but she could not very well ask him, "By the way, can you get me some more coke to get me off with the guy I'm living with?"

Perhaps she could learn to enjoy drug-free sex with this guileless, placid weightlifter. Guiltily, affectionately, she took Rocky's hand and he squeezed hers, gently, the horny ridges of his calluses pressing against her soft skin.

# PART V

# SIC TRANSIT GLORIA

# Chapter 18:  First Place for Losers

Back in Westerville, Rochmann and Gretchen returned to their separate passions.  One evening, when he arrived home after workout, Gretchen met him at the door with a big hug. "It's done!" she exclaimed.  "I fixed dinner to celebrate."  A large bowl of tossed salad sat on the kitchen counter, and spaghetti sauce, redolent with garlic and onion, simmered on the stove.  A linen tablecloth, candles, and two wine glasses graced the table.

"That's great," he said.  "What's done?"

"My thesis, silly.  I handed in the final draft and Schmidlap signed off without a fuss. It's all done. I can't believe it."

"All right!  That's really great."  He set down his gym bag and embraced her warmly.  "I would've taken you out to celebrate if you'd told me."

"Maybe this weekend.  I just wanted to cook for the two of us tonight."  There was promise in her voice.

"I've got some good news, too," he said.  "Chappell has a friend with a condo in Seekonk that we can use for free the weekend of the Nationals.  We won't have to stay in a crappy hotel.  Afterwards we can go up to Boston, or maybe the coast for a few days if you want. You can show me how to sail, like you've always been talking about."

"When is that?"

"Weekend after next.  We can leave Thursday morning, get in that evening, I can rest on Friday and lift on Saturday."

"A week from this coming weekend?  That's graduation.  The graduation ceremony is Saturday.  My parents are coming.  Don't you remember?"

"You're kidding.  I thought graduation was the following weekend."

"Rocky, I can't believe it.  You're on the faculty here and you don't know when graduation is?" she said sharply.  "We talked about it.  You're going to meet my parents."

"The faculty drew straws the beginning of the quarter to see who had to go to the ceremony," he said.  "When I didn't have to go, I didn't pay attention to when it was.  Honest, I thought it was the week after the Nationals. I really want to watch you graduate. And meet your folks. But..." He shrugged helplessly.

"You don't really have to go to this meet." Her voice took on a shrill, demanding tone. "You did good at that Berger thing. Best Lifter and all. And the Olympic qualifying thing is not until next year, right? You're not required to go to this contest." She sounded like a prosecuting attorney.

"Babe, it's the Senior Nationals," he said, as if that explained everything. "I've got to see what I can do against top competition. All the biggies in the U. S. Weightlifting Federation will be there, the people that will be on the selection committee. I have to go." He should have stopped there but he went on. "Why do you have to go to graduation? You get your diploma whether you walk or not."

"You asshole!" she erupted. "My parents are coming. I told you. They want to meet the man I'm living with. Oh, never mind. To hell with you!" She stalked into the bedroom and slammed the door.

He sighed heavily and turned off the burner under the spaghetti sauce. He knocked on the bedroom door. "Gretch, Honey, listen, I'm sorry. Can we talk about it?"

"There's nothing to talk about. You do your thing, I'll do mine."

He stood, listening; there was no sound on the other side of the door. "I mean about being mad," he said at last.

"I'm not mad. I'm just, I don't know, just really, really disappointed."

"Can we talk about that?"

"I don't feel like talking. Maybe later."

Rochmann went into the study, fired up the IIe, and entered his training data. When he finished, Gretchen had returned to the kitchen and was busy at the stove. He tried to give her a hug but she brushed him off. "Let's just eat," she said. "Go sit down while I get this done."

He flipped through channels on the TV in the living room until she called him for dinner. The candles were gone and the wine glasses had been replaced, appropriately, by tumblers of ice water. Both of them made an effort to be civil. He complimented the flavor of the sauce; she inquired how his workout had gone. Later, they sat on the living room sofa, at opposite ends.

"Rocky," she began, "I just don't know what you want from me. Am I just going to get a job, move away? That's the end of it?"

He sighed and looked around the room, at the mossy green drapes she had made for the big window in the living room, at the framed print of Van Gogh's green-complexioned self-portrait she had hung on the wall. Vincent's dead eyes stared back. He thought of Nina's leaping starfish. "I don't know," he said. "What do you want?"

"That is not an answer."

"Okay, okay." He knew, at some instinctual level, what she wanted to hear. Maybe if he just said the words, it would be enough. She was the most beautiful woman he could ever hope to meet. And not only beautiful, but smart, and caring in her own way. He had seen the envy in other men's eyes; Golding, even Chappell, had been smitten by her. And this gorgeous woman was sitting here, on his couch, waiting for him to claim her. But at that same basic level, he knew words would not suffice. It might take more than he could to give. He would be honest with her.

He said, "I really care for you. I've never felt this way about anyone. Next year, after the Olympics, I can begin to think about long-range plans. But right now, what you see is what you get." He kissed her forehead and looked into her dark blue eyes. "I'd like to have you stay here with me. But you've got to do what's best for you."

She looked pensive, then kissed him back, on the lips. "Okay Rocky. I'm sorry I got so upset."

***

"Cheer up, Rock," said Chappell. Rochmann had hardly spoken since they'd left New Jersey. Bill's BMW knifed down the interstate, smoothly cutting past slower traffic. "You did real good. A solid second place in the Nationals is not bad."

"You know what they say about second place. First place for losers."

"C'mon, Rock. You got the same weights you did in the Berger Memorial on second attempts, which is damn good. You looked plenty strong on your third attempts, too, just a little off on timing. You'll get 'em next time, and more. And you were clean." 'Clean' meant he had gone off steroids two weeks before the contest and had flushed his system with diuretics.

"Shit! My 145 snatch attempt wasn't even close. The 190 clean felt okay, but the jerk was way out of the groove. And even if I had made them, so what? Curt White just blew me away. Damn! Six for six. American records! Jesus, it was all over after the snatch-- fucking 15 kilo lead. I mean I hoped, I fantasized, maybe doing those weights next year at the trials. Christ, can you imagine what he'll be doing by then?"

"Yeah, I think he intimidated you a little," Chappell agreed. "But you hung in there. Finished way ahead of the rest of the pack."

"Not by as much as White beat me. His 200 looked easy. Then to rub it in, he tries 205 for another record on a fourth attempt. Unbelievable!"

"Maybe he peaked too early. You'll catch him, Rock. A lot can happen in a year."

Rochmann stared at the cars and trucks that Chappell was picking off, one by one. It was Monday morning and traffic going north was light. "Everybody was setting records, or taking a sh 't at 'em anyway. I wonder what they're on," he mused.

"Probably same as you," Chappell said. "Don't worry. If there's anything new out there, I'll find it." He downshifted to pass a line of lumbering semis, then shifted into fifth gear on an open stretch of highway. The radar detector beeped and he slowed abruptly to 70. "Damn cops," he muttered. "Anyway, like I was saying, I talked to some U.S.W.F. officials, you know, nosing around. Drug testing is going to be beefed up this year, before the Olympics. The I.O.C. is putting the screws to the national committees. They might test during the year, not just at contests. Maybe some new kinds of tests, too. I'll see if I can volunteer to be on the medical committee so I can keep tabs on developments."

Rochmann said, "Well, you better come up with something special, if I'm going to add 30 kilos in a year."

\*\*\*

When Rochmann got home, there was a note from Gretchen taped to the refrigerator: 'Dear Rocky, My parents are taking me on a trip to Europe for a surprise graduation present. Hope you won your contest. See you in about a month. Love, Gretchen.'

"Well, at least she hasn't moved out," he muttered. Then, "Damn, I'm horny." He opened the refrigerator to check its contents, as if satisfying one hunger would take care of the other. Maybe it was a resurgence of his natural testosterone after a long period of suppression by steroids. Maybe it was endorphins generated by the stress of the contest. Or maybe it was a perverse response to Gretchen's absence. But he knew he couldn't wait a month.

He wondered if Nina might be available and tried to recall his last conversation with her, her tone of voice when he told her about Gretchen moving in. Maybe he should have talked to her about Gretchen's 'problem.' If anybody knew about orgasms, it was Nina. Maybe if Gretchen had regular orgasms she wouldn't be so bitchy. But first things first; he had to take care of his own problem.

After a few rings, Nina's voice on the answering machine gave her husband's phone number in the Anthropology Department and numbers of her New York galleries. He called the first gallery and was told that the Feiffers were traveling in South America for the summer.

"Damn! South America. The whole summer!" There was the Oriental Massage Parlor, but getting jerked off, even by a pretty little lotus blossom, wasn't that fulfilling. Perhaps he could talk to mamasan and arrange for something more than a hand-job in the shower.

It turned out that the lotus blossoms were available for activities not listed on the counter-top menu, starting at a hundred dollars a pop. The price of five 'muscle-rubs.' He did a quick calculation of what a vacation with Gretchen would have cost and concluded he could make a few visits and still come out ahead. Cash for coochie--the human mating strategy reduced to its basic elements. While enjoyable, Rochmann felt slightly guilty and looked forward to Gretchen's return.

He received a few airily chatty postcards from Europe for a couple weeks, but after that, no word. He taped the cards to the refrigerator, next to her note.

One afternoon in early July, he was replacing the front brake shoes on the Scout when Gretchen's Accord pulled up behind him at the top of the driveway. He stood and spanked the dirt from his butt, then approached her car, wiping his hands on his jeans. She got out and Mister Lucky stirred at the sight. She wore red shorts and a white tank top, her lithe limbs a smooth, buttery brown, her sun-streaked blonde hair piled atop her head in tumbling curls. Painted red toenails peeked from white sandals.

She retreated a step at his grimy appearance; a hug and kiss were out of the question. He said, "Let me take a quick shower and I'll help unload your stuff." She just smiled and nodded. "There's iced tea in the fridge," he added. Still, she said nothing. "It's good to see you," he said, then went inside.

He did a quick lather and rinse in the shower, thought better of going out naked to greet her, and put on a clean tee shirt and cut-off jeans. Gretchen was sitting at the kitchen table, sipping a glass of tea. He stood behind her chair to hug her shoulders and nuzzle his face in her hair. "It is *really* good to have you back," he said.

She patted his arm. "Sit down, Rocky. I have some news."

From her tone and manner, he got the message that she was going to be leaving soon. He poured himself some tea. While stirring in a heaping spoonful of sugar, he said, with his back to her, "Let me guess. You got a job." He returned the pitcher to the refrigerator, took some ice cubes from a bowl in the freezer compartment, clinked them into the glass, and sat down opposite her. They smiled at each other. Gretchen's sunglasses were pushed up into her hair and her eyes seemed a paler blue than usual.

"Yes, I did," she said. "In New York City."

He'd known this day was coming. It was nothing to be upset about. In fact, it was kind of a relief. He imagined slipping those red shorts down those long, tanned legs. Probably not many more times for that. "That's great. When do you start?"

"Well, I'll be moving right away. In fact, I need to start packing up my things." She waved her hand toward the bedroom.

"I see." Rochmann took a large mouthful of tea, swishing it around before swallowing. "This week?"

She nodded.

"Well," he said brightly. "Make it this weekend and I'll help you move in. I'm pretty good at moving pianos." He jokingly flexed his biceps.

"That's sweet, Rocky, but I've got movers coming for the boxes. Everything's taken care of." Her eyes were wide but she did not look directly at him.

"Can I have your address? I can come visit when I'm, you know, down in the City." He could hear the desperate note that had crept into his voice.

She shook her head, looking down at the table, then up to his eyes with a steady gaze. "Rocky, I'm moving in with Carl. You know, my old boyfriend. We decided it was time to, you know, be a couple."

"Carl?" His voice squeaked. "The guy that was living with another woman?" He did not say, 'The guy that gets you off with cocaine.' He could feel the heat in his face.

She was looking at him so sweetly. "That didn't work out. And Rocky, you and I both know this isn't working either." She reached across the table and grasped his hand. "I really care for you, and I really appreciate everything you've done for me." She continued to look steadily into his eyes and he had to look away, down to her hands that rested atop his clenched fist. He could see her hands but couldn't feel them; he'd never feel her touch again. She was still talking, something about different people, different goals, moving on. His ears rang and his pulse pounded in his neck, in his temples.

Finally, she stopped talking. He sat at the table while she carried some cardboard boxes in from her car and disappeared into the bedroom. He wanted to drive off somewhere but his car was up on jack stands with the front wheels off. He had to install one more brake shoe and bleed the lines before he could drive anywhere. Numbly, he went outside and set to work.

His reaction was senseless, he told himself. If she'd said she was moving to California to take a job and he'd never see her again, he could have bid her a fond farewell. No problem. So what if she moved in with Carl? Gone is gone. But another guy made a difference. He had come in second in a two-man contest, the most basic of human competitions and he didn't even know he was entered in it.

Rage welled up. He looked at his callused hands, blackened with brake dust. He could visualize them ripping off Gretchen's gleaming white top and crimson shorts, leaving filthy black smears all over the perfect globes of her breasts and buttocks. Take her, like a man was meant to take a woman. He stood, feeling the air fill his lungs, the blood fill his muscles. He walked down the driveway, down the street and past the edge of town, into the countryside. He walked until the horizon turned pink and his knees ached and his back and legs were sore with fatigue.

# Chapter 19:  Dick Tracy

Thank God for the weights.  For the remainder of the summer, Rochmann trained more religiously than ever. He seemed to burn with manic energy, doing set after set, rep after rep.  He was off steroids and down about five kilos in bodyweight, and much more than that in maximum lifts, but made great gains in speed, technique, and endurance.

All was going to the plan he and Chappell had devised, except for one thing:  his blood pressure remained high.  No matter what time of day he used the pressure cuff Chappell had given him, or how much he relaxed and did deep breathing before taking the measurement, his blood pressure remained above the point that indicated hypertension.  He did not tell Bill, fearing he might not put him back on the juice when the time came.  Instead, he got a prescription for blood pressure medication from a local doctor.  But the side effects interfered with training, making him dizzy and prone to muscle cramping, so he stopped taking it.  With less than a year until the Olympic trials, training came first.

Thoughts of Gretchen decreased to tolerable levels.  An entire day could pass with no reminder of her.  Nights were more difficult. Whatever their sexual problems, Gretchen had been a cuddler and Rochmann had a hard time adjusting to sleeping alone again.  Now he understood Nina's rule against actually sleeping together; once you got used to it, you were hooked.  He wondered if she and Marvin were sleeping together during their South American trip.

Nina returned at the beginning of fall quarter and they resumed their liaison, but it was not the same.  Rochmann almost resented her easy way with sex, in contrast to Gretchen's struggles.  And there was another, more obvious difference.  Nina seemed to have aged more than the six months could account for.  Compared to Gretchen's lithe limbs, or the drum-head tautness of the lotus blossoms' buttocks, Nina's flesh seemed to have deflated a few pounds-per-square-inch. Rochmann began to look more hungrily at the toothsome coeds in the weight room.  How could he make contact?  "Hi, I'm Dr. Rochmann,

Olympic hopeful.    How'd you like to meet Mister Lucky?"
Ridiculous.

One blonde dolly in particular caught his eye; her hair was more
yellow than Gretchen's, with dark roots, but he liked her hard body
and hard-edged look.  Shiny white leotards seemed painted on her
shapely quads and rounded glutes.  Bright pink accessories demanded
notice:  a pink sweatband held back her tousled blonde mane, thick
pink socks drew his eye to her gastrocnemius, and pink briefs that,
like a baboon in heat, served to accentuate more than cover her
pudenda.  Rochmann watched the rosy triangle disappear into the
crevice between her buttocks as she bent to adjust the weight stack.
The scooped neckline of her leotards revealed the tops of small,
tanned breasts that bulged as she took her seat on the Nautilus
machine, pressing her forearms together in front of her face in
supplication of the goddess of fitness.

Blondie worked with two training partners.   One, a young
woman of heavier proportions, had a pretty, heart-shaped face and
pale skin.  She was decked-out in black leotards with red accents, a
red sweatband in her thick, wavy black mane, and matching red
lipstick.  A large, artfully ripped tee shirt covered her breasts and
torso.  The third member of the trio was a tall, muscular young man,
whose costume was in synchrony with those of his partners--shiny
black bicycle-racer shorts with yellow stripes, and a yellow Gold's
Gym tank top with straps cut to narrow strings.  His hair was black
and curly, shiny from a little sweat and a touch of styling gel.  Like
Blondie, he was deeply tanned, although beach weather was long
past.

Rochmann was doing back squats, deep-knee bends with a
barbell across his shoulders, a simple exercise that could get tricky
with heavy weights.  He had begun his first cycle of anabolic steroids
and was eagerly piling on the plates, exalting in his burgeoning
strength.  He looked around the room for a spotter but did not see any
of the few guys who actually did squats and knew what they were
doing.  Tan-man seemed to be the strongest-looking guy there, but
like most body builders he was top-heavy; his legs, while muscular,

were scarcely bigger than his arms. But he seemed to be on good terms with Blondie. It could be an opportunity to break the ice.

Rochmann walked over to the machine and waited while Tan-man finished a set of pec crunches, or whatever the hell they were called. When he stood up, Rochmann shouted over the din of the tape players, "Can you give me a spot?" and nodded toward the platform in the back where 250 kilos loomed on the squat racks. He looked straight at the guy, but checked out Blondie with a quick glance.

Tan-man seemed momentarily uncertain but, in a show of expertise in front of his partners, said, "No problem."

"I have to wrap first," Rochmann said in a loud voice, pointing to his knee and making a circling motion with his finger, like a tourist speaking to a native who does not understand English. "You can do another set if you want." He meant to indicate there would be a delay before he was ready, but Tan-man followed him back to the platform and stood waiting while Rochmann sat on the bench and wrapped his knees tightly with thick elastic bands.

Rochmann gave instructions, his voice echoing inside his skull, trapped by his earplugs. "I'll do three reps." He held up three fingers. "Don't touch me unless I get stuck, then just give me a little boost across my chest." He demonstrated by crossing his hands on his chest and giving a little upward motion. Rochmann had watched pairs of bodybuilders doing squats--like copulating dogs, one with the bar and the other clasping him from behind, going down and up in tandem, the first grunting in exertion and the second exclaiming encouragement. "Don't touch me unless I get stuck," he repeated.

\*\*\*

"Hey, Traci, you're up," the blonde told her friend.

"Wait, I want to see this." It was an opportunity to openly observe this strange figure that she had been furtively watching. She'd seen him looking their way but suspected most of his attention had been for Jenni, her flashy roommate. Good friends, they shared a dorm room, class notes, and an interest in weight training. Both had replaced the 'y' at the end of her name with an 'i' dotted by a circle, sometimes including a smiley face. But Traci resigned herself to the fact that it was Jenni who drew men's eyes.

The shorter man tightened his belt, chalked his hands, stepped under bar, took a deep breath, lifted it from the rack, stepped back, another deep breath. His face flushed to the roots of his hair, but he did three smooth repetitions, the barbell quivering like the balance pole of a high-wire walker. He replaced the bar on the rack, loosened his belt, and turned and smiled at his spotter. "Thanks," he said.

"Hey, Lou, how much was that?" Traci asked when their training partner returned.

Lou counted the five large plates on each end of the bar--two red, two blue, a yellow--and a couple smaller ones. "About 500 pounds," he guessed. "Strong little dude."

Later, as Traci and Jenni peeled off their clothes in the women's locker room, Traci said, "That weightlifting guy is kind of cute."

"Supergeek?" replied Jenni. She had so many guys after her that she was generally contemptuous of men.

A few guys called Traci, too, college boys who were no different than those in high school. It would be nice to meet a man who knew his way around a woman. Traci said, "I think he's been in the Olympics or something," as if that exempted him from Jenni's derision.

"Yeah, but he's still a geek."

"Why do you say that?"

Jenni enumerated: "Omigod, just look at the way he dresses, those droopy clothes. And he's so short. And he's always by himself. And he smells like a horse. Did you catch that when he talked to Lou? God. He's like a total weirdo." She grinned at Traci. "You probably like that smell. You'd probably like to pinch his butt."

They were both naked, towels wrapped loosely around themselves, walking toward the shower area. "You noticed his butt, huh?" Traci teased back.

They went into adjoining shower stalls and pulled the curtains. Traci soaped her large breasts, feeling the softness of her skin. She envied Jenni's petite size and firm body, but at least in one area she had an advantage over her roommate. Her skin was smooth, her complexion nearly flawless, while Jenni had many blemishes and small acne scars underneath her pancake make-up. For Traci it was enough to allow a friendship; she could not have stood it if Jenni also had perfect skin.

"Why don't you call him up? Ask him for some training advice?" Jenni called over the shower wall, laughing at the absurdity.

"I don't know his name," Traci called back, sharing a laugh at the joke.

"Ask Lou," Jenni said. "He'd know."

***

"Dammit!" Rochmann looked at his watch as he trudged up the hill toward the psychology building in the fading twilight. His legs still ached from the heavy squats he'd done the day before, but that was not the reason for his displeasure. He'd forgotten to bring home the stack of test papers he had to grade that evening. He'd remembered his grade book but left the tests on his desk. The trip to campus and back would kill the better part of an hour. He seemed to be forgetting little things lately, and it was irritating.

"Evening," he said to the three figures walking toward him at a brisk pace, each with a large dog on a leash. He recognized them as the women's basketball coach, the Women's Athletic Director, and the Assistant to the Vice-President for Student Affairs. The nylon fabric of their dark green *Westerville State* warm-up suits made a swishing noise in the crisp, autumn air. The women murmured a brief acknowledgement as they strode past.

"The doggie dyke posse rides again," he said to their backs as they disappeared into the dusk. The trio's evening jaunts with their dogs were a familiar sight on campus. How they spent their nights and what they did with the dogs was the subject of smirking speculation in the men's locker room.

"Dammit," Rochmann said again when his left knee, the one he'd had surgery on, twinged going up the stairs to his office. Payback for those heavy squats, he thought. Nothing's ever easy.

He opened his office door and flipped on the light switch. There was a faint sound in the next room, Golding's office, a muffled thud of something hitting the floor and a brief murmur of what sounded like voices. He froze and listened intently. There was a faint scraping noise and then silence. Had someone broken in? There had been instances of students stealing exams or equipment, or vandalizing the office of a burdensome professor. Rochmann turned slowly and walked quietly into the hallway. He stood in front of Golding's door, holding his breath and listening. Again, a faint scraping noise. As gently as he could, he tried the doorknob; it did not yield.

He fished his key ring from his jacket pocket, trying not to jangle them as he searched for the spare key Golding had given him, then slowly inserted it into the lock, making a slight grating noise. With a quick twist, he clicked the lock, threw open the door, and flipped the switch for the overhead lights.

Golding was leaning back in his chair behind his desk, blinking in the sudden brightness. His shirt was off and his hairy chest and shoulders bristled like the flanks of a boar. A young woman's face also stared, with wide eyes and smeared red lips, a pretty face, surrounded by swirls of long black hair, through which bare white shoulders protruded. The desk hid the rest of them.

"Get outta here!" Golding yell-whispered, "for Chrissake, get out and close the door!"

Rochmann stumbled backward through the door and closed it. Coughing with laughter, he returned to his office. Exclamations of female and male voices came through the wall, in which the female voice seemed to take the lead. There were scraping and rustling noises, a door opening and closing, hurried footsteps disappearing down the hallway, the echoing clatter of the stairwell door, then silence. Rochmann looked around for the stack of test papers.

His door opened and Golding marched in, smelling of musky sweat. His pants were zipped and his white shirt fully buttoned, but black chest hair was visible beneath, evidence of a forgotten undershirt.

"Jesus fucking Christ, Rochmann, what the fuck're you doing! Here I am, finally getting a little action, and you come barging in. Jesus H. Christ!"

Rochmann perched on the corner of his desk, a wide grin on his face. "Calm down, Sam, calm down. Who is she?"

"Who is she? Who is she? What the fuck you want to know who she is? She's pussy, gone, wasted, that's who she is! Asshole!" Golding was not calming down.

"Hey, I'm sorry. I meant you know who she is, you can get in touch with her. She must like you. You can make it up to her."

"Well, if you must know, I don't really know who she is. Asshole. In fact, she was looking for you. If you'd been here an hour ago, that's you would've been getting your knob polished. But no, let me get a little lucky for once and you got to ruin it. Schmuck!"

"What do you mean, she was looking for me?" Rochmann frowned. The face, big-eyed, red-lipped, seemed vaguely familiar.

"I don't know. I come in around five, Sydney's gone, this girl's in the hallway. 'Do you know if Dr. Rochmann is in?' she says. 'He's not here; can I help you?' I say. Well, she wants some information about psychology courses. 'Is Dr. Rochmann your advisor?' I ask. No, she just knew you're a psych professor. Well, I'm just going to tell her to check with advisement, but she's got these big, beautiful bazoombas, so I offer to help. 'I'm a psychology professor, what courses are you interested in?' We go into my office, we talk about courses, we look at brochures, we talk about changing majors, how the curriculum committee, which I chair, would have to rule on accepting her sociology credits. We rub elbows, I compliment her hair, she seems to like compliments, and so on and so on."

Golding regained his composure as he recounted the seduction. "I maybe could find out who she is from the Sociology Department. Her name's Tracy something. You sure you don't know her?"

"Tracy? Like Dick Tracy?" Rochmann asked.

"Yeah." Golding grinned. "That's what I want to do, *dick* Tracy. No, it's her first name."

Rochmann said, "You're a bad man, Golding. The forces of truth and justice will get you for sure. She looked a little familiar but I hardly saw her."

"Well, if you find out, let me know, would you? She's a lot more friendly than, you know, your old girlfriend. Let me have a chance at this one."

"Sure Sam, whatever." Rochmann did not need to be reminded of Gretchen before returning to his empty house.

***

At the weight room the next day, Rochmann paid more than usual attention to the dollies flexing and extending their delectable limbs, as though the raven-haired 'Tracy' belonged to this scene. She was in none of his classes, and this was the only other place where he might have seen her. Tan-man was there, with Blondie. God, she looked tight; you could bounce a quarter off that butt.

He completed the first half of his routine, finishing with repetition deadlifts that left him light-headed, panting and soaked with sweat. He took a dry sweatshirt from his bag and surveyed the room as he changed out of the wet one.

A few steps away from the platform, a young woman also was doing deadlifts, using a little barbell, maybe fifty pounds. He'd noticed her before; she often seemed to be doing some kind of exercise in the vicinity of the platform but she always avoided eye contact. She looked as firm as Blondie, but was different in almost every other way. She wore simple black shorts and tee shirt, nothing tight or flashy. Her skin was dark, not that tanning-salon orange-brown, but a natural olive color. Dark hair, sort of like that girl in Golding's office, but short and curly. The more he looked, the more attractive she appeared. Heavy-lidded dark eyes, a petite nose, full lips with no garish lipstick. She was short, probably would not come much past his shoulder--the polar opposite of Gretchen. He shook his head at the endless variety of female beauty.

Rochmann wiped his face and arms with a towel and did a few stiff-legged toe touches to stretch his lower back. The dark-eyed girl was lifting all wrong, straightening her legs too soon and rounding her back. He could give her some pointers if only he could catch her eye. Absent-mindedly, he chalked his hands even though he was not preparing to do a lift. He squinted at the girl in black, making a fuzzy image. He could visualize his hand leaving a big, white, five-fingered chalk print on the vee of her shorts between her legs. That would get her attention.

# Chapter 20:  Eating Disorder

Gloria looked up at the weightlifter guy stepping off the platform and moving toward her like he was going to say something.  Suddenly, his hand was grasping her crotch, then trailing down her leg.  He crumpled at her feet like someone had pulled the plug on a berserk robot.

She screamed, and kept screaming as though her shrieks would make the figure at her feet disappear.  The clanking of weights and squeaking of pulleys ceased; boomboxes clicked off.  Murmurs turned to shouts as people crowded around the prostrate figure.  "What happened?!" "Who is it?!" "What'd he do?!" "Is he dead?!"

The guy lay motionless, face down, like a heap of rags.  Gloria's yells subsided into sobs and she bent over to cover the chalky handprint on the front of her shorts.  The curious mob elbowed her aside to see what was going on.  "Did he drop a weight on his head?" "Somebody get a doctor?"  "Is he okay?"  She could not answer the random questions and found it difficult to breathe.

Jostled and bounced to the periphery of the crowd, she left the weight room and walked, half-crouched, to the women's locker room.  She pulled on her jeans over the chalk-smeared shorts, grabbed her sweater and jacket, and hurried out of the building.  A siren in the distance demonstrated the Doppler effect.

The bitter wind hit her face and she pulled her unzipped jacket close around her with ungloved hands.  She left her bicycle chained in the rack and walked hurriedly toward the town center, a few blocks from campus.  Streetlights winked on in the gathering dusk, creating black shadows that danced and grabbed at her feet.  Laughing students milled about the neon-lit eateries that offered pizza, submarine sandwiches, hamburgers, and tacos.  Convivial shouts escaped the open door of a bar advertising Happy Hour specials.  She passed by, oblivious to the lights and smells and sounds.

The bells on the door of the Quik-Mart clinked discordantly when she entered.  She blinked in the bright fluorescent light that bathed the place in shadowless whiteness, like an overexposed photograph.  She looked around as if startled by the sudden realization of where she was, then picked up a blue plastic shopping basket and proceeded up one aisle and down the next. There were only a few people in the store but she made sure an aisle was empty before she went into it. She picked out a box of Ho-Ho's, a loaf of white bread, a box of saltine crackers, two small boxes of animal crackers, a large bag of potato chips, and a half-gallon of vanilla ice cream. The brown-skinned clerk rang up her purchases and asked, "Do you want cigarettes?" in an Indian accent. She shook her head and handed him a credit card. While waiting for the transaction to clear, she zipped her jacket and put on the gloves that had been in its pockets. She signed her name, 'Gloria Soares,' in a large, round script, awkwardly, because of the glove. With a plastic bag in each hand, she pushed open the jangling door with her shoulder.

In her dormitory room, Gloria switched on her desk lamp and placed the bags on her bed, the lower of one of two sets of bunks. She was alone, as usual. Three women had been assigned to the room; one had dropped out of school shortly after the quarter started and the other spent most of the time with her boyfriend. Gloria listened intently; there was no sound from the dorm room on the other side of the shared bathroom that completed the suite. Some music wafted from a room down the hall.

She took off her gloves, placing them in her jacket pocket, hung the coat in the closet, went into the bathroom and filled a large plastic tumbler with water, and took a spoon from the bathroom cabinet drawer. She placed the glass of water on the floor beside her bed, and sat down heavily. She sighed deeply but her face remained impassive, as though preparing for an onerous but necessary task, like removing a splinter. On some occasions she might have resisted for a time, building up tension before finally succumbing, but tonight there was no pretense of resistance. She knew what she had to do, and began by dumping the contents of the bags into a jumble on the bed.

She picked up the Ho-Ho's, grasped the cardboard tab and neatly opened the box. The engineering of food packaging for quick and easy access was a small blessing at a time like this. Getting the chocolate morsel out if its individual cellophane wrapper was more difficult, requiring the use of teeth. With great self-control, she took all twelve cakes out of their transparent jackets and lined them up, in two rows of six, on her pillow. The first bite was delicious. It was possible, at first, to savor all the flavors and textures, the gentle crunch as she bit through the waxy chocolate covering, the soft, crumbly cake inside, and the frothy, creamy filling at the center. The second, third, and fourth cakes were devoured with increasing speed, and the last few were consumed by stuffing each one whole in her mouth, barely chewing before swallowing.

When the cakes were gone she took a sip of water and reached for the potato chips. It was time for a change in taste and texture. This bag seemed designed to prevent opening; the plasticized material resisted tearing and was too slippery to yield to her teeth. With a frustrated snort she fetched a pair of scissors from her desk drawer to open the bag. The first chip could be savored like the first cake, the shock of salt grains on her tongue, the crackly snap as the chip broke apart in her mouth, its slow dissolve into a grainy mush as saliva poured forth. Only a few chips could be enjoyed this way, then, as before, her rate increased until she was stuffing handfuls at a time into her mouth, chewing and swallowing as rapidly as she could. She slowed when the bag was about half empty, sated by salt and exhaustion of salivary glands. There was a slight tightness around her middle, as if an encircling arm were gently squeezing. She took a large mouthful of water and undid the belt, button, and zipper of her jeans.

Next, she opened the carton of ice cream. It had begun to melt. She smoothed one of the plastic bags on the bedspread to catch any drips and placed the carton in the center. Dreamily, she spooned the sweet mush into her mouth, sculpting the dissolving block into an ovoid that became steadily smaller. The last of it formed a puddle in the bottom of the carton that she slurped noisily, getting the sticky residue on her knuckles as she scooped out the final dregs. She rinsed her mouth with a swallow of water, then licked the ice cream from her hand and wiped it on her shirt, like a small child.

Sweating slightly, due to the warm room and the caloric effects of eating, she took off her tee shirt and wiped her face and arms. As she did, her foot bumped the tumbler of water on the floor beside the bed, knocking it over and spilling its contents. The interruption of her ritual evoked a sob of frustration; she choked it back, blotted the spilled water with her tee shirt, and walked resolutely to the bathroom to refill the tumbler.

She went through a box of animal crackers, systematically biting off the legs, then the head, of each individual cookie, before letting the round remnant of the body dissolve on her tongue like the eucharist. The faint sweet taste of the crackers provided a refreshing contrast to the cloying sweetness of the ice cream, but eventually the flavor washed out entirely. The saltines provided a similarly faint but salty taste, and she finished half the box, pausing only for sips of water. Her eating slowed. As though underwater, she dreamily cut open the bread wrapper and extracted a puffy white slice. She tore off the crust and stuffed the spongy center into her mouth where it slowly turned into a pasty lump. And then another slice, and another.

With prolonged use, the muscles of mastication become fatigued, saliva output fails, and taste receptors fade. Eating becomes a mechanical chore, like forcing mash down the throat of a *fois gras* goose. The predominant sensation is no longer taste but fullness, a fullness that exceeds mere abdominal tightness, becoming an encompassing pressure, an encircling squeeze like that of a boa constrictor, almost suffocating, but also warm and enclosing, like a cocoon. It is a state both oppressive and comforting. Then there is the first small wave of nausea, like a tickle in the nostril before a sneeze. This is not a sensation to be resisted; as the term 'wave' suggests, it is a sensation to float upon, up and down and up again.

Gloria stood and slowly walked to the bathroom. Leaving the light off, she raised the toilet lid and sat down on the floor beside it. She rode the wave of nausea, becoming dizzy, like a child who twirls and twirls until the world spins around her. The release came, the constricting bonds broke suddenly and all that was inside gushed out. The salty-sweet-sour-bitter fountain became the center of an Archimedes spiral and she hung on to the sides of the toilet bowl to keep from being flung off by centrifugal force.

When it was over, she flushed the toilet and shakily stood and brushed her teeth, avoiding her dim image in the mirror. Then she gathered the remnants of her gastric orgy from the bed. The bread crusts, wrappers, and empty containers were placed in a plastic bag that she stuffed in the trash can beside her desk; the remaining food was placed in the other bag and stored in a bottom drawer of her desk. Her movements were slow and fluid, like a Tai Chi exercise, so as not to disturb her somnolent state.

She returned to the bathroom, turned on the shower, and stripped off her clothes, not looking at the chalk residue that remained on her shorts. Stepping gingerly into the shower stall, her dark skin reddened in the hot water. She sat on the floor of the shower and allowed the scalding water to complete the cleansing process. When she felt like she was about to dissolve, she turned off the water, patted herself gently with a large towel, hung it on the rack, and walked naked to her bed. From beneath the pillow, she withdrew a folded, extra-large, orange tee shirt, emblazoned with *Syracuse University*, pulled it on and slipped between the sheets. She was asleep within minutes.

Gloria did not set her alarm and awakened long after her nine a.m. class was over. Her roommate had not returned. She brushed her teeth, ran a comb through her short, wavy, dark brown hair, and applied a touch of brownish-red lipstick. She removed neatly folded clothes from her chest-of-drawers and dressed slowly in a pair of tight black jeans, a black tee shirt, and a baggy gray *Westerville State* sweatshirt. She tuned her radio to a soft-rock station and sat at her desk, reading the textbook from her missed class, until a quarter to eleven. Then she put on her jacket, a muted beige canvas-like material with a fake fur lining, and a red knit tam, adding a splash of color to her somber ensemble.

The white sun glared from an ice-blue sky, all light and no warmth. Gloria joined the streams of students that flowed from one grey granite building to another. She arrived at the door of the Counseling Center at precisely eleven o'clock.

146

# Chapter 21: Confront Your Fears

D r. Elizabeth Allan, Director of the Westerville State University Counseling Center, gathered her notes for the weekly meeting of the Eating Disorders Group. She met Dr. Susan Koenig in the hall outside her office and together they walked to the meeting room. Susan had volunteered to assist with the group and do research on eating disorders. Dr. Allan had accepted with some reluctance; Dr. Koenig was not trained in clinical psychology and seemed much more interested in research than helping the girls, but she did have some interesting ideas.

"How many do you think we'll have today?" Susan asked. More than a dozen women students had signed up that quarter, but only about half attended any one meeting. Susan was always interested in numbers.

"We'll just have to see." Dr. Allan beamed and nodded as the young women filed into the room and arranged the chairs in a circle. "Good morning, ladies." Dr. Allan's smile was warm and her tone suggested that it really was a good morning. Sounds of jacket zippers unzipping, backpacks clunking onto the floor, and chattered greetings ensued. When all were seated, Dr. Allan said, "All right, who has something to share with us today? Has someone had a success or set-back that we can learn from?"

A petite, dark-haired girl in a gray sweatshirt quickly raised her hand to about shoulder level, then lowered it just as quickly.

"Allllright." Dr. Allan drew out the word as she scanned a list to verify the name. This young woman attended fairly often but had not spoken much. "Gloria," she said. "Thank you. What can you share with us?"

The girl took a deep breath. "Well, I had a relapse yesterday. I mean a lapse." The group had been taught that it was important to distinguish between a 'relapse,' totally giving up and reverting to one's old ways, and a 'lapse,' a bump on the road to recovery.

"I'm sorry, dear," Dr. Allan said. "Can you tell us about it?"

"Well, I, ah, I was assaulted. Sexually. And I, ah, I just sort of lost it, afterwards."

Heads turned and all eyes fixed on Gloria.

"Sexually assaulted," Dr. Allan repeated. "Do you mean you were raped? Did you report it?" If a student had been raped, it was a matter for the police.

"Oh no, nothing like that. I was grabbed. Between my legs." Gloria's voice trailed off and it was difficult to hear her.

"Do you know who did this? Were there witnesses?" asked Dr. Allan. While not as serious, this still could be an actionable offence.

"No, I don't know him. There were lots of people around, but I don't think anyone saw it."

"It was crowded but no one witnessed your being grabbed?"

Gloria nodded. "I don't think so."

"What happened next, dear?"

"I just got out of there, fast. I just left."

"You didn't say anything to anybody?"

"No, I just left. And then I, you know, binged."

It seemed to Dr. Allan as though Gloria was talking about a student party situation, an all too familiar occurrence. Alcohol and drugs flowed freely and sexual groping, and worse, was not uncommon.

"Are you sure he meant to do it?" interjected Dr. Koenig. "If it was really crowded, he may have bumped into you accidentally?"

Gloria shook her head and paused in reflection. "No, it wasn't an accident."

Dr. Allan took charge. "There are three things to consider here. First, we can look at what you could have done in that situation to deal with the emotions you felt when you were grabbed. Second, even if you did not deal with it then and there, we can talk about how to handle your pain without going on an eating binge. And third, although you did have a lapse, we can see about where to go from here. Are you with me on this?"

Gloria nodded and there were murmurs of assent from the group.

"First, let's talk about your feelings. How did you feel when this man touched you? Were you frightened? Angry?"

"I, I don't know. I was just really shocked, really upset."

"That's a perfectly natural reaction. Perhaps you were scared and angry at the same time. Feelings can just kind of run together, don't you think?"

"Yes, I guess so."

"But the fact that you got out of there tells me that you were afraid. Running away from a situation is a natural response to fear. What do you think?" She addressed the group.

"I'd be really angry!" spoke up an overweight blonde girl in a maroon *Harvard* sweatshirt with the logo *VE-RI-TAS*. "If somebody grabbed me, I'd kick 'im in the nuts."

"Thank you, Kaitlin," said Dr. Allan. "Different people have different reactions, and Gloria may have been angry, but I think she was also frightened. Is that right?"

Gloria nodded.

"The important thing is, what do you do with your feelings?"

The girls offered opinions and experiences about slapping men in bars and self-defense training to prevent rape. Dr. Allan brought them back to the matter at hand with the reminder that neither aggression nor running away was the answer. "Remember what we've said about being assertive?" Dr. Allan prompted.

"Yes," said Susan. "In this situation, Gloria would have been safe in confronting this man, letting him know that she was not going to allow such behavior."

Dr. Allan shot a disapproving glance at Susan for jumping in with the answer the group was supposed to come up with. Susan did not seem to notice. Dr. Allan addressed the group. "Now, what could Gloria say and do that would acknowledge her feelings and let this man know that his actions were unwelcome and must stop?"

The other group members joined in enthusiastically, suggesting and rehearsing assertive responses to being sexually accosted. The session passed quickly and Dr. Allan hurriedly asked them, as the hour was ending, to think about the second and third points that she had raised, as homework, to bring to the next meeting.

\*\*\*

Gloria walked out into the clear, cold daylight. That had been an ordeal. For starters, she hated to hear her name announced in public. In a room full of Kaitlins and Kylies, 'Gloria' sounded so dorky. Her big brothers also had old-fashioned names, 'Joseph' and 'Michael' and 'Thomas'--'Joe,' 'Mike,' and 'Tom'--but that was okay for boys. Solid, sturdy names. But for a girl, 'Gloria' definitely marked her as lower class, a name stitched on a waitress's uniform at a diner.

And she hated being the focus of attention. Not like some of the girls, who seemed to relish it. Gloria was glad when they'd gone off on a tangent, rehearsing what she could have said to him. By that time it was too late to tell them he was just laying there like he was dead and she was totally freaked.

Enough food for another binge was in her bottom drawer and she wondered if her roommate had returned to the dorm. No, that was crazy. You can't binge right after therapy. She felt light-headed and her legs wobbled. She plunked down on a stone bench under an ancient oak that defiantly retained its crisp, brown leaves. The wind had died and the pale sun exuded warmth that felt good on her face. She closed her eyes to think. Hadn't she learned anything in the session? One thing Dr. Allan said during the role-plays stood out: 'Confront your fears.' Running away, or covering them up in a binge, just keeps them alive. What was she afraid of right now? Going on another binge. Her stomach rumbled. Okay, the way to confront that was to eat normally. It was lunchtime and she was hungry, so the normal thing to do was to eat a normal lunch. Then she would go to her afternoon classes and she'd be just fine.

Gloria found a table in a quiet corner of the student union cafeteria and set down her tray with a bowl of soup, a cup of yogurt and a banana. Someone had left a copy of the *Sentinel*, the school newspaper, and she spread it out to read while she ate. On the front page, 'Psychology Professor Collapses,' was printed in bold type. There was a blurry file picture of a man in a coat and tie, whose face looked like the man who had grabbed her. Her stomach lurched; she put down her spoon and took a deep breath. "Eat a normal lunch," she said aloud.

She turned to an inside page and forced herself to eat. She read about some terrorist truck bomb killing a bunch of marines in Lebanon. Her brothers had talked about joining the marines, and she was glad they hadn't. It would be just awful if one of them got blown up. There were such horrible things going on in the world, her problem didn't seem that bad. She turned back to the front page and read the article under the picture.

> Robert P. Rochmann, assistant professor in Psychology, was rushed to Westerville Regional Hospital yesterday after falling in the Health & Fitness Center weight room. Dr. Rochmann was an experienced weight lifter but may not have followed the correct policy of using spotters, said Luke Byron, Director of the Center. He is ordering an investigation into the cause of the accident. Dr. Rochmann is in stable condition according to a hospital report. He could not be reached for comment.

My God, the guy was a professor. A professor wouldn't just walk up to somebody and grab them, would he? Maybe it could have been an accident, like that woman with bright red lipstick, Dr. Koenig, had said. No, his fingers definitely had closed on her vulva. It was a grope, no mistake. But he had to be taken to the hospital, so something was wrong with him. It was all so confusing.

*** 

After her afternoon classes, Gloria dropped off her books at her room, retrieved her bicycle from the Health & Fitness Center, and pedaled into town. She locked the bike in the rack outside the main entrance of the hospital and walked up the ramp with a determined step. The automatic-opening glass doors made a wooshing sound, prompting her to exhale the breath she'd been holding.

"Can I help you, dear?" The gray hair and crinkle-faced smile of the woman at the information desk seemed incongruous with her pink-striped volunteer's pinafore. She adjusted her half-glasses and squinted at the computer screen, mumbling to herself as she typed in the name Gloria gave her. "Rochmann, R, O, C, H, M, A, two N's, Robert. Here he is." She looked up. "He's in ICU, dear, intensive care, no visitors. Only family allowed."

"How long will he be there?" Gloria asked.

The woman shook her head. "Doesn't say."

"What's wrong with him?"

The woman looked at the computer screen and then gave her a sympathetic smile. "Are you family?"

Gloria nodded.

"He had a stroke, dear. The ICU is down one level; take the elevator in the Palmer wing." She pointed to the left. "You'll have to sign in down there."

Gloria paused, then turned and walked in the direction the woman had pointed. She crossed the carpeted reception area into a beige-tiled, brightly lit corridor. A doctor in a white coat talking to another in green scrubs hurried past, stethoscopes dangling from their pockets. A man in a brown uniform busily mopped a section of floor that gave off a pungent odor of disinfectant. A nurse trotted past pushing an IV pole, its wheels squeaking like a *Chipmunks* song and her crepe soles chirping in rhythm. Gloria felt invisible. She caught sight of her hazy image reflected in the stainless steel doors of the elevator. To the left was a metal door, marked by a red EXIT sign, with a small window slightly above eye level, its glass crosshatched with chicken wire. She stood on tiptoes and peered in.

"Confront your fears," she whispered to herself, then pushed open the door into the empty, echoing stairwell.

# PART VI

# AWAKENING

# Chapter 22:  A Reasonable Goal

A low, electronic hum filled Rochmann's ears and a phosphorescent haze from a bank of monitor screens provided the only light.  He felt heavy, pressed into the bed like his skin was filled with sand.  He lifted his hand to scratch his head and felt a paper cap covering wires attached to his scalp.

A dim figure rose from a chair in the corner, walked over and pressed a call button clipped to the metal rail of the bed.

"Rocky, you awake?  How're you feeling?"

The voice was familiar but it took a couple seconds to place it.  "Bill?"

Chappell took his hand and squeezed it.  "Yeah, Rock, it's me.  How you doing?"

"What're you doing here?  What happened?"

"You gave us a scare, old man.  But things are looking up.  I'll let the neurologist explain.  Wheeler is one of the best.  You're lucky Westerville has a regional trauma center."

"What happened?" Rochmann repeated.  It was difficult to move his tongue.  Chappell was just a silhouette, with glints of green light reflecting from his glasses.

An overhead light switched on and Rochmann closed his eyes reflexively.  When his vision cleared, a tall, portly black man in a white coat stood over him; he was balding, with a moon-like face, a pencil moustache, and round, wire-rimmed glasses.  Behind him stood a short, plump, white woman, wearing a starched white nurse uniform, tendrils of gray hair protruding from under a traditional nurse's cap.

"I'm Doctor Wheeler," the man announced.  "Do you remember talking to me last night?  How do you feel?"  His voice was deep, with a whispery resonance, like a ballad singer.  Without waiting for an answer, he plugged a stethoscope into his ears and placed the disc on various places on Rochmann's chest.

Rochmann could not recall talking to him.  "What happened?" he asked for the third time.

Dr. Wheeler took a small penlight from his pocket and shone it into Rochmann's eyes, one at a time, peering intently. Their foreheads almost touched and his breath smelled of peppermint. Then he placed his index fingers in Rochmann's palms, long, thick fingers, like brown sausages.

"Squeeze my fingers," the doctor commanded, "hard."

Rochmann's right hand tightened but the left did nothing; there was an odd sensation of pain somewhere on his left side but he could not localize it.

Wheeler went to the foot of the bed and folded back the covers, exposing Rochmann's bare feet. He placed the palms of his hands against his toes and said, "Push against my hands."

The right foot extended but the left did not.

Rochmann exploded. "Have I lost my voice or is everyone deaf! What the fuck happened?"

Dr. Wheeler appeared to have finished his examination. He pulled a stool next to the bed and sat down, his eyes level with Rochmann's. The nurse handed him an open manila folder.

"Mr. Rochmann." Wheeler glanced down at the folder. "Robert, may I call you Robert?" He gave a brief smile. "You appear to have suffered an intraparenchymal hemorrhage, a type of stroke. It has left you with a left hemiparesis, a weakness on the left side. Fortunately, the language areas of the brain seem intact. You may recover some motor function on the left side, or all, or none. We cannot predict at this time. Your efforts during physical therapy, later on, will be an important factor. Do you understand?"

Rochmann nodded.

"You're very fortunate," the doctor continued. "We hope the worst is over, but there is always the danger of further hemorrhage or seizure. We will watch carefully to prevent that, or deal with it if necessary. You are in excellent health, which bodes well for your prognosis. Except for your hypertension."

Wheeler gave the nurse a brief look and she moved quickly to the head of the bed where a sphygmomonometer was attached to the wall. She wrapped the cuff around Rochmann's right arm and proceeded to take a reading.

"How long will it take?" Rochmann's voice was hoarse. "Until we know if I, uh, will recover function?" He looked at Chappell in appeal. "I can't afford to miss much training."

"Rock." Chappell stepped forward and looked down at him. "You're lucky to be alive. Your first goal is to survive this. If you put your training efforts into physical therapy I'm sure you'll overcome the paralysis."

"How long?" he repeated. "Even a few weeks will set me back."

"Rock, listen," Chappell said. "Your priorities have changed. My priorities have changed. God knows I want to see you on the platform in L.A. But now we have to focus on just getting you out of here, getting you up and around. This is not like knee surgery. This is life or death. Wheelchair or walking."

"Dr. Chappell tells me you were a weightlifter," Wheeler added. The 'were' jangled harshly. "Regular exercise is good, but I'm afraid you'll have to pick another activity. Swimming might be good exercise, when the time comes."

Rochmann stared without seeing anything for several seconds. Then he raised his head and squinted at the identification tag on the doctor's lapel. "Raymond, may I call you Raymond? Weightlifting is not an exercise. It's, it's," he paused, sighed, "it's what I am. It's the Olympics. The qualifying trials are in six months. It's my last chance..." His voice trailed off.

"I'm sorry," said Dr. Wheeler. He did not sound sorry, only matter-of-fact. "That is out of the question. A reasonable goal is ambulation. We will work very hard to have you walk out of here."

Rochmann sank into the pillow. Tears blurred his vision.

Dr. Wheeler asked, "Do you have other questions?" He paused. "If you do, please press the call button. Or if you notice any unusual sensations, call immediately. Dr. Chappell, are you going to be here for a while?"

"For a while, yes."

"Good." Wheeler looked down at Rochmann. "I'll check in on you soon. And of course, we're monitoring you closely." He waved his hand at the equipment. "Please call if you need anything." He walked quickly from the room with the nurse, a silent white shadow, behind him.

Chappell sat down on the stool. "Do you remember last night, Rocky?"

It still seemed like night. A very long night. Rochmann closed his eyes. "Not really. Some bright lights, people rushing around. Maybe Wheeler was there, I don't know. When did you get here?"

"Like I said, there's an excellent trauma unit here. Great EMTs. Wheeler was on call and got you figured out and stabilized in record time. You're real lucky. I mean there's a chance you could've died, or ended up a vegetable. My name's listed as your physician, so I got called. Must have been nine, ten o'clock last night. Drove up and got here early this morning, after all the action was over. You were sleeping like a baby."

"My throat hurts," Rochmann said. "Would you get me some water?"

Chappell poured water into a plastic cup from the pitcher on the bedside stand and handed it to him. "They inserted an emergency tube to assist your breathing, prevent aspirating fluid, you know. But you didn't need it for long; you were breathing on your own just fine. You're a horse, Rock, you'll make a good recovery, I know. Just put your training spirit into it and you'll do great."

"Recovery? For what? I wish they had just let me die. That'd be better than, than, this." He waved his hand at his left arm. "Even if I do get so I can gimp around, shit, what'm I going to do? Swimming? I can't even float. Goddammit, Bill, we were so close, just another six months. You know, if this had happened after the Olympics, okay, I'd have had my shot. But this..." Tears welled in his eyes again. "There's no chance things could click into place, you know, in my brain? Just, I don't know, clear up, snap back to normal?"

"You know it doesn't work that way, Rock," Chappell said softly. "You're going to have to change your goal. You can be world champ at stroke recovery."

"Fuck that." Rochmann turned his face away.

"Rocky, 99.999 percent of the world's population has never, ever lifted a weight over their head, and many of them have a happy life. You can too."

There was a long silence. Speaking seemed to take great effort. "Yeah, I know, Bill. But knowing doesn't help."

"It's the grief thing, old man. You know, anger, denial, bargaining, all that. It's normal. Guess you'll have to ride it out until you get to the acceptance stage."

"Yeah, just lie here and accept it. It'd be easier to accept if I was dead." He looked at Chappell and sighed. "I appreciate your coming, buddy. Thanks for being here. I'm real tired. I think I'll sleep some more."

"Okay, Rock. I need to make some phone calls. I was able to get some coverage on short notice before I left, but I've got more patients I need to make arrangements for. You get some sleep and I'll see you in a bit."

Chappell squeezed his hand and turned off the overhead lights as he left, leaving only the glow from the monitors. Noises from the corridor blended with the hum of the machines. Rochmann dozed but was awakened after what seemed like only a few minutes by lights and the clatter of a wheeled cart.

An orderly in green scrubs announced, "Lunch time." He was a brown-skinned man with a gold earring and uneven white teeth that he showed in a wide smile. "My name's Julio. Glad to meet you, mon." He spoke with a musical, Jamaican lilt. "Okay, mon, bland diet, you can feed yourself, right? He cranked up the bed, arranged a tray across Rochmann's lap, and placed the dishes on it. A plate divided into three sections contained a rounded scoop of macaroni on a lettuce leaf, a rounded scoop of tuna on a lettuce leaf, and a puddle of applesauce on a lettuce leaf.

"Looks like they got a good deal on lettuce," Rochmann said.

"Wait'll you see the dessert, mon." The orderly laughed. Sure enough, he placed a small bowl on the tray that contained a square of bright red gelatin on a lettuce leaf. "Here, I got to open your milk and butter your bread." After performing these tasks, Julio asked,

"Anything else?" The patient shook his head. "Okay. Enjoy. I'll be back later."

A half hour later, he returned to clear the dishes and remove the tray, then helped Rochmann to urinate in a bed bottle. He was slightly built but skillfully maneuvered the bigger man's bulk, taking care not to tangle the wires that led to the EEG and EKG monitors.

"You got some serious muscles, mon. You lift weights or somting?"

"Yeah." Rochmann's voice was flat. "Used to."

"I got a cousin, he lifts. He's huge, mon. Goin' to be Mr. New York or somting."

Rochmann did not bother to point out the difference between weightlifting and bodybuilding.

"You need anything else? Want me to bring you a magazine?"

"No, thanks." The exertions of eating and toileting left him strangely tired. "Please turn off the lights. I think I'll take a nap."

The orderly turned the light switch knob, dimming the lights but not extinguishing them. "Catch you later, mon."

# Chapter 23:  Mister Lucky Redux

G loria peered through the glass window of one of the large doors beneath the sign, 'Intensive Care Unit, Authorized Personnel Only.'

"Coming through!" a voice called behind her.

She scrambled to one side as a gurney holding a draped figure, with IV packets swinging from attached poles, pushed by a phalanx of trotting green-clad figures, bumped the doors open and brushed past her.  The doors swung closed and she watched the flurry of activity through the window.  People in white emerged from the glass-enclosed nurses' station and conferred with the green-clad people around the gurney, like bees in a hive meeting foragers returning from an expedition.  The entire group proceeded around the corner past the nurses' station, leaving only a single nurse in the glass enclosure.  This woman sat at a counter filled with trays of folders and charts, with banks of monitors on the wall above her.  Her back was to the doorway and her head bent over some task.

Gloria slipped through the doorway and around the corner.  A chart listing patients' names and room numbers hung on the wall.  Third from the top was, 'ROCHMANN, R., 120.'  Doorways lined the hall with number plaques beside each door.  Number 120 was the third one on the left.  Voices floated from a room further down the hallway.  Gloria eased into the third doorway and stood to one side, pausing while her eyes adjusted to the dim light.

A man lay propped up in a bed across the room.  Gloria moved to the side of the bed, in the space next to the wall, out of view if someone should glance in.  In the light from the open doorway, she could see he was looking at her but could make out no expression on his face.

"Are you Robert Rochmann?"  Her voice barely above a whisper.

"Mm-hmm," he grunted.

The lines she'd rehearsed suddenly left her.  She had a strange feeling of foreboding, a reminiscence more than a distinct memory, of a hospital room from long ago. "I, ah, I want to know why you grabbed me. Yesterday. In the weight room."

He looked up at her, blankly. "What?"

"Yesterday afternoon, in the weight room, you grabbed me. I was very frightened." She recalled from assertiveness training the importance of stating how you feel about a situation. "And angry. It upset me very much. I want to know why you did that. And I want you to apologize." It was also important to request behavior change. "Apologize for grabbing me."

He looked at her for many seconds. "I'm sorry, but I don't remember yesterday," he said in a quiet monotone. "I suppose I was in the weight room. I don't remember. I had a stroke; I don't remember a goddamn thing."

This was an excuse, not an apology. Gloria wasn't exactly sure what a stroke was, something that happened to old people. But she knew he had grabbed her crotch; she had felt his fingers closing purposefully, willfully, on the soft flesh between her legs. She sought to recall the experience, to reconstruct her feelings at that moment. "You grabbed me." Big breath. "Between my legs. It was an assault. I could report you."

The man closed his eyes and sighed, then opened them to gaze at the ceiling, or something beyond the ceiling. "Look, Miss, whatever your name is, I had a stroke. I can't recall anything since--I'm not sure. It's gone. Brain damage. I'm paralyzed. A lifetime of training for the Olympics is gone."

He spoke with great effort, like in those movies where a guy's been shot. Only this was not some actor; this was a real guy that she'd seen lifting an unimaginable amount of weight, and now he was paralyzed?

He made a choking noise. "If I grabbed you, frightened you, I'm sorry. You can't know how sorry I am." He continued to stare through the ceiling, with dead eyes.

It was the empty look she had seen in the eyes of small creatures--birds and rabbits--that she'd found in the woods behind her house, injured survivors of predators or gravity. Again, feelings from childhood nudged at the edge of awareness. Like *Thumbelina* with the meadowlark in her favorite nursery story, Gloria had carried these creatures home, braving her mother's scolding and her brothers' teasing, and attempted to nurse them back to health. The lawn around the maple tree in their yard was pocked by burial sites of coffee-cans containing the tissue-wrapped remains of her failed efforts. But once in a while, a creature responded, thrived in a towel-lined, lamp-warmed shoebox, and with immense satisfaction she'd set it free.

This guy's statement was not much of an apology, and it was obvious that he was much sorrier for himself than for any affront to her, but suddenly the context shifted. She had remained standing while this big, strong man lay at her feet. The fear that seemed always to gnaw at her evaporated. The man lying here was aiming for the Olympics. She had once known a similar desire. He'd fallen, but he had tried. Something sparked within her. Life is a gift. In this gloomy room of humming machines and green squiggles on monitors, this mournful room of accident and loss, Gloria felt wonderfully alive.

There was a muffled commotion out in the hallway, hospital staff rushing back and forth, harried voices. Apparently, the patient they brought in was not doing well.

"My name is Gloria," she said. "I, I'm sorry too, about what happened. To you. I'm sure you'll get better." She leaned across the bed rail and squeezed his hand.

***

The following afternoon, Gloria again peered through the glass window of the doors to the ICU. She carried a plastic bag containing a teddy bear. Nurses and orderlies were in plain view, going about their duties. She squared her shoulders and pushed through the doors.

"Miss, oh miss, where are you going?" A nurse confronted her at once.

"I'm here to see Robert Rochmann."

"This is intensive care, young lady. Didn't you see the sign? No visitors."

She should have rehearsed a story.  "Just a few minutes?" She held up the bag.  "I only wanted to give him this."

"What is it?  We can give it to him," the nurse said, reaching for it.

"Just a couple minutes?  Please?  I need to explain about it."

"I'm sorry, but no visitors are allowed."  The nurse glowered at her.

"Well, let me write something."  Gloria fished a felt tip marker from her pocket, took the bear out of the bag and wrote her name and phone number on the ribbon around its neck.

"Thanks for giving it to him," she said, handing it to the nurse.  It was not a new bear, its brown fur rubbed smooth in places.  "How's he doing?  When will he be able to have visitors?"

"He should be transferred to the main floor in a couple days, if there's no complications.  You can see him then."

***

Rochmann looked up as a nurse entered his room.  "A young lady brought you this," she said in an accusing tone, as though she had uncovered a smuggling plot.  She placed the bear on his bed.

He regarded her vaguely.

"A short girl.  Dark eyes.  Do you know her?"

He shrugged his right shoulder.

"I think she was from the college," the nurse continued.  "Maybe a student?  You're a professor, right?"

He nodded.

"Well, she shouldn't be in the ICU.  No visitors 'til you're out of here."

He nodded again and closed his eyes.  When she had gone, he opened his eyes and looked at the bear she had placed on the bed. Disruptions were tiring.  Any effort at thought or observation seemed beyond his capacity.  He returned to sleep.

***

After three days in intensive care, Rochmann was moved to a room on the general ward that, thank God for small miracles, had no other occupant. His bed faced a large window overlooking the distant hills, covered with dark pines and bare-branched trees that stood out from a dusting of snow like black lace. The row of monitors was gone, removing the electronic reminders that he was still alive.

Bill Chappell came in and pulled up a chair next to his bed. "Good to see you out of intensive care. How you feeling, Rock?"

Rochmann just grunted.

Bill reached across the bed rails and squeezed his shoulder. "Hey, Rocky, amigo, what's going on?"

Rochmann turned to look at him, at the concern in his friend's eyes behind those stylish, tinted glasses. He sighed deeply. "Well, I didn't sleep so good last night. For a while there, all I did was sleep. Guess I'm all slept out. But I can't see the point of being awake."

"Not sleeping so much could be a good thing," said Chappell. "Shows you're ready to move on. Start tackling physical therapy."

Good old Bill. Always the optimist. But it wasn't him with a dead left side. Rochmann gave another grunt.

Chappell kept his hand on Rochmann's chest while he talked. "Another thing, Rock. You need to call your mother. I tried a couple days ago but the number I had was disconnected."

"Yeah, she moved out to Seattle to live with my sister. I'm glad you didn't get through. She'd feel like she had to come out here and that wouldn't do either of us any good.

"You have to let her know what's going on, Rock. There'll be hell to pay if you don't talk to her soon."

"I don't think I could deal with her right now. My sister, either. They mean well, but, you know." He gave a faint, lop-sided grin. "You call her, Bill. You're a doctor, she knows you. Tell her I'm doing good but need rest, no outside distractions or whatever. Get her to promise to stay calm, not insist on coming out, and I'll call her in a few days. Okay?"

Chappell chuckled. "Okay, Rock, it's a deal. Another thing. Your Elieko plates. Want me to pick 'em up from the Fitness Center?"

Rochmann felt like he'd just dumped the weights on his chest, making it hard to breathe. "Just leave 'em, Bill. Let the fucking zombies have 'em."

Chappell squeezed his hand and stood up. "Okay. I've got to get back to the City. Get back to the office. I'll call after I've talked to your mom. I'll be up to see you on Sunday."

"You don't have to..." Rochman started to protest.

"Rock. Hang in there. I'll see you Sunday."

\*\*\*

"Rochmann! How're you doing, ol' man?" Sam Golding was disgustingly jovial. "Everybody in the department sends their best wishes." Golding placed a vase of flowers on the bedside table and a card signed by the faculty. Rochmann regarded the effort to inject a note of color in the sterile cubicle, but said nothing. Golding went on, "We've cobbled together coverage for your classes, but don't think we're getting along without you. We need you back soon, guy."

"It's nice to know I'm wanted."

Pleasantries over, Golding began talking as though on a mission. "You know that girl you caught me with, in my office? Tracy? Well, you were right. I got her name and phone number from the Sociology Department. Called her up, let her know everything's cool. Turns out she'd seen you in the weight room. Seems there's all kinds of scuttlebutt around there, dropped a weight on your head or something. Anyway, we got it together. Man! All she wants to do is fuck. Fuck, suck, everything! It's unbelievable!"

Golding went into more detail than he wanted to hear. When he finally left, Rochmann felt strangely disquieted. Sleep, his usual escape, would not come. He spotted the teddy bear on the bedside table, hidden behind the flowers. There was something written on the ribbon around its neck.

\*\*\*

A young woman answered on the third ring. "Millburn Hall."

"Is this Gloria?" Rochmann's voice was thick, his words almost slurred. He had not spoken much during Golding's visit.

"Gloria Soares? Hold on; I'll see if she's around."

There were muffled shouts and footsteps; eventually a soft voice came on the line. "This is Gloria."

"This is Robert Rochmann. In the hospital? I believe you left me a teddy bear?"

"Oh, yes!" she exclaimed happily. "Mister Lucky. I'm really glad you called. I wanted to explain but they wouldn't let me in to see you. Can you have visitors now? I have to tell you about him."

"Mister Lucky?" He could hardly say the words. What kind of a perverse joke was this?

"That's the bear's name. He's very lucky. I have to tell you about him. Are you out of intensive care?"

She was very enthusiastic. So much energy. Like Golding. So much life swirling around while he lay there, as if in the empty eye of a tornado. This girlish voice exclaiming 'Mister Lucky' was like the flash of a distant firefly. Long ago, it had been verdant summer, with clouds of fireflies signaling their frantic sexual come-ons against a background chorus of cicadas screaming in ecstasy. Now it was dark, silent autumn, with winter looming ahead. 'Mister Lucky.' One small, feeble flash.

# Chapter 24:  Sex Zombie

E ver since he'd first awakened in the hospital, Rochmann had little sense of time.   But now he watched, with anticipation, the progress of the shadows on the hills outside his window as the late afternoon sun formed a vivid, three-dimensional landscape.  Gloria had said she would visit after class and, for once, the temporal order of events held his interest.

She arrived in penumbra of chilled air.  "I brought you these," she said, and fished a cellophane bag of buttermints from her jacket pocket.

"Thanks," he said.  A buttermint suddenly was just what he wanted.  His mouth watered as he tore open a corner of the bag with his teeth and popped one into his mouth.  He offered her the bag but she shook her head and stood there, as if uncertain what to do next.  "Have a seat," he said, gesturing toward the bedside chair.

She hung her jacket over the back of the chair and sat down.  "I'm glad you called yesterday.  How're you doing?"

"As good as can be expected.  I guess I'm out of the woods, for now.  They've started physical therapy..."  He stopped; this was not a pleasant topic.  "Tell me about the teddy bear."

She smiled brightly and reached for the stuffed animal he'd moved from nightstand to the pillow next to him.  The air warmed as she leaned near, and a faint, sweet fragrance beguiled his nose.

"Well, Mister Lucky," she said, sitting the bear on her lap. "When I was a little kid, I don't know, five or six, I was very sick in the hospital.  Scarlet fever, or rheumatic fever, or some kind of fever.  Anyway, I was pretty bad off.  They even had the priest come pray over me.  And my mom got me this bear to keep when she couldn't be there.  She had to go cook for my dad and brothers and couldn't stay at the hospital all the time.  Anyway, all of a sudden, right after I got the bear, I got better."  She nuzzled the bear with her cheek.

"Everyone said I was very lucky, like it was a miracle.  They'd been lighting candles in church, and saying novenas and stuff.  But to me, it seemed like the bear brought me through, so I named him 'Mister Lucky.'  And later, in school, when I'd have tough times, with other kids and stuff, I'd talk to him and I'd just feel better." She stopped and smiled sheepishly. "I guess that sounds pretty silly."

Rochmann shook his head and smiled too. "Not at all. It's very nice, very touching." He could have explained it in terms of conditioned relief. But right now, he was not a psychologist; he was half a man in a hospital bed. "So, you kept him all these years?"

"Well, yeah. When I came to college I put him in with my stuff but just kind of left him packed away." She stared off, as though looking at things packed away. "I forgot about him, I guess. You know, starting college, being grown up. I could have used him though . . ." Her voice faded as if she, too, were retreating from an unpleasant path.

"So why'd you give him to me?"

"Well, you looked like you could use some luck." She hugged the bear again. "It just kind of hit me, all of a sudden. Maybe it was being in the hospital again, the way it smelled or something. It reminded me of Mister Lucky and I thought, this guy really needs some luck." She handed the bear back to him.

He took it with his right hand and held it to his chest. Tears welled in his eyes and spilled down his cheek. He turned his head away, trying to hide his face in the pillow. After a minute, he sniffed loudly and smiled awkwardly at her. Her eyes looked moist, too. He fumbled for the box of tissues on the nightstand, knocking it to the floor. She picked it up and placed it beside him. He blew his nose and wiped his eyes.

"Sorry, don't know what happened," he said in a thin, reedy voice, not looking at her.

She patted his hand. "It's okay. Crying can be good. Maybe your luck is changing already."

\*\*\*

"Well, Rocky, I have some good news and some bad news," Chappell announced on his Sunday visit. "I've been talking to the physical therapist about electrical stimulation. He's willing to work with you on zapping the old muscles, along with the other exercises. Start building some strength for ambulation, you know."

Rochmann nodded, his mouth in a tight line. "Is that the good news, or the bad?"

"That's the good news, or part of it. The bad news is that he thinks you're not trying hard enough. Very passive, he says, just going through the motions. They have to decide about whether to aim toward teaching you to use a wheelchair, one of those motorized ones, finding you an accessible place to live and all that. Or to make an all-out effort toward walking. Of course there's no guarantee, but he thinks you're giving up too soon. Wanted me to talk to you."

"Any other good news?" Rochmann asked in a weary tone.

Chappell said, "As a matter of fact, yes. I've been doing a little research on biofeedback. There's some intriguing stuff on recovery of function. Mostly case reports, nothing systematic, but still fascinating. There's no equipment at the hospital but I could get a machine for you. You'd have to study up and work on it yourself. I brought some articles in case you're interested. Machine's around a thousand bucks--not covered by insurance." He opened his brief case and took out copies of journal articles and placed them on the bed. "What's with the bear?"

"Friend brought it. Said it might bring me luck."

Chappell gave him a quizzical look. "I'll bring you a rabbit's foot next time." He took a copy of *The New Yorker* from the briefcase and sat, quietly reading, while Rochmann looked through the journal articles.

Rochmann was somewhat familiar with biofeedback applications to problems like headache. But 'neuromuscular re-education' was new to him. A half-hour passed in silence. Rochmann laid down the article he was reading and looked at the bear. 'Mister Lucky,' indeed. It was light brown, discolored in places, with gleaming black eyes. Like Gloria's. "Seems pretty straightforward," he said to Bill. "Case reports, like you said, no real control procedures, but pretty neat results."

Just then, an attendant knocked and entered, a large black woman with a wide smile and a maternal, teasing manner. She pulled a wheelchair into the room. "Time for P.T., honey. You wanna walk down there or am I gonna hafta push you again?"

Rochmann said, "You can push me today, Rachel. Maybe tomorrow I'll walk." He grinned at Chappell. "Get me that biofeedback machine, Bill. Might as well give it a shot."

Rachel skillfully maneuvered Rochmann into the wheelchair. "You want your teddy bear, hon?" She shot a grin at Chappell.

Rochmann smiled, looking at the bear, then turned serious. "Hey, Bill. Next time you come, could you bring my workout book? It's in my gym bag, stashed over at the Fitness Center somewhere, probably in the lost-and-found."

"Sure, but why…"

"Tell you later." Rochmann waved his right hand as Rachel wheeled him out the door.

*** 

Chappell was sitting with his briefcase in his lap when Rochmann returned. After the attendant had Rochmann back in bed and cranked up into a sitting position, Chappell opened the briefcase and pulled out a scruffy green book. "Ta da," he said.

Rochmann took the book, its familiar cover mottled with sweat and chalk dust. "Hey, thanks. I didn't mean you had to get it right away."

"Why not? Had nothing better to do for the last hour. And I'm curious why you want it."

Rochmann placed his limp left hand on one side of the book to hold it open and paged through with his right hand to the last set of figures. "I wanted to take a look at my last workout." 'Last workout' echoed in his head as he spoke, slow and low-pitched, like a dragging tape recording. There, listed in his neat script: cleans, high pulls, deadlifts, the numerals marching in orderly rows across the page, the ink blurred in places by dried drops of sweat. His notation, after the last set of cleans, 'Good day!' He did not remember writing, or doing, any of it. He felt engulfed by a wave of icy water and shook his head in a struggle to reach the surface.

Chappell gently touched his shoulder. "Why are you doing this, Rock? Some kind of implosion therapy?"

Rochmann shook his head. "I can't remember my last workout. I thought if I could see, touch something associated with it, it would help bring it back."

Chappell sighed. "Retrograde amnesia, Rock, you know that. Those memory traces were never consolidated. It's just not in there." He tapped his own head. "What's the deal with the last workout?" He pulled his chair closer to the bedside.

"Well, there was this girl, standing next to the platform, and she says I grabbed her crotch when I collapsed."

Chappell emitted a snort of laughter. "That's my boy, Rocko, not going down without a last grab for pussy."

"It's not funny, Bill. It scared her. I must have walked off the platform and stuck my hand, you know, before falling down. How could I do that?"

"Maybe you were just flailing around for support?"

"That's what I thought, but then I would have grabbed her shoulder or arm." Rochmann made a sweeping motion with his right arm, and then a thrusting motion. "Totally different muscles are involved."

"I don't know, Rock." Chappell looked thoughtful. "Who's this girl? How'd you find out about this?"

"One of the weight room dollies; I think I'd seen her around there a few times. She came to the ICU, I guess the day after. I was pretty groggy but I could tell she was upset."

"The ICU? How'd she get in there? Maybe you were hallucinating?"

"She's been back to see me," said Rochmann. "Left me that teddy bear."

Chappell looked at the bear on the nightstand and smirked. "You grab her crotch and she gives you a teddy bear? You always did have a way with women."

"Get serious. Dammit, Bill. She's just a kid. I think she feels sorry for me. But she wants to know what happened. And I do too."

Chappell pursed his lips in an expression of concentration.    "A pretty girl?" he asked.

"Yeah. Cute. Big, dark eyes. Nice, compact body."

"Did you notice her just before it happened?  Look at her with lust in your heart, as Jimmy Carter says?"

"I don't remember, Bill.  That's why I wanted to see this." Rochmann patted the logbook.

"Yeah, that's right.  But you'd seen her other times, in the weight room?"

Rochmann shifted his position, attempting to sit even more upright.  The workout book slid from the bed and fell to the floor. "Yeah, I probably noticed her.  I used to check out all the babes."  He smiled wanly.

"Well, there you go," said Chappell.  "There's this pretty girl next to the platform.  You know you had to be looking at her equipment."

Rochmann said nothing.

Chappell went on.  "So, the last thing on your horny little mind, before the fuse blows, is--pussy."  Chappell laughed with the realization.  "Here's what I think.  The sex circuits are buzzing in your little lizard brain when the cerebral cortex shuts down.  No cortical inhibition.  You probably would have done more than grab if the sensory and motor circuits hadn't shut off, too."

"I don't know, Bill."  Rochmann shook his head.  "That sounds pretty crazy."

"It's the best I can do.  You want me to talk to Doc Wheeler about it?"

"No way.  My neurologist doesn't need to know I go around grabbing coeds."

That evening, after Chappell had left, Rochmann mulled over Gloria's accusation.  She hadn't brought it up during her previous visit, but the idea still bothered him.  What if she told someone?  He was the kind of guy who had difficulty introducing himself to a woman; there's no way he'd walk up and grab her.  Bill was right; the brain lesion was the critical factor.

He called Gloria's dorm. When she came on the line, he said, "Gloria, I've been thinking about what you told me the first time, in the ICU."

"Yes?"

"You know, about my grabbing you when I had my stroke?"

"Yes?"

"Well, I talked to my doctor about it. To see if he had any ideas about what was going on." This was true; strictly speaking, Bill was his doctor. There was silence on the other end. "Is this not a good time? I thought maybe, you know, you were still wondering about it."

"No, this is fine. I'd like to hear what he said."

"I even looked at my training book, at that last session, to see if it would jog my memory." He had to swallow and take a deep breath. "But nothing. It's a medical fact that the stroke wiped out all memory traces."

"Uh huh."

Was she agreeing or being skeptical? He wished he could see her face.

"Well, anyway, what might have happened is that when I saw you in the weight room, before the stroke, I must have seen you since you were close to the platform; well, it probably triggered the sexual circuits in my brain, your being an attractive female and all."

"Uh huh."

"It's a perfectly natural reaction, when a male sees a female," he added quickly. "Ordinarily, the cerebral cortex inhibits all sexual urges, so we never act on them, probably are not even aware of them." He had no idea how this was going over, but plunged on. "But at that moment, I had a stroke and lost all cortical inhibition. I was like a sex zombie for a few seconds before everything shut down."

There was a snicker on the telephone line. "A sex zombie?"

"Well, that's not a technical term. You see, the cerebral cortex..."

"A sex zombie?" She was giggling, though from amusement or nervousness he couldn't tell. "I was assaulted by a sex zombie?"

"Look, Gloria, you see, there is a primitive brain that controls all our basic animal functions…"

He heard laughter and then a sharp inhalation. "Dr. Rochmann."

"Robert, please call me Robert."

"All right, Robert. Would you do something?"

"Sure. What?"

"Would you tell Mister Lucky about the sex zombie? Sit him next to you and tell him, out loud, what you told me."

"What?" He had a Ph.D. in behavioral psychology. He did not talk to teddy bears.

"That's the way Mister Lucky works. You tell him what you're thinking, what you're afraid of or worried about. Just do it, and see what happens. Okay?"

He was silent, trying to picture himself doing what she asked.

"Okay?" she repeated.

"Okay," he agreed.

"Good. Thanks for calling, and I'll see you soon."

# Chapter 25:  Superman and Tinkerbell

One week after her first surreptitious visit to his hospital room, Rochmann smiled happily at Gloria's reappearance. "What's that?" she asked as soon as she'd removed her jacket.

He was sitting up in bed, wearing baggy boxer shorts and a loose tee shirt that had once fit snugly, his muscles melting away like Frosty the Snowman in July.  Between his splayed legs was a metal box, about half the size of a shoebox, with small knobs, buttons, and switches arrayed across the front.  Two cables ran from the back of the box to his thighs, and three wires projecting from each cable were attached to small electrodes placed just above each knee.

"Watch," he said, nodding toward the instrument.  Lighted numerals were displayed on its face, reading 3.7, with a small horizontal row of yellow lights beneath them.  Quickly, the digits counted upward to a reading of 32.6, and the row of yellow lights extended to the right.  The numbers fluctuated up and down around this value for a few seconds, then fell to 2.5 and the row of lights receded to the left and disappeared.

"That's neat.  What is it?"

"EMG biofeedback.  Shows your muscle activity in microscopic amounts."  He wrote some numbers on a small pad of paper.  "Feel this."  He placed her fingertips between the electrodes above his left knee.  The numbers on the machine again jumped into the 30s.

"It moved," she exclaimed.

"Yup.  Yesterday I could only get it into the teens and you couldn't feel any motion.  Been working on it all day and it's really coming along.  Of course, my right leg is a couple hundred microvolts ahead of my left, so I have a ways to go."  He clicked the machine off.  "Say, could you do me a favor?  Could you get me some spiral notebooks, about three or four, and a package of graph paper?  I'll pay you for them."

"Sure, no problem."

He unsnapped the wires from the electrodes, wound up the cables and, with Gloria's help, put the equipment in the bottom drawer of his bedside stand. He covered himself with a sheet and lay back on the pillows with a sigh. "It's good to see you," he said.

She nodded. After a bit of silence, she asked, "Did you talk to Mister Lucky? About, you know?"

He gave an embarrassed grin. The name of the bear, especially from her lips, still seemed strange. "Actually, yeah, I did." Actually, late at night after she'd made her strange request, he had looked at the bear and carried out a silent soliloquy, not going so far as to speak aloud. But he had restated Chappell's analysis.

"And?"

He laughed nervously. "Well, he didn't talk back."

She only raised her eyebrows and looked at him with those dark chocolate eyes.

"Seriously, what I said about failure of cortical inhibition of sexual circuits in the limbic system, I honestly think that's what happened. That's what I meant by 'sex zombie.' I just got a little carried away when I talked to you."

She smiled. "So you're not a sexual zombie?"

He raised his right hand. "Swear to God. Cortical inhibition is firmly in control.

"Okay. If you and Mister Lucky are fine with that, I am too."

Another silence, and then both spoke at once: "So, what's your..." "So how'd you..." They both stopped and laughed. He said, "Go ahead. Ladies first."

"I was just wondering how you got into weightlifting. It seems so unusual for a college professor."

"Well, I was a weightlifter long before I was a professor." Rochmann gazed out the window at the distant hills as if they marked the passage to an earlier time. "It must have been about twenty years ago, I used to stay over at my best friend's house a lot. Practically lived there." He did not say why and she did not ask. "He had a big brother who was a weightlifter. Had their garage set up with a platform, Olympic weights, squat racks, the whole deal. Me and my buddy used to hang out there, mostly to look at the *Playboy* centerfolds his brother'd tacked up." Rochmann stopped. That was a dumb thing to tell a girl whose crotch he'd grabbed.

Gloria smiled reassuringly. "I have three big brothers. You should see the stuff they leave around." She paused, then prompted, "I guess you didn't just look at pictures?"

"Oh, yeah. His brother used to make trips to York, Pennsylvania. That was like the capital of American weightlifting back then. The York Barbell Company. All the greats trained there. His brother had this eight-millimeter camera and he took movies of their training sessions so he could study technique. And he had this film of Norbert Schemansky doing split snatches."

"Split snatches?"

"Well, the snatch is where you lift the bar from the floor to overhead in one motion. What you do is pull the bar up to about chest high and then drop under and catch it overhead. Back then, the popular technique was the split, where one leg goes forward and the other back." He hopped his index and middle fingers apart on the bed sheet to demonstrate.

"So, Norb was our heavyweight champion, a big guy, I mean not ridiculously huge like they are now, maybe two-sixty, two-seventy, just a solid guy. And he has this beautiful, low snatch position, flexible, like a gymnast, only holding three, four hundred pounds over his head. But what really got me in this film was his speed. Norb's wearing this baggy sweatshirt, and he pulls the weight up and splits under it so quick that his shirt stays suspended in mid air! He is so fast, he actually drops out of his shirt. It was like a special effects movie, like one of those stop-action films of a bullet going through an apple or something. I made him show it over and over again, frame by frame. The guy's shirt just hangs there, and his head and arms disappear into it, in just a couple clicks of the projector."

He stared off, as though viewing the film, then looked at Gloria and shook his head. "It's like he really was faster than a speeding bullet. And with this incredible weight, more powerful than a locomotive, you know? Like Superman, only a real guy. It's still the most amazing thing I've ever seen. I started training then, all through high school and college, until, you know..." He waved his hand dismissively. "I gave it my best shot, anyway." His tone and face changed as recall of his inspiration faded into present reality.

\*\*\*

Gloria did not notice his change in mood. She leaned forward in the chair. "I know just what you mean about that movie. I saw something like that when I was little." She spoke rapidly, excited by the chance to share a long-forgotten memory with someone who could understand. "When I was about eight or nine, I saw Olga Korbut on television at the Olympics, and I was blown away."

"That was '72, the Munich Olympics," Rochmann interrupted. "The Black September terrorist attack."

Gloria frowned. "I remember some kind of problem, when all I wanted was to see Olga."

"Yeah, she was certainly the bright spot that year." He shook his head, looking like he was going to say more, but stopped.

Gloria went on. "She was like this fairy princess, like Tinkerbell? But she was a real person, like you said. Here's this actual little girl, with this big smile like she's really, really happy. To me, she looked like she was flying, turning those loops and flips, and I wanted to do that more than anything. I had to be a gymnast."

Rochmann adjusted his pillow to sit in a more upright position. "So, did you?"

"Well, I bugged my mom, begged and pleaded for lessons. There was this little place in Mystic, where we live, this store front where they had a gymnastics club? Some old guy, Ivan, with an accent, and a young woman, his wife or daughter? We didn't have much money for lessons, you know. So I made deals with mom to do extra work around the house, and with my brothers to do their chores, whatever I could do to earn money to pay for lessons. I was older than a lot of the girls, but I was small for my age. I caught on quick and I practiced all the time; I'd go there just to use the mats even if I wasn't having a lesson. It was just so neat to be able to move like that, and I could imagine being on TV."

"That's great," he said. "Did you compete?"

"We had competitions with clubs from other towns. I really was about the best at our gym so I expected to win. Got mad when I didn't and worked even harder. After a couple years, I started winning trophies and ribbons. I remember one meet, I got this little gold medal for winning the floor exercise. I thought I was really on my way to being the next Olga."

Rochmann was nodding and smiling like he really understood. "What happened?" he asked.

"Well, I got to go to a regional meet. I rode with this other girl, Bridget, and her mother? There were kids from all over, teams with matching uniforms and everything, and they were talking about the Olympics and the best gyms in the country to train for them. I didn't win anything, or even place, but I got higher scores than Bridget. So later that summer, it turns out that Bridget and her mom were going to move to Florida, or Texas, or someplace, where this famous coach trains girls for the national team? They were pretty rich. I think her dad owned a car dealership or something. Her mom drove this big fancy car, white with white leather inside."

"Money talks."

"I mean, I'm shoveling snow and mowing lawns and ironing my brothers' shirts and washing their cars to pay for lessons at this cruddy little gym that doesn't have decent equipment? And Bridget's going to train for the Olympics? And to make it worse, she's this snotty kid, with blond curly hair, who knows I'm from the wrong side of the tracks. I mean, I'm better than her athletically, but her mom makes her these fancy costumes with sparkly sequins and all. And she wears make-up and has this big smile, all these little hand flutters and stuff. And the judges just love her, she's so damn cute."

She fluttered her hand in imitation of Bridget, then continued. "So, I just quit. I went back a couple times, but finally gave it up. When I hit junior high, I got into cheerleading. Gymnastics gave me an edge and I even got to be captain of the squad my junior year in high school. That was sort of neat. I mean I got to hang with the snooty kids even if I was from the poor side of town."

She stood up suddenly. "Could I have some of your water? All this talking makes me thirsty."

"Sure, help yourself."

Gloria did not want to talk about high school, about the costs that had gone with her hard-earned status. Cheerleaders were expected to date the boorish football and basketball players. This meant hand jobs, blowjobs, going all the way. There were pressures to smoke pot and snort cocaine in post-game parties. The other cheerleaders taught her about bulimia to cope with the munchies and the changes puberty brought. It had been too much and she'd given it up her senior year and concentrated on her grades. This brought her a college scholarship and a means of escaping.

Gave it all up, that is, except the bulimia. This habit accompanied her to college, a way of calming herself that, paradoxically, produced a festering unrest that continued in a cycle of tension and release. It had been an almost welcome ritual to sustain her that first year away from home. But she knew she had to stop, and had joined the Eating Disorders Group the beginning of her sophomore year. Just having to tell the group about a binge was enough to curb the beast, though the urge was still lurking whenever a boy talked to her, or she thought about getting fat, or class pressures built up. Or that time in the weight room.

She looked at Rochmann. He was lying back with closed eyes, as if exhausted by their revelations. Her last binge seemed like another life, a bad dream from which she'd woken. She'd had no urges all week and decided not to go back to Group. She didn't want to be reminded of the past. The past was gone: Olga and Bridget, cheerleading and bulimia. Mister Lucky looked at her from the nightstand. Well, some links to the past were good.

# Chapter 26: Walking Out

Dr. Wheeler stood next to Rochmann's chair, watching the numbers flash on the biofeedback equipment. "So how's the biofeedback going?" he asked. "I understand you're making good progress in P.T." He looked at the chart he was carrying. "You can stand and bear some weight on the left leg now. " He turned a couple pages. "It's been what, almost three weeks? Blood pressure is controlled with meds. Looks like time to move to the rehab ward."

"Sounds good to me," said Rochmann, clicking the machine off. "Would you like to see some data?"

"Of course," said Dr. Wheeler. He seemed amiable, less formidable than usual.

Rochmann fumbled, one-handed, in the drawer of the nightstand, pulled out a folder containing sheets of graph paper, and handed it to the doctor. "These are summary data, where I've plotted the highest microvolt level reached in each session, across training sessions, for each muscle group. The little arrows indicate where motion was first detected. You can see pretty steady increases. There are comparison values for my right side, which are way higher, but the left is getting there."

The numbers were almost as satisfying as those he'd once inscribed in his green workout book, microvolts rather than kilograms, but at least they were moving in the right direction. That direction no longer pointed toward Los Angeles, but to his little house on a side street. The goal was not a medal on the victory podium but getting back to square one, the place everyone took for granted, using two legs and two arms. The numbers carried him along.

"Hmm, interesting," said the doctor as he leafed through the pages. "But how do you know it's the biofeedback, and not just that you're getting stronger with time and physical therapy?"

Rochmann smiled. "Good question." He proceeded to show Wheeler how, by focusing on one muscle group at a time, and leaving others untrained, he was able to isolate the effects of biofeedback, replicating with one muscle group after another. Overall, there was an improving trend, but a noticeable acceleration when biofeedback was added. "It's called a multiple-baseline, a way of showing experimental control in an individual case. You don't need large groups of subjects and statistics to do valid research. You can do it with one person."

"You don't say." Dr. Wheeler examined the graphs more closely. "You've been busy," he finally said with an approving nod. "Tell you what, after you walk out of here, we'll hire you back as a consultant."

"I'll think about it." Rochmann laughed at the joke.

\*\*\*

The frequency of Gloria's visits also increased. They found much to talk about in sharing childhood stories. Both were the youngest child, probably unplanned they concluded, with an absent father and an unhappy, distant mother.

"I didn't know my dad very well," Rochmann told her. "He was in the Army, in Korea, when I was a little kid. My mom worked in an office, and my big sister, Louise, was supposed to watch me. Mostly, she bossed me around."

Gloria laughed. "Yeah, I know about that. My big brothers treated me like a servant."

"So, my dad got out of the service when I was about twelve. He opened a garage. That was pretty neat, because I was really into cars, anything mechanical. Then, one day a hydraulic lift collapsed and killed him. My mom took it really hard, all depressed and everything. Louise was gone; I think she'd just gotten married and moved out to Seattle. That's when I started hanging out at my friend's house. The kid I told you about with weights in the garage? That's when I got into lifting."

Gloria took his hand. "Your father's killed by a collapsing watchamacallit, and you take up weightlifting?" Her brown eyes looked at him intently.

Rochmann frowned and was silent for several seconds. "You should be a psychologist," he said finally. "I just felt like it was something to do, a place to go. But I didn't feel that devastated. Not like when I, you know, when this happened. I suppose that sounds cold but I guess I wasn't that close to my father. He was like this really nice guy who came to visit, and then was gone."

"My father's still alive," said Gloria, "but, to be honest, I don't feel very close to him, either. He runs a fishing boat and is gone most of the time. And when he is in port, well, he drinks a lot. Hangs out with other Portuguese fishermen. And he's not very nice to my mom."

Now it was his turn to squeeze her hand. Gloria smiled and said, "He doesn't beat her or anything. He's just, you know..." She shrugged.

He felt like hugging her. Instead, he asked, "How does he treat you?"

"Mostly ignores me. I'm just expected to help mom, you know, wait on him." Still smiling, she said, "My brothers, when they were still at home, were just like him. Women are expected to wait on the men. Do all the cooking, cleaning, picking up after them."

Rochmann laughed. "Sounds good to me. Where do I sign up?"

Gloria waved her hand at the room. "You got all that right here.

The grin left his face. "Yeah, that's right. Actually, I don't mind cleaning, and I am a good cook." He sighed. "When I get out of here, I'll fix you a nice dinner. Stir-fry is my specialty."

"Deal," she said. "And if you like fish and garlic, I can cook all kinds of stews."

After a month of hospital food, this was one more reason to get his walking shoes on. Despite her youth, Gloria seemed like some ideal version of a big sister. She examined the graphs he kept and cheered on his progress. She brought him treats: dark chocolate and cashews and pizza slices. And she even started calling him 'Robby,' as his mother and sister had done, before he'd become 'Rocky' to Chappell and passing women.

*** 

For Gloria, without thinking about it, visiting Rochmann had become part of her routine, like classes and exercise. She no longer went to the Fitness Center but used the equipment in the basement of her dorm. And she no longer went to Group; urges to binge had vanished and her problem seemed so paltry compared to his stroke recovery. They were like *Hansel and Gretel*, abandoned by their parents, and now he was trapped, not by a wicked witch but by a malfunctioning brain. And she was helping him escape. She'd done some reading on stroke and decided maybe she'd be a physical therapist rather than a veterinarian.

Though she felt comfortable talking with him, she never brought up her eating disorder. Once, she'd come close, asking about his weightlifting in high school, wondering how he'd handled those years so troublesome for her.

He had told her, "I trained as much as I could. My buddy wasn't into it like I was. I went out for the wrestling team; I was small, and pretty strong compared to the other guys. But the coach didn't want me to lift weights--supposed to be bad for growing kids, he said. The crazy thing was, we were supposed to lose weight to wrestle in a lower weight class. Kids in the middle of their growth years are supposed to diet and lose weight. Looking back, it was crazy. But when you're a kid, you know, you go along."

This was an opening to share her own experience with dieting and all the rest, but she just sat, stroking the teddy bear's fur. "Yeah, I know," was all she said.

***

On a clear, mid-December morning, sunlight poured through the window like a spotlight on Bill Chappell as he packed Rochmann's belongings. Dr. Wheeler had performed his final check-up and signed the release papers earlier that morning. Waiting for Chappell, Rochmann had sat motionless, thinking of neither past nor future, just watching the shadows of objects in the room as the sun rose higher. It was impossible to see the shadows move yet, inexorably, they shortened. When Chappell arrived, Rochmann said little. Plans had been made and nothing, really, needed to be said.

The quiet was broken when Rachel, the attendant, entered with a wheelchair. "You ready, honey? Time to wheel you out of here."

"I can walk," Rochmann said, nodding toward the aluminum-tube, four-point walker, like those used by geriatric patients, that stood next to his chair.

"Regulations, honey. You gotta ride outta here."

"I've been walking up and down these halls for days," he protested.

"Them's the rules, baby. Don't argue. Now set your butt in here. Don't make me pick you up."

They proceeded down the hall, a little parade led by Rochmann in the wheelchair, holding the biofeedback equipment on his lap with the teddy bear peeking over the top of the box. Rachel, behind him, pushing, her dark, round face wreathed in a huge smile. Chappell brought up the rear, carrying a larger box and the walker. Christmas decorations were fastened on some of the doors and a large artificial tree stood in the lobby, hung with decorations made by children in the pediatric ward. People moved through the lobby on their own trajectories, taking no notice of the occasion. A gray-haired woman in a pink pinafore at the information desk, smiled vaguely.

Chappell helped Rochmann put on a padded ski jacket and gloves, then held the walker steady while he stood. The glass doors wooshed open and they made their way slowly down the ramp. It was bitter cold and a slight dusting of glittering snow, little more than a heavy frost, coated cars and buildings. The parking lot had been salted and swept dry. The sun in the pale blue sky glinted from the windows and snow-covered surfaces with an eye-stabbing glare.

"Here's your ride, Rock," said Chappell. He opened the trunk of a gray Ford Taurus and loaded the boxes. "It's an automatic. Leased it until you can handle the clutch on the Scout." He closed the trunk. "The best thing is, you won't have to worry about parking spaces." He indicated the blue handicapped sign dangling from the rear-view mirror. "Want to drive?"

"That's okay," Rochmann replied. "You drive. Not even sure if I remember the way home."

Their silence resumed on the trip as if, by saying nothing, the future was held at bay. Rochmann stared out the window. It was six or seven months since he'd last ridden with Bill, returning from the Nationals. A half year and a whole lifetime. Chappell stopped the car at the curb. "Your driveway looks kind of slick," he said. "Wait here."

Chappell slipped several times as he made his way up the incline to the garage. He emerged with a broom and worked his way down the edge of the driveway, clearing a path in the icy powder. He went back to the garage and got a large coffee can filled with rock salt that he sprinkled on the path.

He opened the car door. "There, that should do it." He was breathing heavily and his face was red from the cold and exertion. "Take it slow. Don't want any broken bones."

Rochmann cautiously made his way up the salted path, with Chappell staying close behind but not touching him, like he was spotting for a heavy squat. Rochmann had practiced only on slight inclines and it was hard work to get up the slope of the driveway. He, too, was breathing hard as they entered the screened back porch. Chappell moved ahead to unlock the kitchen door, opened it, then stood back while Rochmann negotiated the single step upwards.

The kitchen appeared familiar, yet somehow different, like the face of a friend one has not seen for a long time. The ship-cabin tidiness seemed to emphasize its emptiness. There was the stale odor of unused rooms.

Sunshine streaming in from the window over the sink made a bright patch on the floor. The surfaces of the counters shone with a muted luster under a smooth coating of dust. A pile of unopened junk mail lay on the kitchen table. Chappell had brought him the bills and cards and letters when he visited the hospital, and dumped the rest here. Rochmann clanked the walker over to the coat hooks behind the door and removed his jacket, unaided, and hung it up. "Be it ever so humble," he said.

"Hungry?" asked Chappell. "I got a few groceries for when you get back. Some frozen meal things. And look." He walked over to a large black metal cabinet taking up most of one counter top, barely fitting beneath the cabinets. "Ta da! It's a microwave oven. Can heat things up quick and easy. Here's the manual." He indicated the pamphlet next to it on the counter.

"Thanks, man. Not really hungry right now."

"It's a pretty clever gizmo. Thought you'd be interested in it."

"Yeah, thanks. I'll check it out later."

Rochmann shuffled through the kitchen, into the living room. Along one wall, below the large window, his Eleiko plates were stacked in squat cylinders of red, blue, yellow, green and silver. On the windowsill were several small flowerpots containing shriveled brown stems and leaves, their shadows magnified on the stack of weights like twisted gnomes.

Chappell followed his gaze. "I know you said to leave 'em in the weight room," he said. "Couldn't do it. Couldn't let the zombies get 'em." He smiled. "Never can tell, you might need 'em. Or at least you can sell them," he added quickly.

"It's okay." Rochmann parked his walker and sat down heavily on the sofa across from the weights. "Tired," he said.

"It's been quite a morning," agreed Chappell. "I've got to get your stuff out of the car. And finish cleaning off the driveway. You should call your landlord and make sure she gets someone to keep it cleared when it snows. And the sidewalk and front steps. It'll be a while before you can shovel."

"It'll be a while before I can do anything."

Chappell said nothing and left to finish the tasks. When he returned, Rochmann was dozing on the couch. Chappell touched his shoulder and told him, "I'm going to fix us some lunch. You need to pack a suitcase for Seattle. We'll go to the airport after we eat."

Rochmann sighed, then smiled up at his friend. He had agreed to spend Christmas with his sister and mother, the price for their not coming out while he was in the hospital. "You're right. Things to do, places to go, people to meet." Using the walker for support, he stood up. "Let the games begin."

# PART VII

# PENULTIMATE

# Chapter 27:  First Kiss

Rochmann shuffled cautiously across the cold, wet tile of the Fitness Center natatorium.  Baggy black nylon trunks drooped to his knees and a white tee shirt loosely covered his shrunken torso.  He used a four-point cane around campus as a precautionary measure but he'd be damned if he was going to use the clunky thing here.  He looked around for Gloria.

Holiday Break was over.  Gloria had called the previous day, as soon as she had returned from Connecticut, to see how he was doing.  He told her that the physical therapist recommended a pool-walking regimen and she said she would meet him here.

A sense of déjà vu had gripped him as he drove to the Fitness Center.  Walking from the locker room into the natatorium was like a dream where you turn a familiar corner and a strange, disorienting passageway suddenly looms.  He had never been in the pool and looked around uncomfortably, like a hick in Grand Central Station.  Shouts, splashing, and the springing sound of diving boards echoed and re-echoed off the tile walls.  Chlorine-scented mist tickled his nose; he sneezed and almost fell.

"Hi," Gloria said, taking his elbow.  Startled, he turned quickly and almost slipped again.  She held his arm tightly to keep him upright.  "Didn't mean to scare you."  She laughed.

"Hi, yourself," he said.  "Nice to see you." Her skin was several shades darker than his pasty white hide.  She wore a shiny, black, high-necked swimsuit that completely covered the small bulges of her breasts.  The back of her suit was cut away, revealing surprisingly muscular trapezious and erector spinea; the legs were cut high, showing the sides and bottom of her round gluteous; her quadriceps were thick and sturdy.  A soft mound bulged where he had...  He shifted his gaze and met her eyes.  "So, how's your classes?"  Had she noticed him looking at her?

"Only had a couple so far," she replied.  "How's yours?"

"Managing okay.  It's good to have something to do."  There was, in fact, plenty to do.  What he lacked was an organizing principle.  Training not only had filled twenty-plus hours each week, it was the centripetal force that had held his life together. Now, he had no center. He went to physical therapy and did his exercises, but walking did not seem as compelling a goal as the Olympics. In a clutter of ambiguous and delayed possibilities, Gloria was a welcome, immediate presence.

They reached the edge of the pool and he hesitated. He could not jump in and climbing down the chrome ladder looked daunting. Gloria seemed to sense his confusion.

She said, "Tell you what. You sit down on the edge and slide in, and I'll catch you." Gloria jumped in while he slowly lowered himself into a sitting position and dangled his legs in the water. She looked up at him, expectantly, her wet hair in dark, shining curls around her smiling face, her dark eyes wide with encouragement. He slowly slid downward and then fell forward as his feet hit bottom. She caught him with a semi-hug, laughing as if it were a great accomplishment.

"Let's start slow," he said. They turned and began walking in the waist-deep water, the wall on his right, Gloria on his left.

She did not take his arm but stayed beside him, her hip and thigh sometimes brushing his. Mister Lucky stiffened like a bowsprit. Great! First he grabs her crotch and now, the first time they're back at the Fitness Center, he gets a woody. Rochmann glanced down to see if it was noticeable through the splashing water. It was the first stirring of sexual feeling he'd had in months. Progress, perhaps, but most inconvenient.

They reached the end of the lane and he paused to catch his breath, leaning his elbows on the side of the pool, shielding the front of his trunks from view.

"How're you doing?" Gloria asked.

"Great," he said. "Let's pick up the pace on the next lap."

He splashed ahead quickly and tried concentrating on the pressure of water against his legs, but Mister Lucky seemed like a permanent fixture, so hard it almost ached. What if this lasted until it was time to get out of the pool?

Gloria swam a few stokes to catch up, crossing in front to get to his side. "Hey," she said, "you're really going to town."

Her buttocks bumped against him as her feet settled to the bottom of the pool. Rochmann stumbled forward, as if he had tripped, and pushed her away, quickly searching her face for any reaction.

She showed no change of expression. "Sorry," she said, laughing. "Let's go." She took his arm and encouraged him forward.

That moment of alarm did the trick. Mister Lucky wilted as quickly as he'd arisen. But the glow remained.

They spent half an hour walking briskly from one side of the pool to the other, talking about--what? Their trips to visit their mothers. Her brothers' scrapes with the law. Rochmann had meant to count the number of laps but when time was up, he found that he had not done so.

He climbed clumsily up the chrome ladder, doing the work with his right leg and arm. As he reached the next-to-top rung, he suddenly began trembling from fatigue and cold. Gloria scrambled out of the water and rushed to help him. He made it over the top and stood hunched, wracked with shivering spasms.

"You're blue," Gloria said, and hugged him tightly around the waist. She guided him to the bench against the wall where their towels lay, helped him sit down, and began vigorously drying him off. He took deep, diaphragmatic breaths to stop the shivering. "Let's get in the hot tub," she said, indicating the spa that bubbled nearby.

The edge of the spa was raised slightly above floor level, with broad tiled steps and a chrome railing that led down into the water. It stopped bubbling as they approached and two female students climbed out, their skin a bright pink. Gloria turned the timer knob and the water began churning again. Rochmann descended the steps slowly, clutching the rail, the water painfully hot to his chilled skin. The pool had space for about a dozen people but they had it to themselves. Gloria sat a few inches away, her knees grazing his thigh. She smiled, although her brow remained furrowed. "How's it feel?" she asked.

He gave a big sigh and slid down so that the water frothed around his chin. "Great," he replied. "I feel like an ice cube in a glass of hot tea."

Too bad he hadn't known about this before. It could have saved some trips to the massage parlor. The massage parlor. How long since he'd been there? Mister Lucky began to stir. He glanced at Gloria but she, too, had stretched out, with only her face above the water, eyes closed. The bubbling, foamy water made viewing below the surface impossible and he closed his eyes and returned to images of the lotus blossoms. But then he recalled his emaciated body. 'Mister Muscle Man' was now 'Mister Gimp Man.' His erection faded as the timer dinged and the water stopped bubbling. He opened his eyes and sat up. Gloria looked at him and smiled.

"Okay?" she inquired.

"Yeah, I'm cooked."

She watched solicitously as he made his way up the steps, then got out quickly and handed him his towel. "These are soaked. Need to get some dry ones in the locker room."

"Right," he said. "Meet you in the lobby?"

***

He was surprised to see her waiting for him when he emerged from the locker room. How different from the always tardy Gretchen. "How about some dinner?" he said. "I owe you, big time."

"You don't owe me anything." She smiled. "But okay. I've got my bike and can meet you. Where you want to go?"

"My car has plenty of room. Why don't you put your bike in the trunk and we'll go together."

Rochmann eased out of the handicapped parking space by the entrance, close to the spot where he probably had been loaded into the ambulance. "What do you like to eat?" he asked. "Italian, Chinese, Mexican?" Westerville, a college town with many students and faculty from the City, had a variety of good little ethnic restaurants.

"I like it all," she said. "Anything's better than cafeteria food. You pick."

194

He chose The Parthenon, which, despite its grand name, was a little family-owned café with homemade Greek and Italian dishes. He had taken Gretchen there once but she preferred more elegant fare.

"Would you like some wine?" he asked, looking at the wine list.

She grinned. "Can't. Underage. Wouldn't want to get you in trouble."

God, it was true. She was just a kid. To make matters worse, he spied a familiar figure at a table further back. Susan Koenig was seated across from an older woman whose tweed suit and sensible shoes marked her as another professor. They sat chatting over coffee and did not seem to notice him. The empty plates pushed to the center of the table indicated they had finished their meal and would be leaving soon, having to walk past the booth near the entrance where he sat. Perhaps Susan had already seen them when they entered. But why should he care? There was no law against going to a restaurant with a young woman.

He had a glass of the house red and Gloria had a diet Dr. Pepper. He ordered the dolmas--succulent lamb and rice with aromatic spices, rolled in grape leaves. Gloria was not familiar with many items on the menu and, taking no chances, ordered spaghetti and a small green salad. She tried a taste of the dolmas and exclaimed over the flavors, saying she would have to order it next time. Next time. An encouraging note. Rochmann sampled her spaghetti and told her he could do better.

The table where Susan had been sitting was cleared. He hadn't seen her leave. Perhaps she had not seen him, either.

The servings were not large but he had to pass on dessert, though baklava and cannolli were both on the menu. Nor could he finish the half serving of spaghetti that Gloria left. When he'd eaten out with Gretchen, he routinely finished her meal, along with appetizers and desserts, two or three times the amount he'd just eaten. His appetite was just another item in a long list of diminishments. His shoulders sagged and he walked out of the restaurant with a more pronounced limp and shuffle than when they had entered.

"Tired?" Gloria took his left arm as they walked to the car.

"Yeah. The pool and dinner seem to have added up."

195

They said little on the drive to her dormitory.

"Thanks," she said cheerily when he stopped in front of the entrance. "Don't get out. I can get the bike."

She hopped out and went to the rear of the car, then wheeled her bicycle to the driver's side. He pushed the button and the window whirred down.

"Really nice dinner," she said. "See you at the pool on Wednesday?"

"Ah, yeah. Wednesday, same time."

"Good!" She leaned her face through the window and, surprisingly, kissed him lightly, a brief but warm pressure of her lips on his, and then she hurried away.

\*\*\*

Seated at her desk, Gloria got out a sheet of paper to write her mother and let her know she'd arrived safely back at school. She wrote a couple times a month and, since talking to Rochmann, had become more sympathetic to her mother's situation. There was so much she hadn't told her mother and she struggled to think of things she could safely say. Her mother always wanted to know about her friends at college. In the middle of her sophomore year, Gloria still had no close friends, until 'Robby.' Certainly none of the girls in the eating disorder group; they reminded her of the over-privileged, self-centered girls in high school, and she wanted to avoid the one thing they had in common. She got along well enough with kids in the study groups that formed in some of the harder classes. Afterwards, they might go out for pizza or a movie at the student union; sometimes, a nerdy guy would ask her out for coffee.

Her mother had warned her about boys: "they only want one thing." If she only knew. But her mother also expressed the hope that, at college, she would meet the "right sort of boy." By this, she meant one on his way to becoming a doctor or banker or at least an office worker, someone whose hands did not smell of fish and who could put her in a house big enough so you didn't hear the toilet flush whenever anybody used it.

What could she tell her mother about Rochmann?  What could she tell herself?  Why had she kissed him?  It was just a sisterly, cheer-up kind of kiss.  He'd said he was tired, but she had seen the dejection in his eyes and feared his old melancholy was creeping back.  She just wanted to tell him to be strong, that things would be better, but the words hadn't come.  Instead, the kiss happened.  She smiled.  It felt right.

# Chapter 28: The Real Robby

G loria thought Wednesday at the pool went much better. Rochmann did not appear to become nearly as fatigued as the first time, and seemed generally in better spirits. Afterwards, he took her to the same restaurant so she could try the dolmas. He ordered shish kabob and, although he'd regained some use of his left hand, she had to help get the meat chunks off the skewers. She enjoyed helping him, though he obviously was conflicted about it, seeming both reluctant and grateful. He said he'd cook dinner for her on Friday and she agreed. When he drove her back to the dorm he stopped in the driveway, short of the well-lighted main entrance, and turned to face her. He put his arm around her shoulder and drew her toward him. They kissed briefly, tenderly, with trembling lips and a little tongue.

Back in her room, Gloria again sat at her desk, her heart pounding and her head a little dizzy. She looked at the sheet of paper on which she had written 'Robby' at the top. She drew a line down the center, then labeled the left side, 'Like,' and the right side, 'Dislike.'

Under 'Like,' she immediately wrote, 'Eyes.' He had the purest blue eyes imaginable, like that actor her mom was so nutty about, Paul Newman. Her mother had taken her to a lot of Paul Newman movies, probably to keep her company, Gloria realized later. She hadn't cared for the movies that much, but there was always a close-up scene that focused on Newman's soulful eyes and she could sense what her mom was feeling. Rochmann had eyes like that. Eyes so different from the hard, dark eyes of her father and brothers, so different from her own; strange she should find them so attractive.

Next, she wrote, 'Smart.' She could talk to him about any of her classes and he always had something interesting to say. He was really into the space program and told her she could be an astronaut, like Sally Ride. Intentional or not, he prodded her to think about the world outside Westerville and Mystic.

'Listens.' She felt really comfortable talking to him. She hadn't told him any of her deep secrets, like what went on in high school or her eating problem. But she knew she could, and that he would understand.

'Tough.' She had seen him in the gym before the accident, lifting unimaginable weights; his ferocity and intensity had been scary but fascinating. Then she'd seen him totally helpless and defeated. Now, some of that toughness was coming back. Not a lot, but she could see it was still there, under the surface.

'Needs me,' she wrote next, then scratched it out. That was too strong. She felt good about helping him, and that he appreciated it, but she could tell he was a little wary, as if resistant about depending on her. She remembered the way his face brightened whenever he saw her. 'Likes me,' she finally wrote, but that didn't quite capture it, either. The warmth of his kiss came back to her but she immediately turned to the other column.

Under 'Dislike,' she wrote, 'Old.' She'd figured out that he was twelve years older than her. Not that much, really, about the same as her oldest brother. But his age would be the first thing her mom would notice, what anybody would notice, if they--if they what? If they were a couple? A ripple of panic rose in her stomach, that old urge she hadn't felt in months. What was she doing, making this list? An impulse to crumple the page and yank open the desk drawer where she kept her food stash washed over her. It took a couple seconds to remember she'd thrown out her stash. Instead, she took slow, deep breaths--like Rochmann said he did to calm down--and pictured his blue eyes.

She returned to the list. What else did she dislike? 'Sad,' she wrote. He'd told her that he was depressed but didn't want to take pills; depression was a natural reaction to loss and he'd just work through it. She knew he was getting better but there still were times when he got really down. Everyone got down, or upset, or a little crazy once in a while. It was only human.

She sat back, looked at her list and grinned. "I really, really like a sad old man," she said aloud.

\*\*\*

After the pool session on Friday, Gloria went with Rochmann to his house for dinner. She'd been amazed when he talked about cooking. At home, cooking, like house cleaning, was women's work, carried out in the background for the convenience of her brothers and, when he was home, her father.

She watched him place a large, bowl-shaped pan on the stove, he called it a 'wok,' and remove several plastic containers of cut-up vegetables from the refrigerator. He asked her to take the tops off the containers since he couldn't grasp things with his left hand very well. He poured a little peanut oil into the wok, and most of the rest of the bottle into a saucepan, and turned on the burners.

"Want something to drink?" he asked. "I got you some diet Dr. Pepper."

"Have any beer?"

"Sure, I have just the thing." He said nothing about her age.

He retrieved two green bottles of Tsingtao from the refrigerator and popped off the caps with an opener under the countertop. He handed her one and clinked the top of his bottle to hers. "Two billion Chinamen can't be wrong," he said, and took a deep swallow.

She took a sip and looked the label. "This is good. Chinese beer? I didn't know they made beer." She wished she could take those last words back; she sounded like a kid.

He only smiled and said, "Live and learn."

He drained the sauce from cubes of marinated pork into a small bowl and dumped the meat into the wok, where it sizzled and gave off a tangy aroma. Gloria observed as he added the veggies and stirred, first the hard ones, then the soft ones. It wasn't as spectacular as that Japanese restaurant where the chefs juggle knives, but still interesting. He mixed some cornstarch into the marinade sauce and poured it over the vegetables, turned down the flame, stirred everything together, and covered it with a domed lid.

"Watch this," he said, tearing open a cellophane package of rice noodles with his teeth. He took a handful of the thin white threads and dropped them into the pan of hot oil. They sizzled for a few seconds and then made an almost audible *poof*, expanding into a twisted ball, like stiff white yarn. He lifted them from the oil with chopsticks and placed them on a paper napkin, then dropped another handful into the oil and repeated the performance.

"Wow!" Gloria laughed aloud. "That's neat."

She set out plates and opened two more Tsingtaos while he put the hot food on the kitchen table.

"Dig in," he said. He showed her how to use chopsticks, placing the sticks in her hands and closing her fingers around them. Maybe it was just an excuse to touch her, but she liked it. Chopsticks were clumsy at first, but she caught on quickly. They talked about cooking and she said she would show him how to cook Portuguese food.

"What kind of music do you like?" he asked. He agreed with her on the *Eurythmics* and the *Police*, but didn't care much for Cyndi Lauper or Madonna. Neither of them liked *rap*--those rhyming chants mixed with record-scratching that seemed to be spreading from New York City to all over. And they both thought that Michael Jackson was over-hyped. She liked some of the music from his era, the *Beatles* and the *Rolling Stones*. He said mostly he was into jazz.

After dinner, she helped him wash the dishes, then, with more Tsingtaos, they went into the living room. This was the most beer she'd drunk since high school. But it seemed natural, sophisticated, not like that furtive pressure to go along with the other kids.

Rochmann turned on the table lamp next to the sofa and said, "I got a new tape deck; been taping some of my favorite albums." While he was fiddling with the stereo, she peeked under a blanket that covered a pile of lumpy objects beneath the large front window. His weights were stacked there, like giant tinker-toys. She dropped the corner of the blanket and returned to the sofa as he pushed a button and adjusted the volume. A thin, reedy tone filled the room, shimmering, like flickering firelight. He flopped down beside her and, with effort, put his left arm around her shoulder.

"Wow! Who's that?"

"Miles Davis," he said, "*All Blues*."

"Cool; gives me goose bumps." She snuggled closer and looked into his blue eyes as he turned to kiss her.

He was a good kisser; she'd have to add that to her list. She felt relaxed and warm, like she had in the spa, not just her muscles but deep inside. She drank more beer and floated on the music; it was melancholy, yet sensual, with an undertone that thrummed with her pulse. His mouth moved to her ear, sucking her earlobe and nibbling on the little gold stud, tonguing deep inside. God, it was like the nerves ran from her ear to her most intimate center. She gasped and pressed closer into him.

His right hand was under her sweater, caressing her bra-less breasts. She'd always felt self-conscious about her small breasts but they seemed to fit his palm perfectly. He bent to kiss them and she sat back. "God, I'm burning up," she said. She took off her sweater and tee shirt and dropped them on the floor, then pulled his face to her breasts, stroking his hair and caressing his ears while his tongue played with her hardening nipples.

He slid down so he was sitting on the floor, his tongue circling her navel. Then his hand was on her belt buckle, pulling it loose. A decision point, but everything was flowing so smoothly that the decision seemed made long ago. He was fumbling, one-handed, with the button of her jeans. She reached down and undid the button, unzipped the fly, and, wriggling her hips, together they removed the tight garment. He took the waistband of her panties in his teeth and pulled. Giggling, she scooted down and helped slide them off. Still holding them in his teeth, he sat back, growling, then tossed them aside with a jerk of his head. She spread her knees apart.

Centuries ago, in high school, she had listened in disbelief to what some of the nastier girls said they liked to do. And she had given in, reluctantly, to the demands of loutish boyfriends. Now, she eagerly awaited whatever Rochmann was up to. Or down to. The tingles that she'd felt from his kisses on her ear and breasts were like little drops of rain compared to the storm that gathered inside her. She heard herself panting and saying 'Oh God,' over and over, but mostly she just felt this ball of lightning expanding until she couldn't stand it, then expanding even more, until she exploded in convulsive waves. She opened her eyes, feeling a great need to be held.

Rochmann's face came into focus; still sitting on the floor, he had moved beyond the arc of light cast by the lamp.

"C'mere, you," she said huskily, reaching out toward him. He clambered up and sat beside her, gathering her naked body in his arms. "God!" was all she could say.

He kissed her, his mouth wet with her own juices, setting off those electric tingles again. She reached down to the front of his pants and felt a hard lump. "Ooh, we have company," she said, rubbing the swelling, then undoing his belt and zipper. She took hold of his sweater and undershirt to pull them over his head.

"Wait," he said, and reached over and snapped off the lamp, leaving only the glow from the kitchen.

"Why'd you do that?" she asked.

"I'd rather not be under a spotlight. I look so awful."

"Robby, you look fine." She stroked his cheek and ran a finger over his lips.

He kissed her. "You're sweet, Gloria. But I know how bad I look."

She smiled. "I think maybe you have body image issues."

"Yeah, well, it's not an image. It's really me, or what's left of me."

"Robby, those big muscles were like a suit of armor. You were kind of scary, you know? Banging and clanging around. Maybe it's like that armor is gone and the real Robby can come out."

"Yeah, well, maybe I don't know who that 'real Robby' is."

She kissed him gently. "Let's find out."

# Chapter 29: The 'L' Word

With Gloria's assistance, Rochmann removed his clothing, but the interruption and talk of body image changed his mood. Gloria said nothing, only snuggled closer. Her warm mouth on his, her inquiring tongue, her smooth skin, her sheer availability, eventually brought Mister Lucky back to life. Rochmann leaned over the arm of the sofa, opened a drawer of the lamp table, and retrieved a condom. He tore open the foil packet with his teeth and, with his one good hand, extracted the little circlet and attempted to unroll it over the head of his penis. It stopped--damn thing must be wrong way around. He flipped it over and tried the other side. It still would not unroll. He tried to feel, between thumb and forefinger, which way was up, but once again his resolve, and all else, failed.

Only a year ago, he'd been on a mission to seduce the beauteous Gretchen. Then, he had been so sure of himself, so cocky after that 400-pound clean-and-jerk, that he'd been amazed when she put him off, so full of testosterone that he'd had to seek relief at the massage parlor. Now he couldn't even get it up for this teen-ager. What a sorry excuse for a man. "This isn't working." His voice cracked. "I'm sorry. I really want you. But Mister Lucky just isn't cooperating."

"Mister Lucky? The teddy bear isn't cooperating?" Her eyes were wide with bewilderment.

"Ahh, no." He gave a choking sigh. Embarrassment compounded his humiliation. There was no way back; just plunge ahead. He could kiss this relationship goodbye. "What I mean is, that just kind of slipped out. You see, a long time ago, I started calling--it," he made a sweeping gesture with his hand toward his flaccid penis, "Mister Lucky. You know, for when I 'got lucky.'"

"You named your thingy?" She was grinning.

"Yeah, I know it sounds stupid. It's sort of a joke. But that's why I was so amazed when you told me the teddy bear's name. It was like the weirdest coincidence in the world."

She snuggled closer. "So when I told you about 'Mister Lucky,' you thought I was talking about your thingy?"

"No, no. But it reminded me that I had one. I'd had so much bad luck, the name of the teddy bear kind of gave me hope that I could get lucky again. Not sex, exactly. I hardly thought about sex. Just that something good might happen." He gave an audible sigh. "I know I'm not making sense."

She kissed him gently and placed her warm hand on Mister Lucky. "That's okay. I know what you mean."

They kissed. After a while, she worked her way down, following the route he'd taken earlier with her. She was not as expert as Nina, nor as professional as the lotus blossoms, but her amateur enthusiasm was much more arousing.

She stood, straddled his lap and whispered in his ear, "We don't need that rubber thing; I'm on the pill, to regulate my period." She slowly eased herself down, making little gasping noises. He grasped her perfect globes and became lost in her heat, her musk, her motion.

***

While Gloria was in the bathroom, Rochmann picked up their clothes that lay scattered on the floor and draped them on the arm of the sofa. In the back of the bedroom closet, he found his old blue bathrobe and a short, white terry-cloth robe that Gretchen had left. He gave this to Gloria when she emerged and went in to use the facility himself.

He came out to find her standing in the darkened living room in front of the window. The robe, which had barely covered Gretchen's butt, reached halfway down Gloria's thighs. He came up behind and hugged her to his chest, rubbing his cheek against her still-damp curls.

"Look at that," she said, "outside the window." Snow lay thick on the roof of the house next door. Around the street lamp, clumps of white swirled like goose down from a titanic pillow fight. An unbroken grey-blue blanket hid all demarcations of streets and yards, and a pinkish glow suffused the horizon where the lowering sky captured light from the town and reflected it back in a luminous fog.

"I guess you're stuck here until the spring thaw." He kissed the top of her head.

"Mmm," was all she said, wriggling her bottom against him. They stood staring at the silent, snowy cocoon that slowly enveloped them. "I better call the dorm," she said at last. "I didn't sign out for an overnight."

"Phone's in the kitchen, on the wall next to the back door." He watched the silhouette of her small figure as she walked into the light.

She dialed a number and waited. He heard her say, "This is Gloria Soares. I'm snowed in and I'm staying at a friend's house." She paused, then read off his phone number."

Rochmann put on another tape, more upbeat than the plaintive Miles Davis that had started the evening. Hanging up the phone, Gloria called from the kitchen, "Who's that?"

"*Weather Report*, their *Heavy Weather* album; I think it suits the occasion. Why don't you bring a couple more beers. Let's celebrate."

*** 

Rochmann awoke in a tangle of bedcovers, with Gloria a warm bundle in his arms. Gray, diffuse light from the bedroom window indicated that the snowstorm continued. He nuzzled her neck and inhaled the salty-sweet fragrance of their lovemaking. They had not been fucking or screwing or getting it on, but making love. He sighed contentedly and hugged her closer. She turned to face him, her full lips opening in a smile, her dark eyelashes parting like a curtain on the future. "I love you," he said.

"Mmm, I love you, too," she murmured.

At her reply, he realized what he'd said. The 'L' word, a word he'd avoided since high school, wary of its powers to ensnare and entangle. An older boy had told him of its magical powers to get a girl to put out--a code word, a polite way of saying you wanted to fuck. It took a couple of painful experiences for Rochmann to learn that girls did not hear it that way, that it was much more complicated. There were expectations of telephone calls, of sitting together in the cafeteria, of spending time together and not talking to other girls. He discovered there were derisive hoots from his buddies if he complied with these expectations, and tears and recriminations if he did not. Thankfully, sex in college was much more casual. And even with Gretchen, the word had not felt appropriate. He reserved the 'L' word for phone calls on Mother's Day.

And now, he had said it to Gloria, without calculation, without analysis. Her presence evoked this reaction as naturally as sunshine unfolds a rosebud. He said it again, his tongue savoring the words like chocolate. "I love you."

They spent all that Saturday together, naked, making love. The gunmetal sky was pocked white with falling snow, but they shut out even this feeble light. They closed the blinds and turned on all the lights in the bedroom, the bulbs glowing in the old-fashioned glass ceiling fixture, the bedside lamp, even the closet light, warming the room in golden incandescence.

Gloria was like no other woman. She needed no thick muscularity to inspire her, no cocaine to turn her on, and no cash on the countertop to induce her to yield her supple body to him. Those three little words summed up everything.

The snowfall ended sometime Saturday night. On Sunday morning, the heavens cleared to a bright blue and the earth glittered like an ice palace. Snow-clearing machinery clattered by that afternoon and, before dark, they dug out the Taurus, throwing snowballs at each other and laughing like school children on holiday. They drove to her dorm that evening and sat in the driveway, kissing long and passionately before parting, reluctantly, as though they would not see each other for weeks. "See you at the pool tomorrow," she said, giving Rochmann a last kiss through the open car window, "Mister Lucky."

# Chapter 30:  Lucky's Gym

On a Friday evening near the end of January, Rochmann reclined languidly on the sofa with Gloria.  Teaching, physical therapy, and biofeedback practice provided a comforting structure to his days, and Gloria added warmth and color to his evenings.

"It's chilly," Gloria said.  She got up and grabbed the blanket that covered the stack of weights under the window.  Returning to the sofa, she nodded toward the weights and asked, "Do women do Olympic lifting?"

"Hmm?  What'd you say?"

"I said, do women compete in Olympic lifting?"

"Uh, yeah.  It's actually just kind of getting started.  Some meets have a female division, and there's even a woman's national championship the last couple years.  But they're not in the Olympics.  Why?"

"Do you think you could teach me?"

Rochmann turned to look her in the face.  "It's not really a good sport for women.  I mean, it takes a lot of raw strength."

"C'mon.  You told me how much it involves coordination and technique."

"Yeah, well what I mean is, it's not very feminine.  Gives you thick muscles.  You wouldn't want to look like me."  He sighed.  "Like I used to."

"Robby, I'm not a guy, in case you haven't noticed.  Why would weightlifting make me look like one?"

The female bodybuilders in physique magazines were pumped so full of steroids that they looked like miniature Schwarzeneggers.  Female Olympic lifters were much rarer, and they looked okay in the few pictures he'd seen.  The sport probably hadn't been around long enough for them to get really juiced.  This was not a topic he wanted to discuss with her.

"Well, it's still a lot of hard work.  Why would you want to do that?"

Gloria snuggled close and drew the blanket tighter. "I've been thinking about missing my chance as a gymnast. It's too late for that, but maybe lifting is something I could do. I like working out and it would give me something to shoot for. Besides, where would I ever find a better coach?"

Rochmann inhaled the sweet fragrance of her hair and traced the muscles of her back with his fingertips. "I've never coached anyone," he said, and then fell silent. He had not wanted ever to see a barbell again. But the gleaming chrome bar beneath the window seemed to whisper, 'touch me, touch me.' His rehab workouts with pulleys and dumbbells were boring and he wondered how it would feel to try the complex motions that had once been as familiar as walking. He knew he could never lift anything heavy again but he could at least play with the weights if he trained Gloria.

"I couldn't go back to the Fitness Center weight room," he said. "I think it would really bring me down."

She kissed him softly. "Yeah, I can see that would be weird. For both of us." She sat up and pointed at the floor in front of them. "Why not here? I'll bet if we moved the furniture around, there'd be room."

"Hmm." Rochmann stood and surveyed the room. "We could move the sofa and stuff into the spare bedroom. I'd have to build a platform; put a brace under the floor so we don't crash through into the cellar." He grimaced as the past and the future pulled at him. "I suppose it could be done."

"Oh Robby!" She jumped up and gave him an enthusiastic kiss. "That would be so cool."

The next day, they went shopping. Rochmann's left leg was strong enough to operate the clutch in the Scout, and they filled the back with planks from the lumberyard. He bought a little barbell set because his 20-kilo bar was too heavy for some beginning exercises. For lifting shoes, Gloria got a cheap pair of boy's leather shoes that they took to a shoe repair shop and had extra heels put on to give proper support and balance. If she stuck with it, he promised, he'd order her some real lifting shoes from Europe. He also had the shoe-repairman cut down one of his old lifting belts so it would fit her petite frame. He insisted that she wear an ordinary sweat suit to train in, rather than her previous costume of shorts and tee shirt. This would keep her muscles warm, he explained, and allow him to concentrate on the business of coaching rather than get distracted by her tight little buns. Rochmann had thrown out his old sweat clothes, so they each got a few sets of industrial gray sweatshirts and pants. "We look like the *Saggy Baggy Elephant*," she said, laughing, when they tried them on later at home.

From the sleeves that he cut off his sweatshirts, Gloria sewed an outfit for the teddy bear and perched him on top of the stereo in a corner of the living room, facing the platform. By Monday, 'Lucky's Gym' was ready for business.

\*\*\*

Gloria was a natural. Her agility and kinesthetic awareness allowed her to learn quickly the intricate nuances of maneuvering her body around the bar's trajectory. Her strength built steadily. "You must be part Bulgarian," Rochmann teased.

Her tenacity surprised him. Often, he had to hold her back rather than urge her forward. "It takes a lot longer to build tendons than muscles," he said. "Don't want you tearing a knee." He massaged her aching muscles after workouts, recalling Mrs. Ang's techniques, though these sessions often served as foreplay. And he re-worked his computer program to chart Gloria's progress. Sometimes a heavy feeling weighed on him as he entered the numbers and inspected the trend lines, but nostalgia decreased as the weeks went by.

Rochmann lifted the bare bar in order to demonstrate technique. His left hand still could not grasp tightly, and his left arm and leg was weaker than the right, but he stuck with it as another form of therapy. Gradually, his balance and strength improved and he began to add a little bit of weight to the bar. He had to resist the impulse to try to keep up with Gloria's progress.

In early March, he said, "How'd you like to get some meet experience? The New England Open is coming up. They should have some women lifting. Pretty low key. Be a chance to get your feet wet. See how you like competing."

"You think I'm ready?"

"Your technique is excellent and it might be time to see how much you can do. Set a baseline for future reference. It would just be to give you some meet experience; no one expects you to blow anyone away the first time. Besides, I think it's the weekend after winter quarter is over, the start of spring break. After the meet, maybe we could get away on vacation. You want to go to Florida with an old professor?"

Gloria frowned. "I think I'd like to try competing," she said. "And I'd really like to go somewhere with you, but my mom's expecting me home over spring break. I haven't told her about you, about us," she added.

"Don't want to get you in trouble with your mom." It sometimes was difficult to remember how young she was. "Or have your big brothers come after me."

She laughed. "It's not that, exactly. I think it's time to tell them. It's just probably best that I don't start off going away with you on a trip, you know, first thing. They're pretty traditional."

"Of course, Sugar Babe." He hugged her tightly. "One step at a time."

"Okay, sign me up for that meet," she said.

***

When the entry form arrived, they went over it together after a workout. Rochmann said, "We need to decide what class to enter you in. I haven't paid attention to your body weight; wanted to see what your natural weight was after training for a while. Do you know what you weigh now?"

She looked surprised, then turned away.

"Gloria?"

"Oh," she said. "I was just thinking. I used to be about 110 but I haven't checked lately." Her tone brightened. "Why don't I sit on your face and you guess my weight?"

"Okay. But we can't do that at weigh-in." He kissed her ear.

"I'll weigh after I take a bath," she said. "Take one with me?"

They made love in the tub. Then, calmly but insistently, she told him to leave the bathroom while she weighed herself.

"One-twelve," she announced, emerging from the bathroom, wrapped modestly in a large towel. "I've gained a couple pounds."

"That's not much. We'll have to put some meat on you. The two lowest classes are 48 and 52 kilos, around 106 and 114 in pounds. Makes no sense at all to go down, so you can gain some and still make 114 easy. We may eventually want to go up to 56 kilos."

"Gain weight?" She looked alarmed.

"Gloria? What's wrong?" He embraced her.

"Robby, I've got to tell you something."

Just then, the timer in the kitchen dinged, signaling that the chicken and vegetables baking in the oven were done. "Let it wait," he said. "What's going on?"

"Let's go sit down." She led him into the kitchen and they sat next to each other at the table. "Well," she began slowly, "I used to be bulimic. You know, binge eating and throwing up?"

He nodded and took her hand.

"Then it all went away, right after I visited you in the hospital. It was like I wasn't worried about how I looked, how fat I was, compared to your problems. Or I think that's what it was. I mean, the urge to binge just sort of left me after I started seeing you. When you didn't want me to look at you the first night, you know, because you thought you looked bad, I just so understood how you felt because I used to feel the same way."

"You're beautiful," Rochmann said, and moved to kiss her.

She put her finger on the tip of his nose and gently pushed his face away.

"I'm serious," she said. "Just now, when we started talking about weight, gaining weight, I got a flashback of that old urge. Just a twinge, but it was upsetting because I thought I was totally over it."

He reached out and stroked her hair. "How do you feel right now?"

She closed her eyes, as if better to look inside. "I feel good that I told you. It was sort of like a secret and I didn't know how to bring it up. I don't feel any urge to binge right now, this minute." She opened her eyes and sniffed. "Well, I do feel hungry, but it's a normal hungry. I mean it is dinnertime, and I just worked out, and that chicken smells really good, so I should feel hungry, right? That's another thing. When I had it bad I wasn't able to tell an urge to binge from being hungry, and just feeling hungry scared me that I'd go on a binge. It was very confusing. I finally had to eat just certain things at certain times so I wouldn't lose control. That's a strategy I got from some girls at Group. I went to an eating disorders group on campus where we talked about it. It helped some, I was able to get control but it never went away totally."

"Tell me about control," he said.

"Well, there's a real struggle for control between yourself and this urge to binge, which I guess is just another part of yourself. They talked about that at Group, the leaders, about parts of yourself that were fighting for control. Your unconscious and all that. I don't remember the details; it was pretty complicated."

"Just tell me about your own experience, not what other people told you about it."

She took a deep breath and placed her hands on the table. He covered them with his.

"Well, a binge is like totally losing control of yourself, giving in completely to all these feelings of taste and smell and everything." She paused. "Sort of like sex, in a way, just totally getting lost in feelings. Only sex, with you, anyway, doesn't leave me feeling awful and fat and guilty afterwards. After a binge you just have this terrible bloated feeling that you have to get rid of, take back control, you know? So you throw up and feel better, nice and calm, if you don't think about what you've done. But at least it's over with and you can get some sleep and get on with your life." Another pause. "It was sort of like an orgasm, throwing up. That sounds sick, doesn't it, but there's all this tension and then a big release. You know, a couple of times I tried masturbating when I got an urge. It seemed to help a little but it wasn't as satisfying. I never said anything about it at

Group and nobody else ever brought it up. That's really sicko, isn't it?"

"Not at all," he said. "It makes sense. People often use eating, or drugs or sex, to deal with stress. It can be real comforting to just give up the struggle, give in, let yourself go. The problem is when that leads to more stress down the road and you just set up a vicious circle. Some people use sex like that, a sex addiction. And other people are the opposite, and have trouble with sex when they can't let go." Like Nina and Gretchen, he thought.

"That's not my problem, letting go, with you anyway. You don't think I'm a sex addict do you?" She sat back and looked at him, her eyes wide.

"I should be so lucky."

"No, seriously. You don't think I'm substituting sex for binge eating do you?"

"Well, you said the urges went away right after you saw me in the hospital. That was a long time before we had sex. And tonight, you got an urge right after we had sex, when gaining weight was brought up. I think where weight is concerned, that's a stimulus that causes this reaction, a gut reaction that you call an 'urge.'"

"Hmm, could be," she said, "but I don't feel anything right now when you say it. Gaining weight. Gaining weight. Nope, don't feel a thing. A little hungry, though. Let's eat dinner."

# Chapter 31: New England Open

Gloria gazed out the window of the Scout, at the road winding through the Massachusetts hills. Snow remained in shadowed woodland patches but the bright afternoon sun hinted at spring. Rochmann had suggested that she sleep on the trip but she was too keyed up. She hummed along to the *Steely Dan* tape on the cassette player that Rochmann had installed. She tried to imagine the contest but kept her questions to herself. Her companion seemed lost in his own thoughts, not saying much since the last gas stop.

The sky glowed pink as they pulled into the parking lot of a Motel 6 and she waited while Rochmann got their room. He returned to the car and drove to a high school gymnasium. Inside, a handful of men were constructing lifting platforms at one end of the basketball court. The sounds of hammering, mixed with bantering voices, reverberated from the hard surfaces. Gloria hung back a bit as Rochmann walked up to an older man and clapped him on the shoulder.

"Dennis, you old dog," he said. "How's it going?"

The man turned and grabbed his hand, pumping it as though trying jerk his arm from its socket. "Rocky! How're you doing? You lifting? Heard you were injured."

"Yeah, retired from competition." His mouth formed a tight line for a moment, then he smiled and motioned for Gloria to come closer. "I'm coaching now. Dennis, this is Gloria Soares. This'll be her first meet. Gloria, this is Dennis Clark. He's running the show."

"Glad to meetchya," Dennis rumbled, shaking her hand as vigorously as he had Rochmann's. "You got the Rock here coaching ya, you'll do all right. We got six, seven girls entered, so you should have some good competition. About twenty, twenty-five guys. What class you in?"

"Fifty-two, I think." Rochmann answered for her. "You got the official scale available so we can check weight?"

"In the men's locker room," Dennis replied. "The wrestling team scale. Should be pretty accurate, but it's in pounds."

"Can we use it?" he asked.

"Sure. Shoo out anyone in there. Mildred'll weigh-in the girls in the morning. Eight o'clock. Lifting starts at nine."

"Mildred's his wife," Rochmann told her. To Dennis, he said, "How is Mildred? You guys healthy?"

"Like a couple 'a horses." Dennis laughed. "Old horses, but still pulling the plow. What about you? Tear your knee again?

"Worse. Had a stroke. I'm lucky to be alive."

"No shit!" Dennis exhaled like airbrakes on a semi. "And you're so young. You gonna' come back?"

Rochmann shook his head, then put his arm around Gloria's shoulder and pulled her close. "My run's over. Trials are in a couple months and I'll be too old in another four years."

"Too old, hell! Remember Ski in '64?"

Gloria felt his hand tighten. He said, "Yeah, well, guys like Schemansky come along once a century. Besides, I can't risk another brain blowout. I'm happy just coaching." He gave her shoulder another squeeze, then dropped his arm. "Let's go check your weight."

On the way to the locker room she said, "Schemansky, he was the one in the film you told me about in the hospital, right? The guy so quick he dropped out from under his sweatshirt?"

"Yeah. Norb." His voice caught on the word and he said nothing further.

Gloria weighed a half-pound under the class limit and Rochmann took her to a restaurant for a small steak, salad, and baked potato. Back at the motel, he explained his Spartan theory of sexual abstinence. But she insisted that a little poke would help her sleep; she promised to lie real still and let him do the work so she wouldn't use up any energy. They slept soundly, cuddled like puppies in a box.

The next morning, he checked her weight on the bathroom scale he'd brought, and told her she could have a banana and half cup of yogurt, with more to eat and drink after weigh-in. He bustled around, getting ice for the cooler and double-checking her equipment, while she sat on the bed and flipped through the Saturday morning television cartoons.

"Settle down, 'Rocky,'" she said affectionately, trying the name Dennis had called him. "You're making me nervous."

"Yeah, it's like I'm the one competing." He sat beside her on the bed. "You know, you don't have to call me 'Rocky.' That was my old life. I've got a new one now, with you. 'Robby' is just fine." She nodded and kissed him on the cheek, then turned back to the television.

\*\*\*

Gloria lined up with five other women on the platform while Dennis read their names and weights over the public address, but she didn't really hear much. Her face felt warm, her palms were sweaty, and her heart was pounding. She took slow, diaphragmatic breaths to calm down, like Rochmann had taught her.

A skinny blonde high school girl on her left was also in the 52-kilo class. On her right was a muscular black woman in the 56-kilo class. Two women were in the 60-kilo class: one, a tanned, heavily made-up, big-breasted, bleached blonde; the other, a pale, mousy-looking woman. There were no entries in the 67.5 or 75-kilo classes. A pear-shaped teen-ager made up the heavyweight class. Each woman stepped forward, when her name was called, to a smattering of applause from the sparse audience of friends and family.

Rochmann met her in the warm-up area, behind a partition from the competition platform. "Okay," he said, "you stretched good before the introductions. There's about six attempts before your opener, so we'll just follow what's on the bar. Leave your sweats on until your last warm-up. How do the shoes feel?" Her new Adidas lifting shoes, white with red stripes and straps across the instep, had arrived only the week before.

She sat passively, though her stomach churned, while he wrapped strips of adhesive tape around the second joint of her thumbs and middle fingers, where the bar abraded the skin. "I feel nauseous," she said.

"That's good. It means adrenaline's pumping. Take a sip of Gatorade and breathe slowly."

The mousy woman began the snatches with just the 20-kilo bar, resting on blocks to give it proper clearance from the platform.

Backstage, Gloria did three repetitions with the bar. "Perfect!" Rochmann said.

The woman took 25 kilos for a second attempt and Gloria could hear her husband shouting encouragement, as though she were attempting a world record. Gloria gave Rochmann a stern look and said, "Don't yell at me when I'm out there."

The woman finished with a successful 27.5 kilos. Her husband rushed out to join her as she left the platform, and they both laughed and hugged as though she'd given birth to a son.

The skinny girl in Gloria's weight class started with 35 kilos. She was coached by Dennis, who turned the announcing and scorekeeping duties over to Mildred. The girl had a good squat technique, her wiry arms and legs folding and extending like an animated stick figure. The tanned blonde followed with a power-snatch, hauling the bar to the overhead position with neither a split nor squat under it. They both called for 40 kilos for a second attempt.

Rochmann loaded 40 kilos on the bar behind the curtain for Gloria's final warm-up. She stripped off her *Westerville State* sweat pants and shirt, dark green and gold with a snarling bear emblazoned on the front. Beneath, she wore a plain black leotard and a white tee shirt. She chalked her hands and stepped up to the bar. "Butt down, head up, back flat," she heard him say. The barbell flew up and she caught it overhead in a solid squat. "Piece of cake," he said. "Remember, slow off the platform."

And then she was on the platform, in front of an audience and all alone. The months of practice, the warm-ups, all focused on this moment, on two seconds of effort. She bent and grasped the 45-kilo barbell, head up, butt down, slow off the platform.

"Three white lights, that's a good lift." Dennis's voice came over the p.a.

Rochmann stood by the scorer's table, grinning and making the thumbs up sign. He mouthed the word, "fifty?"

Gloria returned his grin, nodded in assent, and almost skipped back to the warm-up area. The black woman walked past and gave her a deliberate smile, as if issuing a challenge. Highlights gleamed on her dark skin, accentuating the curve of muscles in her shoulders and legs. Her bright yellow lifting suit looked spray-painted on: two button-hard nipples, the indentation of her navel surrounded by a brick wall of abs. Gloria watched the woman rip the barbell off the platform with only a slight step back as she caught it overhead.

Gloria put a towel over her shoulders, sat down on a folding chair, and closed her eyes. She rehearsed the sequence of movements for her next attempt, like Rochmann had taught her and like she used to do for her gymnastics routine.

The chair next to her creaked and she opened her eyes to see the black woman plop down. "That is so neat, the way you squat under the barbell. How'd you learn to do that? You got a coach, right? That old guy, he's your coach?" She went on and on, how she did bodybuilding and powerlifting too, how she could deadlift 325 pounds, all the contests she had won.

"Gloria Soares, 50 kilos, second attempt." Her name crackling over the p.a. startled her. She hurriedly chalked her hands and rushed to the platform. How much time did she have left? She looked over to where Rochmann was standing; he just smiled and nodded for her to go ahead.

She tried to focus; she had done this weight in practice. Piece of cake. The bar was up, she was under it, but it didn't stop, arcing back and crashing down behind her. She felt like she'd been punched in the stomach, and tears stung her eyes.

Dennis's voice on the p.a. said, "No lift; she'll probably take that again for her third attempt."

She felt Rochmann's hand on her shoulder as he guided her behind the partition to the warm-up area. "It's okay," he was saying. "Plenty high enough, you just swung it a little. You'll make it easy on your third."

"But I've done 50 in practice," she protested. "I know I can do more. That girl was talking to me and got me distracted." Gloria nodded toward the platform, where the muscular black woman pulled on the barbell with a mighty heave and ducked under it with a little stagger.

"Press out," said Rochmann, "but they'll probably give it to her. She'd be good if she learned some technique."

219

Gloria did not like the way he was studying the figure in the tight, yellow suit. "I can beat her," she said. "I want 55 for my third."

"Sweetie, she's not in your weight class. You're not competing against her," he said in a soothing tone.

"I don't care. I want to do more than her. Fifty-five. I'll tell Dennis myself."

He took her by the shoulders and massaged her tense trapezius. His lips twitched in a slight smile. "Fifty-two-five," he said. "You go sit down over there, away from her, and get your head together."

Rochmann returned from the scorekeeper's table and sat next to her to keep away intruders. Neither spoke. When her name was called, he walked with her to the chalk box. While she chalked her hands, he said quietly, "Slow off the platform, don't yank it."

The barbell felt heavy as it came off the platform, much heavier than her previous attempt, but there was no time for reflection, just look up, shrug and under. The weight was overhead in just the right spot. Gloria stood and waited for the referee's down signal before allowing a grin.

Rochmann gave her a big hug, then handed her her sweat pants and shirt. "Picture perfect," he said. "Put these on; you need to keep warm."

They took chairs off to the side and watched the black woman in the yellow spandex attack 55 kilos. The barbell barely reached the top of her head and she struggled to press it to arm's length. "They can't give her that one," he said, and three red lights came on.

"I beat her," Gloria murmured in a satisfied tone.

Rochmann patted her thigh. "You're half way there," he said.

Sixty kilos was loaded for the heavyweight girl's opening effort. Her face was resolute as she strode to the center of the platform. Gloria could imagine the taunting she had endured from school kids over the years. 'Fatty, fatty, two by four.' Now the she stood defiantly in a tight blue nylon lifting suit that revealed the roll of fat around her midsection and the dimples in her legs. She bent to grasp the barbell, belly pressing into the flesh of her thighs. The bar slowly rose from the floor, accelerated, and in a flash, she was under it. She stood easily, the same calm expression on her reddened face. She had found her niche.

"Dang, she's fast," Gloria said, joining in the applause.

Rochmann eyed the heavyset girl with what could be the same look he'd given the black woman. Gloria couldn't be sure. "Lots of potential," he said.

The big girl did 65 kilos easily for a second attempt, but lost 70 behind her on her third.

"Ten-minute break until the clean and jerks," Dennis announced, and switched on a tape of the *Rolling Stones* 'Satisfaction.'

"Let's warm up," Rochmann said. "Take a caffeine pill, drink some Gatorade, and some honey."

"I don't think my tummy would like that."

"It's not about your stomach; your muscles need fuel. It's easy to let down after the snatches, but now's the time you need to move some heavy weights." She did as instructed while he rubbed her quads and traps with a pungent ointment that made her eyes water and her skin feel hot and cold at the same time. He swatted her butt and said, "Let's do it."

The clean-and-jerks went much the same as the snatches, with the women lifting in about the same order. Gloria made 60 kilos on her first attempt, as did the black woman and the large-breasted blonde. Their second attempts with 65 kilos were similarly successful. Gloria was pleased that her squat-clean technique allowed her to keep up with the bigger, stronger women, who employed a crude, power-clean style.

Rochmann insisted that she take 67.5 kilos for her third attempt, while the others called for 70, and she agreed with some reluctance. Her arms trembled as she held the weight overhead and she let it crash to the platform when the referee gave the down signal, almost collapsing with it. Rochmann rushed to steady her as she staggered from the platform. "You used every drop in the tank. Way to go," he said in her ear.

As before, they took chairs to one side and watched the other women complete their lifts. Fatigued but strangely exhilarated,

Gloria did not even mind when the black woman muscled up 70 kilos. "If I was that strong, I could do a hundred," she said.

Rochmann squeezed her knee. "I'm sure you will."

The heavyweight girl did 80, then 85 kilos, before missing with 90, and the women's contest was over.

Mildred announced names and totals for each class while Dennis handed out the awards, little medals on red-white-and-blue ribbons. He ceremoniously placed these around each woman's neck and gave them a hug, his reward for running the meet. "And, according to the Schwartz formula, the best-lifter award for the women's session, goes to..." Mildred paused for dramatic effect, "Gloria Soares."

Elated, Gloria accepted a small trophy of walnut-colored wood with an engraved plate stating, 'Best Lifter, Women, New England Open, 1984.' Incongruously, a gold plastic figurine of a man doing a deadlift adorned the top. The other women shook her hand and hugged her as she left the platform.

"Not bad for starters," Rochmann said. "New personal records, first place, and best lifter."

She dug the teddy bear out of her workout bag and hung the gold medal around its neck. "Mister Lucky comes through again," she said, kissing its nose.

"What about me?" he asked, laughing.

She gave him a sly smile. "I don't know about the other Mister Lucky. I'm awfully tired."

***

Back at the motel, they lay naked and spent in a tangle of sheets and pillows. "That's about the neatest thing I've ever done," she mused. "When's the next one?"

Rochmann nibbled at her ear. "Give me a little while and I'll see what I can do."

She swatted at him playfully. "You're awful. You know what I mean."

"Don't know exactly. I think the women's Nationals are after the Olympics. I'm pretty sure your total here will qualify. You're off to one heck of a start."

She turned on her side and looked deep into his blue, blue eyes. "Robby, do you really think I could do it? Compete at the national level? Go to the Olympics?'"

He looked past her, staring at the ceiling. "You won't win the Nationals this year. Just qualifying is a hell of an accomplishment. Next year, with a lot of hard work and a little luck, who knows? The Olympics in 1988? To be honest, getting a new sport added is very difficult. But there's a lot of interest worldwide; they've already had a women's World Championships. After the boycotts of Moscow and Los Angeles, adding a women's section might help in putting Humpty-Dumpty together again."

"Well if they do, I want to be ready."

That afternoon, Gloria boarded the Greyhound bus for Mystic in high spirits. She had a lot to tell her mother over spring break. She blew kisses through the window to Rochmann, standing next to the terminal, as the bus pulled away in clouds of black exhaust.

# PART VIII

# THE FAT LADY SINGS

# Chapter 32: The Conduct Code Committee

**"W**eatherman's being nice to us," Rochmann said cheerily as he walked by Sydney's desk. "A great way to start spring quarter." Gloria had called him early that morning to say everything had gone great with her family visit and she'd be over to work out at his house after classes. He resisted the urge to take Sydney's hand and waltz her around the office. She looked up and nodded, but said nothing.

From his cubby in the warren of faculty mailboxes, he extracted a stack of mail and walked, with only the slightest trace of a limp, to his office. He tossed most of the stuff that had accumulated over break into the trashcan. A white business envelope with the *Westerville State University* logo gave him pause. The typed address read:

> Robert P. Rochmann, Ph.D.
> Assistant Professor
> Department of Psychology
> CAMPUS

Campus mail usually was sent in pale green envelopes that could be reused. This looked very official. He read the letter inside:

> April 2, 1984
> Dear Dr. Rochmann:
> You are requested to attend a meeting with Dr. Corcoran
> and selected members of the Conduct Code Committee.
> The meeting is scheduled in the Psychology Department
> Conference room at 4 p.m., Monday, April 2. This time
> does not conflict with your class schedule but if some urgent
> matter prevents your attendance, please inform Dr.
> Corcoran at once.
> Sincerely,
> Dr. Frances X. Corcoran
> Chairperson, Department of Psychology

"Crap," he muttered. This would delay seeing Gloria and interfere with their workout. He thought about telling Corcoran he had other plans but decided he should start participating more in academic bullshit. Corcoran had covered for him while he was in rehab, after all, and he should be nice to his boss. He would go home at lunchtime and leave Gloria a note that he'd be late. A ringing class bell startled him. He snatched up his briefcase and hurried out.

After class, he stopped in the outer office. "Sydney, what's with this meeting with Corcoran this afternoon?" She had typed the letter and knew everything going on in the department.

She just pursed her lips, raised her eyebrows, and shook her head. "Can't really say."

"Maybe it's an April Fool's joke?" he asked with a smile.

Sydney looked at him sternly. "Certainly not."

Continuing down the hallway, he stuck his head in the open door of Golding's office. "Sam, you hear anything about the Conduct Code Committee? They looking for new members or something?"

Junior faculty were routinely drafted to serve on the committees that grew in academia like mushrooms in the forest. Administrators made the decisions but committees were constructed to give the appearance of faculty input and to do the dirty work of handling some of the teapot tempests that regularly bubbled up in the internecine world of college politics. Committee service was helpful for new faculty in career building, earning them recognition as good university citizens. Rochmann had avoided participation because meetings interfered with training. Maybe Corcoran had noticed.

Golding looked up from a book. "No, I haven't heard anything. Maybe they're looking to screw somebody."

The Westerville State University Conduct Code, a document printed in eight-point type, took up several pages in the students' *Catalog of Classes* and the *Faculty/Staff Handbook*. It was doubtful anyone actually read it except for the members of the Conduct Code Committee, who regularly revised the code to meet the latest trends in political correctness. Large sections dealt with 'hate speech' and 'sexual harassment,' in efforts to rid the university culture of its Euro-male hegemony, though this was not stated explicitly. It cautioned faculty to be circumspect in any discussion involving politics, race, religion or sex.   Among students, it was used to curb fraternity hazing, alcohol-induced dating gaffes, and placing the Confederate flag in dormitory windows.  Complaints against someone violating some part of the Code could result in hearings and disciplinary action.

"Yuck.   Hate to have to sit through some poor bastard's inquisition," Rochmann groaned.

"Let me know what happens."  Golding smirked.  "It could be entertaining."

***

At four o'clock, Rochmann knocked on Corcoran's office door. "Come in," the Chairperson said with great enthusiasm, shaking his hand vigorously.  Frances X. Corcoran was a tall, thin man with long silver-white hair and a thick white moustache under a beaked nose. In a tweed jacket and vest, he looked like someone's English uncle. "Right on time.  Not everyone's here yet.  Come back and have a seat. Coffee?"

Corcoran led him into the conference room that adjoined his office.   A large ovoid table, resembling an oversized mahogany surfboard, filled the center of the room.  On the far wall, a bookshelf, containing rows of volumes in colored leatherette binding with gold trim, lent a scholarly aura.   One shelf held a water pitcher, a large silver coffee urn, stacks of styrofoam cups, small boxes of sugar cubes, sugar substitute, and creamer packets.  The room was equipped for serious conferencing.

Pale, afternoon sunlight slanted through the open venetian blinds of two tall windows at the end of the room, silhouetting a seated figure.  Corcoran said, "This is Dr. Feiffer, from Anthropology, Chair of the Committee."  The silhouette nodded slightly.

Feiffer?  Nina's husband?  Rochmann squinted to make out the man's facial expression, his pulse quickening.  Was this about Nina? He hadn't heard from her in months, not since his stroke.  He'd never called her.  Was she pissed?  No, that was not like her.  Had her husband found out about their relationship?

"And this is Dr. Beste, from Athletics."

Rochmann had not noticed the woman seated on his left. The brown conical helmet of hair identified her immediately as the Women's Athletic Director, though she was not wearing the warm-up suit he was accustomed to seeing her in. Her white, shirt-like blouse with a black string bowtie gave her a mannish appearance. She also nodded, her unpainted face showing no sign of recognition.

"Did you want coffee?" Corcoran asked again. "Please, sit anywhere."

"No coffee, thanks." Rochmann moved to the right and took a seat across from Dr. Beste.

"Ah, here's Dr. Koenig, whom you know, I'm sure," Corcoran said as Rochmann's colleague entered the room, a cloud of citrus perfume preceding her. She pursed her bright red lips, nodded mechanically, and took a seat at the end of the table opposite Feiffer. He could see Beste and Corcoran, across the table from him, without turning his head, but looking at Feiffer and Susan would be like watching a tennis match.

"Would you like some coffee, Susan, er, Dr. Koenig?" Corcoran asked. She shook her head with an economy of movement that indicated she had more important business. "Well, then we can get started. This is an informational meeting of an investigatory subcommittee of the Conduct Code Committee, am I right?" Corcoran looked at Feiffer, who gave a slight nod. "Robert, Dr. Rochmann, as your Department Chairman, er, Chairperson, I am here on your behalf. On subsequent meetings you are free to have myself or another faculty member of your own choosing to accompany and advise you." Corcoran's warm, empathic voice, almost unctuous in tone, contrasted sharply with the demeanor of the others.

Rochmann stared at Corcoran. Investigatory subcommittee? He looked again at Feiffer for some sign of cuckoldry anger, but the man looked bored, staring into space as if waiting for a subway train.

"Dr. Feiffer, as Chair of the committee, would you please proceed," Corcoran concluded.

Feiffer sat forward and cleared his throat. "Thank you, Dr. Corcoran." His voice was deep and rumbly, with the faintest trace of a Germanic accent, reminiscent of Henry Kissinger--a voice of authority. He looked straight at Rochmann. He wore thick tortoise-shell-rimmed glasses that, against the backlight of the window, hid his eyes. His jacket was unbuttoned, showing a broad expanse of white shirt over a surprisingly thick chest, with a silk moire tie, giving him a very European look. He placed both arms on the table, surrounding the stack of manila folders in front of him, his chunky, manicured fingers curled in repose. A thick wedding band gleamed on his left hand, balanced by a heavy, Byzantine-looking ring on his right.

"Dr. Rochmann, as you know, when you sign your yearly contract of appointment with Westerville State University, you sign an agreement to abide by its Conduct Code. Our purpose here today is to inform you that we are investigating the possibility that you are in violation of that code, specifically Article Six, Section Two." He opened a folder and read: "No person with a faculty appointment shall have a relationship that can be construed as sexual, including cohabitation, with any person enrolled as a student, excepting those who are married or in a legally recognized relationship."

He looked up with no change in expression. The breath went out of Rochmann like the man had jumped on his chest.

Feiffer continued. "It has come to our attention that, in the past academic year, you cohabited with a female graduate student, who has since graduated and left the area. Now it appears that you have taken up with a young undergraduate female, a sophomore I believe." He looked down at the papers as if to confirm this. Still looking down he continued, "Furthermore, there are reports of what seems to be sexual activity occurring in your departmental office after office hours."

Rochmann saw Corcoran glaring at him, all signs of his earlier solicitude vanished. "Now just a minute," Rochmann interrupted. "This is ridiculous. Who's making these charges?"

"This is not an evidentiary hearing," Feiffer said coolly. "This meeting is simply informational, to inform you that these matters are under investigation. You will have ample opportunity to address the evidence at the proper time."

"'Informational?' Well, I'd like some information," Rochmann said. "I'd like to know how this has 'come to your attention.' I'd like to know who's complained about my relationships. Don't I have a right to face my accusers?"

"This is not a trial, Dr. Rochmann, where one faces one's accusers," Feiffer said in a quiet, even tone. "The question is, or will be, have you violated the Conduct Code that you contractually agreed to abide by? The Committee will decide if the evidence supports such a conclusion and will make recommendations to the appropriate administrative bodies about consequences." He nodded at Dr. Corcoran. "As I said, at this time we are simply informing you of this issue. There is no need for you to affirm or deny anything at this time. We will schedule a meeting in a few weeks at which time we will present the results of our investigation and listen to your statement. In the meantime you should closely read the Conduct Code and perhaps discuss it with Dr. Corcoran, or another senior faculty who is familiar with such matters. That person can accompany you to our next meeting to offer advice, or make a statement, or whatever seems appropriate to your interests."

"So, you won't tell me who's making these charges, or the 'results of your investigation' until this next meeting?" He looked from Feiffer to Corcoran and back. "Sounds like I need a lawyer."

"You will be given a written summary of the results of our investigation prior to the meeting, with sufficient time to allow you to prepare a response," said Feiffer. "I must tell you, these proceedings are under the jurisdiction of the university and lawyers are not permitted at our meetings. You may, of course, consult an attorney, but you will find that the university has every legal right to hold its faculty to their contractual agreement. This has been taken to court several times and the university has never lost." Feiffer seemed smugly satisfied at this record of success. "The university has every right to assure its students, and their families, that they have a safe environment to pursue their studies, free from sexual exploitation."

Sexual exploitation! How about your wife sucking me dry? After me to fuck every chance she got? Rochmann didn't say this. Maybe this had come about because he'd stopped seeing Nina? Had she tipped her husband off about Gretchen? And Gloria? Nina seemed to know every sexual act that occurred on campus. But jealous? Not Nina. Had Feiffer found out about their affair? He'd have to call Nina.

"Dr. Rochmann?" Feiffer was speaking. "I said, do you have any other questions?"

"Ah, no. Not at this time."

"Well if you do, please discuss it with Dr. Corcoran, or whomever you select for your advisor. Please do not contact me, or other members of this committee, as we will be conducting an independent investigation." Feiffer nodded toward the women. Rochmann turned to look at them with an embarrassed glance. Their expressions remained somber, cold, accusing. "That will be all, then. You may leave," Feiffer said.

Rochmann withdrew like a ghost, leaving his body to the vultures.

*** 

When he had gone, everyone leaned forward, as if on cue from a conductor's baton. Feiffer spoke. "There are three aspects to this matter, and I have apportioned them among the three of us. The most serious, in my opinion, is the matter of sexual congress in his university office." He paused. All nodded, again on cue from the invisible conductor. He looked to the woman on his right. "Dr. Beste, will you take charge of this? You said you have personally seen this Rochmann enter the psychology building after usual business hours, is that right."

"Yes," she replied, "a couple of times, late last fall."

"And Dr. Corcoran, you have reports from the janitorial staff that they have heard voices and other sounds suggesting, ah, sexual activity, emanating from his office at about this time?"

Corcoran cleared his throat. "Yes, the janitors reported hearing, um, such noises in Dr. Rochmann's office."

"On more than one occasion?" Feiffer asked.

"Yes, at least two or three times."

"Dr. Beste, since Dr. Corcoran is not a part of the investigative committee, you will get a statement from him and then follow up with the janitorial staff."

"Very good," she replied, writing some notes on a legal pad.

"Dr. Koenig?" He looked to the woman at the far end of the table. "It seems that another serious matter is a relationship with an undergraduate, and you've said this person may be psychologically vulnerable?"

"Yes. A girl in our eating disorders group stated that she had been sexually assaulted." She spit the words out with distaste. "Right after that, she dropped out of group. Later, she's been seen in the company of Dr. Rochmann, quite often I believe. I've checked with her dorm R.A. and found that she is spending weekends at his house."

"Right," said Feiffer. "Will you follow up on that? Get specifics. Document everything. You know the procedure?"

"Of course," she said in a voice that let everyone know she was not a rookie.

"The last matter, cohabiting with a graduate student who has left the area, is not so serious as these others, but I think it may establish a pattern." He paused and the women nodded. "I will pursue this aspect, and, of course, collate and summarize all our investigations. Does this seem an equitable arrangement?"

Everyone murmured assent.

"Does a month seem reasonable time period to complete our inquiries?"

Again, agreement.

"Very well, I will entertain a motion for adjournment."

"So moved," said Susan.

"Those in favor," he said in a perfunctory tone. "We are adjourned. Please keep me informed of your progress."

# Chapter 33: The Sex Police

In his office, Rochmann punched the first few digits of Nina's home number, then hung up. Maybe Sydney was listening in. "Fuck 'em," he muttered, and completed the call.

After the first ring, Nina's recorded voice informed him that Marvin could be reached at the Department of Anthropology and she could be contacted through her New York gallery. Rochmann replaced the phone with a *thunk* and sat with his elbows on the desk, palms pressed into his eyes. Voices and footsteps sounded through his closed door as the inquisitors filed down the hallway. He waited until all was quiet, until Sydney had turned out the lights and the outer office door clicked shut. Then he grabbed his coat, made sure his door was locked, and went home.

Gloria had begun her workout, her sweatshirt already damp under the arms. Trying to make his voice light, he said, "Hi, Honeybuns. Sorry I'm late. How's it going?"

She rushed to embrace him. "They make you work overtime first day of classes?" she asked, then squinted at him. "Something wrong?"

He kissed her wet forehead. Her sweaty musk mixed with the sweet scent of her shampoo; he wanted to carry her into the bedroom immediately. It had been more than a week since he'd put her on the bus to Mystic. "No big deal," he said. "I missed you."

She pulled back and looked him in the eye. "You're upset. I can tell. What's going on?

"Why don't you finish your workout and then we'll talk. What're you doing today?"

"Pulls. Nothing complicated. It can wait. I can't train when something's bugging you.

"Excuses," he chided her. "If you want to be national champ, you have to train no matter what."

"Just tell me what's going on and I'll decide."

"Do your next set before you cool off. I'll change clothes and we can talk between sets."

He emerged from the bedroom in his sweat clothes and sat on the floor. "I feel better already," he said, grunting as he stretched to touch his toes.

Gloria plopped down beside him. "Okay, what's going on?"

"Welll." He drew the word out as he touched his elbows to the floor between his splayed legs, hands clasped behind his head. He sat up. "You've heard of the Conduct Code? It seems I'm being investigated for making love to a certain sophomore." He squeezed her thigh affectionately.

"What?" Her voice rose with incredulity. "Are you serious? Why does anyone care what we're doing? It's nobody's business!"

"My sentiments, exactly," he said. "I don't know who's behind this. But the Conduct Code does prohibit faculty from having sex with students. Or even the appearance of a sexual relationship, or some such happy bullshit."

"That makes me mad," she said. "I don't need a damn Code to tell me who I can and can't have sex with."

"Well, let's see you channel that anger into your training." His voice was calm. "It'll be okay."

They continued to discuss the matter between sets. Gloria wondered how they could prove they were having sex and Rochmann said her signing out of the dorm and giving his phone number gave the 'appearance' of hanky-panky. Her eyes widened with alarm when he mentioned his contract next year could be withheld.

"You're going to lose your job because of me?"

"That's not going to happen. Somebody just likes to throw his weight around. Committees have to find something to do. Meetings will be held, reports will be written, people will get some cheap thrills, I'll get a slap on the wrist, and they'll be on to the next poor bastard. It's nothing to worry about, Sugar Babe. Besides, the thought of taking advantage of a helpless little undergrad makes me horny. How many more sets you have?"

After he'd returned from taking Gloria back to the dorm, Rochmann called Chappell and filled him in.

"I can kind of see their point," Chappell said. "It's like doctors screwing their patients. A big no-no."

"Whose side are you on? Gloria's not in any of my classes. Neither was Gretchen. There's no contingency at all, not even the possibility of one. Besides, it wasn't just sex. Gretchen and I were pretty tight, you know, and I'm really serious about Gloria."

"Okay, okay. I know you weren't trading grades for pussy, but you've got to see their side if you're going to defend yourself."

"Yeah, well basically I think maybe someone's out to get me. Feiffer's the committee chair. You know his wife and I were screwing around until my stroke. Maybe he just found out and is coming after me."

"Holy shit! You never told me about that."

"Yeah I did. Nina, the woman I met just after I got here."

"Who? The cocksuck queen? She's the wife of the Conduct Code chairman? Not a smart move, buddy boy." He laughed.

"Well, I didn't know it at the time. Besides, there's nothing in the Code about faculty wives," Rochmann said with his own rueful laugh.

He explained that Nina was in the City, and asked Bill to call the art gallery and have her phone him.

"Sure thing, buddy," Chappell said. "Glad to help. How're you doing otherwise? Keeping up with the exercise? Biofeedback?"

"Yeah. Aerobics, stationary bicycle, light weights with Gloria. Don't do biofeedback on myself any more but I've started consulting with Wheeler and the P.T. department at Westerville Memorial with some stroke patients. Pretty interesting. He has friends in Albany and we're looking for some grant money."

"That's really neat. Be careful with those weights, man. Don't want you popping another cork."

"Don't worry. I'm not straining myself. Blood pressure's good. If this Conduct Code doesn't kill me, I'll be okay."

\*\*\*

At noon the next day, Rochmann stuck his head in Golding's office. "Let's go to lunch. Got something you'll be interested in. The sex police are after me."

They huddled at a table in a corner of the faculty dining room at the student center, and Rochmann told him the latest developments. When he got to the accusation of having sex in his office, Golding drew back and stared. "Why do they think that?"

"Well, I talked with Corcoran. He's agreed to be my 'advisor' or whatever they call it. Sort of a corner man, patch me up between rounds while the others flail away at me."

Golding just sat, not eating, waiting for him to continue.

"Anyway, it seems the janitors heard noises in my office that sounded like someone going at it. They reported it to Corcoran but then it stopped. When Feiffer contacted him about Gloria, they put two and two together and decided we'd been doing the nasty in there. But," Rochmann sat back triumphantly, "it couldn't have been me. When you look at the dates of the janitor reports, it was when I was in the hospital. I have an iron-clad alibi."

Golding nodded slowly. "So what does he think was going on?"

"I have no idea. Maybe it was rats. Maybe it was other cleaning staff." He looked closely at Golding. "Maybe it was some other professor and his hottie using my couch? You still have a key to my office don't you?"

Golding's face flushed. He opened his mouth as if to speak, and then closed it. Finally, he croaked, "Did you say that to Corcoran?"

"Nooo," Rochmann said, laughing. "I wouldn't do that. I'm just happy they've got a story I can poke holes in. They're only interested in it to hang me. I got Corcoran to promise not to say anything about the dates, as my advocate. Then when they bring it up, I can prove they're full of shit and they'll drop it like a hot potato."

Golding let out a long sigh. "That damn couch of yours. You never used it for..." He stopped. "You know, I'd never let you take the rap. I mean, I'd've stepped forward if I had to. But you know, it could mean my job, my marriage..."

"It's okay," Rochmann said. "There's no reason to say anything about you. Just be careful. The sex police are everywhere."

\*\*\*

The following Monday night, the phone was ringing as
Rochmann got home after dropping off Gloria at her dorm. He
dragged over a kitchen chair and sat down before answering.

"Rochmann here."

"Rocky. How are you?" Nina's low voice was almost a whisper.

"Nina. I'm good. How're you doing?"

"Excellent, Rocky, just excellent. I met your friend, Dr.
Chappell. Very nice man. Very charming. I'm so glad you asked
him to contact me."

"You met him?"

"Oh yes. He came round to the gallery this weekend. We had a
nice talk. Very knowledgeable about art. Most congenial."

"Yeah, Bill's a happenin' dude. He gave you my message?"

"Yes. I've been meaning to call you for months. I heard about
your--your accident. I feel so bad that I didn't call, but time just gets
away from me. You know me, running in a dozen different
directions. You sound fine. Have you quite recovered?" Nina
sounded almost as though she were affecting an English accent. It
must be her city voice, he decided.

"I'm doing well, thank you. I'm not competing any more but
have no real impairments in everyday activities. I'm very lucky."

"Well yes, I suppose you are. But I know how much competing
meant to you and I'm so sorry. Life is all about changes, though, and
I'm sure you're very resilient."

"Yeah, life goes on. I'm doing fine, except for one thing that I
wanted to talk to you about."

"Yes, Bill told me. Something about Marv and the Conduct
Code Committee investigating your affair with a coed?"

"Well, it's, ah, more than an 'affair.' We're quite serious about
each other. What I wanted to ask you about was, well, I don't know
why I'm being investigated. I realize it's against the Code, but these
things usually don't arouse any attention unless there's a complaint. I
was wondering if Marv, maybe, has found out about us, you know,
and was, ah, getting back at me?"

There was an abrupt, choking laugh on the line, and then a gasp. "Oh Rocky, Rocky my dear. No, I'm sure Marv does not know a thing about us. And even if he did, he would not do anything so childish. We are quite accepting of each other's, ah, explorations, even if we don't care to know the details. I'm sure he would not be vindictive if he knew you and I had a 'past.' But it could, ah, make it harder for him to be a neutral observer."

"Neutral observer?"

"Oh yes. You know Marv is a cultural anthropologist."

"Yes?"

"Well, I don't know a great deal about his work, the details, any more than he knows the details of my art. But I do know his general interests. For example, why he's chair of the Conduct Code Committee and runs these investigations."

"Why is that?

"Well, he sees the university campus as a small, self-contained culture, with all kinds of traditions and so forth. Much more convenient to study than Samoa or the Amazon jungle. Chairing the Committee, he can actually participate in setting up some of the rules. And then he observes what happens when people run up against them, how the system handles it, and so on. He's written quite a bit on university cultures. Maybe you should look at some of his books. I know he tries to stay neutral and see how the various roles play out. He doesn't try to influence the outcome, just records what happens."

"So the Conduct Code is his little cultural experiment?"

"Oh no. He doesn't have that much control over it. He's mostly an observer. You never know, you might end up as a case note in a book a few years down the road, appropriately disguised, of course. That would be remarkable, your playing a part in the work of both us."

He recalled Nina's exclamations over the powerful 'emotional impact' their couplings had on her artwork. "I'd just as soon not be his lab rat, but I guess I'm stuck with it. I appreciate your telling me this."

"Well, you can be sure that Marv will be completely fair. I wish there was some way I could help you, but I'm sure you understand that's impossible. I do hope everything works out for you and your sweetheart."

"Thanks, Nina."

"Bye, Rocky."

He hung up and then called Chappell to thank him.

"Well, I should thank you," Chappell said. "Quite a woman. Most talented."

"Yeah, she said you went over to the gallery. Hey, you guys didn't..."

"Well, things just kind of happened. You know how it is. You really know how to pick 'em, Rock."

"She picked me. And it sounds like she picked you, too."

"Well I figured you were done with her, being all in love with Gloria and everything. You're not upset are you?"

"Nooo, not upset. Not surprised either, knowing you two. Have fun."

"You too, Rock. Anything else I can do, just let me know. Keep me posted on the trial."

"Will do, Jocko. Take care."

The next day, Rochmann went to the library and checked out the latest book by Marvin L. Feiffer, titled *The University as City-State*. Feiffer's conceit was that universities are modern versions of city-states, like those in medieval Italy, replete with political struggles, class conflicts, and expensive wars in the guise of intercollegiate athletics. It was entertaining but no help in planning a defense. Even if Marvin was not looking for revenge, he might be bringing charges just to collect data. Rochmann felt like one of Galileo's spheres, hurtling downward from a twisted ivory tower.

# Chapter 34: Robert's Rules

N ear the end of April, a registered letter arrived, detailing the charges and evidence of his wrongdoing under Article VI, Section 2 of the Campus Conduct Code. Rochmann and Gloria read it together.

The first charge was that he had cohabited with an unnamed graduate student during the spring and summer quarters of 1983. There was a copy of a letter from his landlady, whom he had notified in accordance with the terms of his lease. This showed that he had 'willfully disregarded said Article' and was evidence of a 'pattern of such disregard.'

He had already told Gloria about Gretchen and she just said, playfully, "You've been a bad boy."

The second charge was a report that there had been 'voices and sounds suggestive of sexual activity emanating from the office assigned to Robert P. Rochmann on at least three occasions.' In her statement, Dr. Charlene Beste reported an interview with the cleaning staff and noted that she herself had seen Rochmann entering the psychology building after business hours during fall quarter.

Rochmann explained how this was bogus, since he was in the hospital when the reports were made. Gloria only laughed about doing it in his office and said she'd like to try it some time.

The third charge was that he was cohabiting with an unnamed sophomore on weekends beginning winter quarter, 1984, continuing to the present time. A written statement from a dormitory Resident Assistant verified that the young woman in question had signed out every weekend with Rochmann's address as her destination. Another letter stated that the unnamed student was 'particularly vulnerable to exploitation, having an eating disorder and other psychological problems.' It was signed by 'Susan Koenig, Ph.D., Clinical Associate and Co-Facilitator of the Eating Disorders Group.'

"Susan," Rochmann muttered. "I should have known."

"I could tell you some things about her," said Gloria.

"What do you mean?"

"Well, if anyone made me feel exploited, she did. She was after us all the time to fill out these dumb questionnaires. Lots of questionnaires over and over again, and some of them were really long. I don't think Dr. Carter knew about all of them."

"Eating disorder questionnaires?"

"A couple were about eating. Most were about feelings, you know, anxiety, depression, stuff like that. And some were just weird. This one had hundreds of dumb questions, like, I don't know, 'people should wash their hands more often,' true or false, or 'I have never told a lie.' On and on. It took hours."

"Sounds like the MMPI," he said. "She was probably measuring personality factors."

"Well, we were there, you know, to work on our eating problems, things that upset us, not to have our personalities measured. But we had to do them in order to stay in the group. This one girl did this big test, the MPI? Just goofed around with it one time, you know, marked the answer sheet any old way without reading the questions? I guess Dr. Koenig could tell. She really came down on this girl and she got so upset she quit the group. Another time, a girl tried to ask how these tests were related to our problems, but Dr. Koenig just cut her off. Dr. Carter was really nice and helpful, but Dr. Koenig could be a bitch sometimes."

"Did you sign anything about being in a research project?"

"No, I don't think so. We signed up for the group, but there wasn't anything about a research project."

***

Gloria did not go back to the dorm the night before the hearing, even though it was a weeknight. She called the RA to report where she was staying. "See if they add that to the list," she said, defiantly.

"My little tiger." Rochmann laughed and hugged her.

"It's not funny. People prying into our life."

"Sickies have to get their kicks, too."

"Not with me, they don't."

"Really, Sugar Babe, it's my ass they're after. Your name's not even mentioned, remember? It doesn't affect you."

"If it affects you, it affects me. They're using me to get to you and I don't like it one bit."

He kissed her. "After the stroke, and losing my chance for the Olympics, this committee bullshit is nothing. I have you, we have each other, and it's all good."

"It's still not right," she said.

\*\*\*

Perhaps it was the two additional people, or the fact that he had been there before, but the conference room seemed much smaller this time. The windows, dark with rain clouds, contrasted with the harsh light from the fluorescent fixtures buzzing vaguely overhead. Susan Koenig's cloying citrus scent made the room even more oppressive.

Dr. Feiffer sat at his place at the head of the large oval table, his wide paisley tie giving him a jaunty look. To his right, sat one of the new people, his secretary. A spare, unsmiling woman, her gray hair in a twisted knot atop her head, she looked as though she could take notes at Judgement Day.

The other new person sat on Feiffer's left. A plump, black woman, her face was somber but, unlike the secretary, that did not seem to be her habitual expression. She was swathed in bright multi-colored fabric, with a matching turban, and hung around the neck and wrists with chains of beads made of ivory and carved wood. Feiffer introduced her as Dr. Marcella Mkabe-Jones, Dean of Student Life, a neutral participant in accordance with the arcane percepts of the Conduct Code. As one of the few African-American administrators, Rochmann figured she was much in demand to add diversity to campus committees. He could only hope she was not soured by these impositions on her time.

Drs. Beste and Koenig sat next to the secretary, across the table from Mkabe-Jones. Beste wore an almost military looking jacket, matching in color and style her brown helmet-hair. Susan seemed the size of a linebacker in her thickly shoulder-padded suit jacket.

Corcoran, to the left of Mkabe-Jones, looked like a shadow in his suit of funereal black. Rochmann took the seat next to Corcoran, across from Susan. She was the person to keep an eye on.

Corcoran busied himself making sure everyone had been offered coffee while Feiffer completed the introductions. Finally, in his Kissinger-accented baritone, Feiffer intoned, "Let us begin." He read the charges, everyone following along in their own copy, then raised his gaze to Rochmann. All eyes followed. "Dr. Rochmann, you may make an opening statement."

He cleared his throat. "First, I would like to address the charge that I was having sex in my office." He opened a manila folder. "I have here a letter from Dr. Clarence Wheeler, Chief of Neurology at Westerville Regional Hospital, that states that I was a patient in the hospital, from October 19, 1983, when I suffered a stroke, until December 22, 1983, when I was discharged from rehab." He pushed the letter across the table to Susan, giving her a cold look. She glanced at it and passed it to Dr. Beste, who in turn pushed it back across the table to Dr. Mkabe-Jones, who passed it to Feiffer, who gave it to his secretary.

While the letter completed its journey, Rochmann continued. "I also have a letter from Dr. Corcoran that states I was on medical emergency leave of absence during this period." He passed this across the table to Susan. "If you will compare these dates to those of the reports of noises from my office, you will see that I was confined to the hospital during the time of the alleged sexual activity." He sat back with a satisfied smile.

Susan glared at Corcoran. "Why didn't you inform us he was gone at the time of the cleaning staff reports?" she asked.

Corcoran shrugged. "I didn't pay close attention to the dates. I just turned the reports over to Dr. Beste."

The mention of Beste cued Rochmann to continue. "As for Dr. Beste seeing me enter the psych building after hours last fall," he looked at her with a friendly smile, "I have sometimes seen Dr. Beste and her associates walking their dogs around campus in the late afternoon, and I freely admit returning to my office sometimes after work hours. But, I don't see how that is in any way relevant to this matter."

The fluorescent lights hummed. Susan looked as though she were sucking on a lemon peel.

"Any additional comment on this point?" Feiffer finally asked. More silence. "Very well. Do you have a statement regarding the other issues?"

Rochmann took a deep breath. "As to my relationship with an undergraduate woman..."

"Girl," interjected Susan.

"Excuse me?" Rochmann said.

"She's a girl; she's only a teen-ager."

He appealed to Feiffer. "She's twenty, but please, can we not get into a debate as to when a girl becomes a woman?"

Feiffer looked at Susan. "There will be ample time to discuss Dr. Rochmann's statement," he said. "Let us get it on the record first." He nodded for Rochmann to continue.

"The young woman in question visited me in the hospital. I had not known her prior to that time. This was a period of, uh, great difficulty for me. In fact, I was very depressed. This young woman was very understanding, very kind. When I was released from the hospital we continued to see each other and fell in love. I challenge anyone to show I exploited her." He looked directly at Susan.

"Is that your statement on this charge?" asked Feiffer.

"It is."

"The floor is open."

Susan pounced. "You say you didn't even know each other and she just came to visit you in the hospital? You're a total stranger and she just happens help with your 'depression?' That makes no sense."

"Well, she may have known who I was," he replied. "But I didn't know her."

"How would she know you?"

"From the weight room, in the Fitness Center. We both worked out there."

"But you had no relationship at all?"

"No."

"I still don't understand." Susan looked around the table.

"If I might," said Dr. Corcoran. "Dr. Rochmann is fairly well-known around the campus as an Olympic athlete, isn't that right? You're training for the Olympics?"

"I was, before my stroke."

"Yes," added Dr. Beste. "He was a regular at the Fitness Center. Many people there know who he is."

Susan sighed. "All right, she might've known who you are, but why did she come to the hospital?"

"Well, you see, when I had my stroke, it was in the weight room. She was standing nearby and I kind of fell on her. It, uh, kind of frightened her and she wanted to ask me about that."

Susan's eyebrows raised in an expression of sudden insight. She licked her thick red lips as she thumbed through papers in the folder in front of her. "What date did you say that happened?"

"October 19, of last year."

"Ah, here it is," she announced. "On October 20, Gloria, er, this girl, told the eating disorders group that she had been sexually assaulted. Sexually assaulted! Just how did you 'fall' on her, Dr. Rochmann?"

"I had a stroke," he said in even tones. "I was unconscious. I have no recall of the events immediately before and after the event."

"How convenient," Susan went on before he could continue. "So we have this young girl, who has a very weak ego, low self-esteem, severe social anxiety, not to mention distorted body image, who is working out with weights." She scowled in distaste. "How appropriate. Then, this 'well-known' weightlifter 'falls' on her..."

There was a disturbance outside the room and everyone turned as the door opened. Gloria walked in, with Sydney hovering behind her. "I told her she could not come in here," Sydney said. "She just pushed by me."

Gloria looked at them with a defiant smile, her dark eyes shining, her curls glistening with rain. She carried a dripping yellow plastic raincoat and her tight, black jeans were wet from the knees down. She dropped her soaked backpack heavily to the floor.

"My name is Gloria Soares," she announced. "I'm the person this meeting is about and I figured I ought to be here. I would've got here sooner but I didn't know where it was." Her eyes sought out Rochmann. "I didn't tell you. I didn't decide to do this until just a little while ago."

Corcoran smiled reassuringly at Sydney and, with a small wave of his hand, bade her leave the room. "Thank you, Sydney. We'll take care of this."

"No, no, no," Feiffer was spluttering. "No visitors, no participants that we were not informed of in advance."

"I am not a visitor. You all are talking about me, me and Robert, and you should say what you have to say to my face, and I should get a chance to answer."

She pulled out the chair next to Rochmann, kicked her backpack under the table, and sat down. He shook his head, an amazed smile on his face, and squeezed her hand.

"This will not do," said Feiffer. "If you do not leave, we will have to adjourn the meeting and continue at another time."

"Well, I'd just come to that meeting, too. You might as well get it over with. What's so secret that you don't want me to know, anyway?"

"Proper procedure requires that all participants be named in advance of the meeting." Feiffer sounded like Moses on Mt. Sinai. "We would be violating our own rules if we allowed someone to just appear, no matter how relevant they might be."

Dr. Mkabe-Jones spoke up. Her voice had faint traces of the Caribbean, in marked contrast to Feiffer's Teutonic diction. "I may not be up on my *Robert's Rules of Order*, but can't someone make a motion about changing the procedural rules, and if it carries, we can follow the new procedure?"

"I believe that is essentially correct," said Feiffer, looking at his secretary, who had spent a lifetime attending university meetings. She nodded.

"I make a motion for adjournment," Susan interjected.

"What?" asked Feiffer.

"A motion for adjournment. According to *Robert's Rules*, it takes precedence over all other business."

Feiffer did not blink. "There is a motion for adjournment on the floor. Is there a second?"

# Chapter 35:  Psychological Disorder

R ain beat a staccato tattoo against the murky windows in counterpoint to the steady buzz of the fluorescent lights. Feiffer cleared his throat and repeated, "Is there a second to the motion to adjourn?"

Susan shifted slightly in her chair, nudging Dr. Beste with her elbow.  The Athletic Director moved her arm out of range, patting her lacquered coiffure as though a hair had budged from its assigned position.

"The motion dies for lack of a second," Feiffer pronounced.

M'kabe-Jones spoke up.  "I make a motion that we allow," she turned to Gloria, "what's your name again, Miss?"

"Gloria Soares."

"That we allow Miss Soares to attend this hearing of the Conduct Code Committee, and that she be allowed to make a statement on matters related to her.  How's that?"

"So moved," said Feiffer.  "Is there a second?"

Corcoran raised his hand.  "I second it."

"Discussion?" asked Feiffer.

"I think it is a very bad idea," began Susan, then stopped. "Before we go on, I think the visitor should not be here listening to this discussion on whether or not she can attend the meeting."

"Good point," said Feiffer.  He and his secretary exchanged whispers and then he addressed Gloria.  "We must go by our existing rules of no outsiders until such time as that rule might be changed for this meeting.  I'll have to ask you to leave the room.  If the motion on the floor is passed, you may return."

"You can wait out in the reception area," Corcoran said gently, "by Sydney's desk.  I'll inform you of the vote."

Gloria turned to look at Rochmann.  He nodded.  She pushed her chair back from the table and stood.  "Okay, but however the vote goes, you need to hear from me."

As soon as the door closed, Susan spoke.  "As I said, I think her being here is a bad idea.  There are, well, psychological issues that we just can't bring up in front of her."

"And why is that?" Rochmann asked.

"Well, it's like if a group of doctors wanted to discuss a patient, they would have a professional meeting without the patient to arrive at a diagnosis. It wouldn't do to have the patient hear all the back and forth of their discussion."

"But this girl is not a 'patient' and we are not here to diagnose her," said M'kabe-Jones.

"Well, she has been a patient of mine, in a way, at the Clinical Center. As I started to say before she burst in here, she has a number of vulnerabilities that make her especially susceptible to exploitation."

"I wasn't aware you had a license in clinical psychology," Rochmann said.

"I don't need a license in clinical psychology to see that certain test scores are in the pathological range," Susan retorted.

"You're not presenting test scores," he persisted. "You're making inferences regarding 'vulnerability' and 'psychological disorders' that seem to suppose expertise in clinical psychology, which I don't believe you have."

Susan's voice was cool and condescending. "I work closely with Dr. Elizabeth Carter, who is a clinical psychologist. I'm sure she would agree with my assessment of this person."

Rochmann shuffled through the papers in his folder as though looking for something. "I don't see any statements regarding Gloria's so-called psychological disorder from Dr. Carter, or anything telling us that you're her proxy. Are you saying that you became a clinical psychologist by virtue of working with one?"

"I could easily get a statement from Dr. Carter. I could show you the test results of this girl, her MMPI profile indicating weak ego strength, borderline personality tendency, her high social anxiety, low assertiveness scores, depression..." Susan's voice rose in pitch, as though someone were turning up the treble.

Rochmann interrupted, still thumbing through the papers, his tone curious. "I don't see any test scores. Here's some reports by housekeeping staff, here's a statement from my landlady, nothing from Dr. Carter..."

"Dr. Rochmann, I have a Ph.D. in psychology. I have extensive experience in personality research. I am offering my professional opinion to the Committee." Susan spoke as if that ended the matter and looked at Corcoran and M'kabe-Jones for support.

"Research?" Rochmann asked. "These personality questionnaires were part of a research project?"

"Well, yes," Susan said slowly. "I'm looking at personality characteristics of subjects with eating disorders."

"Subjects? Did these 'subjects' sign informed consent forms agreeing to personality research? I believe all such research requires approval by the Committee for Human Subject Research, and all participants need to sign statements that they've been informed about the project and agree to participate in it." Rochmann turned to Corcoran." Isn't that right?"

"That's true." Corcoran looked at Susan, his white eyebrows raised questioningly.

"This is just a preliminary investigation," Susan said. "It's not a formal research project, just a pilot that might lead to a proposal." Her voice became louder and more shrill. "I have done nothing wrong. I'm not the one on trial here. Here's this, this, *man*," she spat out the word, flinging her hand at Rochmann, "who has sexually assaulted a young girl, who took advantage of a girl with psychological problems, and you're looking at me like I'm wrong for exposing this, this violation of campus decency." She was almost shouting.

Dr. Beste put an arm around her shoulder as though to calm her, but Susan shrank away. "Don't touch me, you, you..." She began gasping for air.

Beste withdrew her arm, her face pink.

"I think we could all use a break," said Corcoran. "I propose we call a recess."

Susan had withdrawn an inhaler from the satchel next to her chair and took a couple hits as Corcoran spoke. "I'm fine," she said with a weak wave of her hand.

"We have a motion on the floor," said M'kabe-Jones. "I, for one, would like to hear from the young lady. I suggest we call the question and then take a recess."

Feiffer's gaze swept the group like the beam from a lighthouse, and then he turned to his secretary. "Would you please read the motion."

The imperturbable gray lady read from her notes in a flat monotone, "It has been moved and seconded that Gloria Soares be allowed to attend this hearing of the Conduct Code Committee and make a statement on matters that pertain to her."

"All those in favor signify by saying 'aye'," intoned Feiffer.

"Aye," chorused Beste, Corcoran, and Jones.

"Those opposed?"

"Nay," Susan said.

"The motion is carried. We will recess for ten minutes and reconvene with Miss Soares in attendance." Feiffer pushed his chair back from the table and stood.

\*\*\*

The group reassembled with Gloria taking the chair next to Rochmann. When all were settled and called to order, M'kabe-Jones leaned forward, peering around Corcoran and Rochmann at Gloria, and spoke in her euphonious accent, "Young lady, would you tell us how you met Dr. Rochmann?"

Gloria nodded. "Well, I'd seen him a lot in the weight room, in the Fitness Center?" She ended her statements with an upward inflection, as though asking for agreement, but showed no other signs of nervousness. "Where we used to work out? But not together. We didn't even know each other then. And this one time, when he had his stroke? I was standing close by and he kind of took a step toward me and just collapsed, kind of grabbing me when he fell?"

Rochmann sat with eyes closed, both hands resting on the table. Gloria gave the hand closest to her a quick squeeze, then continued.

"I didn't know he had a stroke or anything. I didn't know what was happening. It was real scary, everyone crowding around and it was like, I don't know, just crazy in there, everyone yelling, 'what happened! what happened!' I kind of freaked out and just got out of there and, well, I guess you know that I used to have an eating disorder, bulimia?"

She glanced at Susan with a quick, grimacing smile, then turned back to the placid face of M'kabe-Jones. "Sometimes when I used to get upset, I'd go on a binge, and I did it that night. That was the last time, you know. Anyway, the next day we had group, and anybody that binged had to talk about it and problem-solve with the group? And I said that I'd been sexually assaulted, on account of where he grabbed me when he fell."

She reached out and again touched Rochmann's hand. He still had his eyes closed, breathing slowly and deeply as though meditating.

"The group talked a lot about men, how they're all the time after women, and date rape, and women as sexual objects, and all? So it seemed something like that happened to me? Anyway, one of the things Dr. Carter taught us was to confront your fears. So I found out Robert's name, and that he was in the hospital, and that seemed like a safe place to confront him."

M'kabe-Jones interrupted with a summary. "So, Dr. Rochmann collapsed in the weight room and grabbed you in a way you felt was sexual. And you went to confront him about it in the hospital. After you talked to him, did you still think he'd assaulted you?"

Gloria shook her head. "Oh no. Not at all. He had gone into a coma when he collapsed and didn't know what was going on. When I saw him in the hospital, he was like, paralyzed on one side? And really, really sad."

Now she placed her hand atop his and left it there. Rochmann opened his eyes and gave her a faint smile.

"You know, he was going to be in the Olympics and then he couldn't even walk. I felt so bad for him. So I went back to see him again. And we talked, and, you know, got to know each other? And when he got home from the hospital we started spending more and more time together, and, well, I just love him to pieces."

The group sat in silence. Susan stared at the row of books above M'Kabe-Jone's head, as if willing them to tumble from the shelf.

"Well, that's quite a story," said M'kabe-Jones at last. "I don't have any more questions."

Feiffer cleared his throat. "Yes. Well, does anyone else have any question for Miss, ah, this young lady?"

Dr. Beste spoke up. "You said you used to have bulimia. What do you mean by that?"

Gloria said, "It seems like it was another life. I don't even have any urges any more. I think about my weight once in a while, but that's normal, I guess."

Dr. Beste continued. "Do you spend weekends with Dr. Rochmann, at his house?"

Gloria nodded. "Actually I'd like to move in with him but, you know, my dorm and everything is paid up through spring quarter, so I stay there during the week."

"I have no more questions." Dr. Beste sat back.

Feiffer gave Susan an inquiring look but she ignored him.

"Very well." Feiffer looked at Rochmann. "Do you have anything else to say? There is still the matter of, ah, cohabiting with another student last year."

"I don't deny that." Rochmann shrugged. "I had a relationship with a woman who happened to be a graduate student in another department. She completed her master's and we've both moved on."

"Anybody else? Dr. Corcoran?" Feiffer asked.

Corcoran cleared his throat. "Well, I suppose I could add that I've never received any student complaints about Dr. Rochmann, for sexual harassment or anything at all. All his teaching evaluations have been very favorable."

Feiffer's searchlight gaze again swept the room. "All right then, if there is nothing else, that concludes this part of the hearing. The two of you may leave and the Committee will remain to make a decision on this matter. Dr. Rochmann, you will receive a written copy of our conclusions in a day or so."

Gloria took her backpack from under the table and, when they were in the hallway, unzipped it, "I know it'll be okay." She took out the teddy bear in his sweat suit, her gold medal around its neck. "Mister Lucky is looking out for us."

\*\*\*

Corcoran happily served coffee to Drs. Beste and M'kabe-Jones while Feiffer gazed out the rain-streaked window. Susan moved to the end of the table opposite Feiffer. When everyone was seated again, Feiffer said, "The floor is open."

"Well, I saw no sign of vulnerability or coercion in that young lady," stated M'kabe-Jones. "She seemed very self-assured. In fact, it was pretty gutsy for her to show up and tell her story." To Susan, she said, "She seems to have improved substantially since you administered your tests. Perhaps the relationship with Dr. Rochmann has been good for her?"

"I agree," said Beste. "I see no evidence that Dr. Rochmann pursued or manipulated her. She may have been touched by his disability, no pun intended, but that hardly seems a matter of his taking advantage of her."

"The fact remains," Susan said in cold, even tones, "that a member of the faculty had a sexual relationship with a student, in direct violation of the Conduct Code. Furthermore, this is a pattern he's displayed since he arrived at the University. How they met, however 'touching,' does not alter that fact." To M'kabe-Jones, she said, "She may appear to be very together right now. But what happens when he 'moves on,' as he admitted he's done with a previous student? I predict she'll be right back where she was before, probably worse than ever."

"My, aren't we cynical," Mkabe-Jones said.

Susan ignored her. "This committee must find that Dr. Rochmann has violated the Conduct Code by having sex with a student. Both he and the girl admitted that. The only question is what consequence to apply for his violation. I propose that, at least, the Committee have a letter of censure placed in his personnel file."

"Now hold on," said M'kabe-Jones in a serious tone. "Nobody said they were having sex. They said they were 'in love,' but we have no evidence they are having sex."

"Come on, you can't be serious!" Susan's voice became thin and tight. "They're 'in love,' they're spending weekends together, you can't believe they're not having sex."

"I don't know," said Beste. "Maybe it's chaste love. Maybe they're waiting until they're engaged, or after they're married. No one has seen them in the act. Or heard them, either, we know that much for sure." She grinned and tapped the leave of absence form with her finger.

Susan looked down the length of the table at Feiffer. "The Code says gives the appearance of a sexual relationship or something like that?"

Feiffer recited, "Article six, section two: No person with a faculty appointment shall have a relationship that can be construed as sexual with any person enrolled as a student, excepting those who are married or in a legally recognized relationship."

"Construed as sexual," Susan said triumphantly. "You have to construe their relationship as sexual, even if they haven't said it in so many words. And he admitted cohabiting with another student last year."

"Construing is in the eye of the beholder," M'kabe-Jones' voice was soothing, as though speaking to a child. "I don't construe it that way at all. In fact, I move that we find no violation of the Conduct Code on the part of Dr. Rochmann."

"I second the motion," said Beste.

"You can't!" shrilled Susan. "This is a travesty! You're the Chair!" she yelled at Feiffer. "Tell them, they can't just ignore the Code like that!"

"I have a motion and a second," said Feiffer calmly. "Further discussion?"

"This, this is not right!" sputtered Susan.

"Please call the question," said M'kabe-Jones.

"Those in favor signify by saying aye," said Feiffer.

The vote was recorded as three in favor of the motion and one abstention. Susan slammed the door as she stormed from the room, but she did not actually say 'nay.'

# Chapter 36: The End of the Beginning

"So you're really leaving?" Golding walked around the cardboard boxes stacked neatly on the floor of Rochmann's office and leaned against the desk. Rochmann was taking books from a shelf and packing them into an open box that sat on the old, red velvet couch.

"Yep, Wheeler made me an offer I couldn't refuse. I'll be doing biofeedback research with stroke patients and, icing on the cake, making a good bit more than I do here."

"That thing with Susan didn't have anything to do with it, did it? You came out of that smelling like a rose." Golding smirked and the desk chair creaked as he plunked himself into it. "I hear Corcoran didn't renew her contract for next year."

"Really?" Rochmann continued to pack.

"You knew Corcoran had to eliminate one of the untenured positions for next year, because of budget cutbacks."

"No shit."

"You didn't know about the cuts?" Golding's voice squeaked with incredulity. "You really should go to faculty meetings more often."

"Well, I was gone a lot. And I've been pretty busy since I got back."

"Ignorance is bliss." Golding chuckled. "You really lucked out. Since you and Susan were the last hired, one of you would have to go." He sat back and looked thoughtful. "Of course, if they'd followed up on that noise thing, it could've been my nuts in a vise. I really need to get my tenure dossier together."

"Yeah, you should," was all Rochmann said.

Golding lowered his voice conspiratorially. "You know, Susan buddied up with Sydney and I think she found out about the budget cuts way last year, before Corcoran said anything. And Sydney probably told her about the janitor reports of screwing in your office. I don't know how she found out about Gloria, but you guys were pretty open so it wasn't that hard. She put two and two together and thought she had you nailed. Lucky for me."

"Yeah, well, I'm just glad it's over."

"You're not going to miss all this?" Golding waved his hand at the empty shelves.

Rochmann just shook his head.

Golding got up to leave. "Yeah. Well. Hey, before you go, would you give me a hand moving this couch into my office?"

***

Nineteen-eighty-four circled toward the summer solstice and the lawns of Westerville were chartreuse blankets speckled with dandelions, like tiny mirrors reflecting the yellow sun. It was a good day to be outdoors. As a compromise, Rochmann and Gloria had opened the windows to let the light and breeze into the room while they worked out. Gloria concluded a particularly strenuous training session and sat, exhausted, on the sofa in the bedroom office while Rochmann punched her training data into the Apple IIe.

"The Olympics start pretty soon, right?" she asked.

"End of July."

"We'll have to watch it on TV. Can't wait to see the weightlifting."

Rochmann exhaled audibly. "They never show much lifting. Just the superheavies, probably. If an American does well they might show him, but it's not likely, even with the Soviets gone. None of the hotshots from the Nationals last year even made the team." He wondered if the drug tests had caught them but said nothing. So much had changed since his second place in the Nationals a year ago, it seemed another lifetime, another person. For an instant he wondered how he would have done if only... But in a way, it was a relief not to have been there, not to worry about drug testing.

Gloria was saying, "Do you really think they'll have women's weightlifting in 1988? God, that'd be so neat."

Rochmann got up from the computer and sat beside her on the sofa, giving her quadriceps a gentle squeeze. "If they do, you should be in top form by then."

"No, really, do you think they'll have it?"

"Well, it's hard to get new a sport added. But women's lifting is really taking off, so there's a good chance. You could still be National, or even World Champion, even if it's not the Olympics."

She stretched to give him a kiss on the cheek. "I want to shoot for the Olympics, just like you."

He said nothing but put his arm around her shoulder and pulled her close.

"Are you sorry you're not going?" she asked. They both looked straight ahead, staring in parallel through the open window. The thin curtains fluttered outward, as though the room had sighed.

Finally he said, "Yeah, it's tough. But it'd be a thousand times worse without you." He tightened his hug. Another silence. "You know, in the best of all possible worlds I would have made the Olympic team *and* be in love with you. But since I can only have one, I'm glad I got you. Just call me Mister Lucky."

Gloria gave him another kiss, then snuggled close while he sat in silent reverie.

A metallic clank sounded from the front room. "The mail," Gloria said, jumping up. "I'll get it." She came back with the usual sheaf of junk mail and catalogs. "You got something from U.S.W.F.," she exclaimed, extracting a large envelope and tearing it open. "It's the information about the Women's Nationals." She shuffled through the enclosures. "They're going to be in September, after the Olympics."

"What are the qualifying totals?"

She pulled out the page listing the amount needed to qualify in each weight class. He stood and they examined it together.

"You made it! I thought that New England Open would do it. That's great!"

"Just barely." She was less enthusiastic. She turned to another page. "Here's the U.S. records. Dang! Look. They're doing almost double body weight clean-and-jerk in my class."

"You'll get there, Babe. You've only been training a few months. Hell, it took me years before I did double body weight. And I'm a guy."

"Years. By that time the records will be way higher than they are now." Her voice had a plaintive note.

"Gloria, Sweetie. You qualified for the Nationals in your very first meet, after only training a couple months. You're off to a great start. You might set a record some day, but it's not going to happen overnight. You have to strengthen bones and tendons, refine your motor patterns, build up fast twitch muscle fibers, even get injured and recover from it. It's a long road."

"I know, I know. But I haven't been making much progress lately."

"You can't expect to keep going at the pace you started out, Babe. Plateaus are normal. We'll change your routine, work on your weaknesses. You have plenty of time."

"Weaknesses are right," she said in a petulant tone. "I can barely front-squat what the clean-and-jerk record is. I know I can't set records right off but I want to be respectable at the Nationals. Do better than just make the minimum qualifying total."

"You will, Sweetie, you will."

She shuffled through more of the papers. "Look, here's the results from last year. I'd be next to last. I don't know, Honey. What else can I do? I mean I'm working really hard now, aren't I? I'm not going to have to wait until I'm thirty, am I? I couldn't do what you did for all that time." Tears welled in her big brown eyes.

He hugged her and nuzzled the dark curls atop her head, still salty damp from her workout. Then, taking her hand, he led her to the sofa and sat her down. He sat beside her and twisted around to look directly into her face, those sad eyes. He said, "Sugar Babe, that desire is what will make you a champion, but it's going to take time and hard work. There's no short cuts."

"What about steroids?" She gave a knowing look, eyebrows arching.

He inhaled sharply but continued to hold her gaze. "What about them?"

"I know that lots of people use them. Even though they're not supposed to. That black girl at the contest, the one with all the muscles, remember?"

Rochmann smiled and nodded. "Yeah, the girl that was bugging you; all power and no technique."

Gloria grinned. "In that tight yellow suit. I know you noticed her 'technique.' Anyway, she came up after the meet and we talked; she's really nice. One thing she said was, she takes steroids, just to give her a boost sometimes. Couldn't I do that?" Her face grew serious. "You've got to know about steroids, all the years you were lifting."

Rochmann sat back on the sofa and looked up at the ceiling. This was one secret he'd kept from her. He had told her about Gretchen and Nina, and his buddy, Bill Chappell, of course, but not what Dr. Jock had supplied him with. He remembered Golding asking him about steroids that afternoon in front of the television, how he'd defended their use, athletes pushing their limits, taking risks. How did he feel about Gloria taking risks?

"Well, for one thing, it's against the rules," he said, tentatively.

"Rules are made to be broken." She gave him a conspiratorial smile. "Like the Conduct Code."

A girl after his own heart. Still, something protective stirred within him. Something more than just the rules made him pause, though he could not put it into words. So he just continued on the track he'd started.

He said, "You get caught breaking the rules, there's consequences--you get banned from competing. And they're doing more and more testing, more sophisticated, so it's more likely you'd get caught."

She just pursed her lips, raised her eyebrows, and shrugged as if to say, 'so what.'

He went on. "Steroids in women have real masculizing effects, too, you know. It's a form of testosterone, after all."

"You like muscular women," she interrupted. "I saw the way you looked at that black girl. I wouldn't mind having muscles like that." Gloria did a mock double-biceps flex pose.

"I like muscular *women*, not guys with no penises. Some women get really scary-looking, like physique-ohs with breast implants. And it's not just muscles. There's facial and body hair, voice changes, acne. Ovulation problems. It's not pretty."

"I don't want to overdo it," she said. "Just once in a while, to get past the plateaus. Couldn't we try it, as an experiment?"

Thunder rolled faintly in the far distance and the curtains at the window fluttered inward on a cooling breeze. Rochmann felt the shadow of excitement he and Chappell had shared when, at about the same age as Gloria, they'd embarked on their steroid 'experiments.' He knew Dr. Jock would be more than eager to test the effects of male hormones on a willing female subject. Probably want to measure the length of her clitoris. Rochmann shuddered.

"Robby? Earth to Robby, hello-oh," Gloria said in a playful tone.

Rochmann hunched forward, elbows on knees, and spoke, as if to the floor. "I took steroids, off and on, for more than ten years. And it was great, I admit, setting one personal record after another, winning contests, dreaming about the Olympics. But you lose most of your gains when you go off them, and you can't tolerate going backwards. You get addicted to moving heavier and heavier weights, and you *need* the drugs to help you do it. It's like your value as a person is measured in kilos, and any decrease means you're worth less." He recalled faking his blood pressure data to assure his supply of steroids, and lapsed into silence.

Finally, he sat up and turned to look into her eyes, big and solemn. "It wasn't until I met you, when I was weak as that teddy bear," he waved his hand at Mister Lucky, sitting on the desk next to the computer, "that I began to feel I could be worth something as a person. That there's something worth working for besides the Olympics."

Gloria nodded, a quizzical frown on her face. "You think I should stop lifting?"

"No, Sugar Babe. You have natural talent and you should do it as long as it's enjoyable. Just don't get consumed by it. You're going to be a veterinarian, remember?"

She smiled. "Or a physical therapist."

"Or a physical therapist." He took her hand and gently kissed the calluses on her palm. "And maybe, down the road a ways, Missis Lucky?"

Her chocolate eyes widened, and her plumy lips parted before she pressed them to his. "Maybe," she whispered.

Printed in the United States
79690LV00001B/1-99

9 781601 452047